SUPERNATURAL™

JOYRIDE

ALSO AVAILABLE FROM TITAN BOOKS:

SUPERNATURAL™

JOYRIDE

JOHN PASSARELLA

SUPERNATURAL created by Eric Kripke

TITAN BOOKS

Supernatural: Joyride
Print edition ISBN: 9781783299362
E-book edition ISBN: 9781783299379

Published by Titan Books
A division of Titan Publishing Group Ltd
144 Southwark St, London SE1 0UP

First edition: October 2018
10 9 8 7 6 5 4 3 2 1

To receive advance information, news, competitions, and exclusive offers
online, please sign up for the Titan newsletter on our website: www.
titanbooks.com

A CIP catalogue record for this title is available from the British Library.
Printed and bound in the United States.

For my mother, Billie May Passarella, for making a bigger house a home, for her encouragement and support, and for helping me learn to weather the storms.

ONE

Determined to lose twenty pounds in two weeks to fit into the undersized suit he purchased for his cousin's wedding, Jeremy Merten had cleaned caloric house, tossing out all the junk food from his refrigerator, freezer and pantry. No temptation, no excess in his diet. Or so he thought. He'd lasted two full days before the cravings became insistent. On the second night, he dreamed of an island of potato-chip flower petals and pretzel-stick vines, ice-cream streams winding through chocolate-chip cookie bushes. Nacho shale surrounded bubbling hot springs of gooey cheddar, while a grove of donut trees filled the other end.

Jeremy decided he shouldn't have gone cold turkey. He needed some kind of "in case of emergency, rip open shrink wrap" snack on hand. Having one or two items in the house should be enough to keep the junk-food demons from invading his dreams with visions of forbidden-calorie islands. After watching the evening news and gnawing absently on his thumbnail through the weather forecast and sports scores, he decided he'd head to Moyer's Gas-N-Sip minimart to stock up on a few items: a bag of chips and some jerky. That was it. Emergency rations.

He grabbed his keys and jumped into his car for a quick drive.

No going overboard this time. Snack-sized bag of chips and some jerky. That'd be it. He nodded, proud of his restraint. For a few minutes. Then he frowned. Chips and jerky covered the salty side of the junk-food equation. He should probably grab something sweet also. Maybe a box of mini powdered donuts. Good idea, he decided. Bite-sized sweetness. Less chance of overindulging. Add a single pint of ice cream—plain old vanilla—and that would round it out: all his snack bases covered.

Sparse traffic on the state road this time of night, past Jeremy's usual bedtime. He yawned at the thought of putting so much distance between his head and his hypoallergenic pillow. Truck headlights loomed ahead, approaching fast. "Pack of gum," he said aloud, talking to himself to stop himself from drifting off. "Sugar-free, though. No cheating." Gum would take care of the oral fixation.

He glanced at the dashboard clock: 11:59.

Almost a new day, he thought. "New day, new you." Of course, he wouldn't eat any of the G-N-S snacks. Just having them in the pantry—or the freezer, in the case of the pint of vanilla ice cream—would get him through the next week and a half.

From behind him, he heard an approaching rumble. Glancing in the rearview mirror, he saw a single headlight approaching at maybe twice the speed limit. Motorcycle rider.

For some reason, bikers always seemed impatient, and as that thought was running through his mind, two things happened simultaneously. The motorcyclist swooped into the left lane to pass him. And the digital clock readout changed to 12:00 AM.

Jeremy's field of vision immediately shrank, swallowed by an occlusion of shadows rushing in from the edges to extinguish all light and awareness. For a flickering, panicked moment, he fought against the loss of consciousness. Before darkness claimed him, he recognized that his car had drifted toward the center of the state road—or possibly the approaching semi had drifted into his lane—and felt the jarring impact of the speeding motorcycle ramming his car from behind like a giant hand shaking him awake.

Already unconscious when his bike struck the rear bumper of Jeremy Merten's SUV, Steve Swauger catapulted toward the oncoming tractor trailer while his motorcycle spun on its side, spraying an impressive rooster tail of sparks across the state road.

Slumped unconscious behind the wheel of the semi, Loretta Papenfuss never saw Swauger's body strike and roll across the asphalt before half her complement of eighteen tires pummeled his lifeless body. Buster, her long-haul companion, an excitable Bichon Frise, awoke in his carrier behind her bench seat and barked in alarm. Loretta remained unconscious when her truck collided with Jeremy's SUV and drove it backward, metal screeching against metal, before shoving it aside. Buster lost his footing several times, but continued to bark in distress as the truck veered off the road, lumbered up a grassy embankment, plowed over a white picket fence and punched a prodigious hole through the side of a white split-level home, inches from the bed of a septuagenarian couple who remained asleep throughout the entire incident.

As debris fell in loose and sporadic clumps across the mangled cab and starred windshield of Loretta's truck, Buster's cries of alarm grew quieter, as if realizing that nobody, least of all Loretta, was paying attention. Listening to the familiar rumble of the truck engine, he settled down in his cushioned carrier, chin on his paws, eyes wide and uttered a low, disconsolate whimper.

A few miles away and a couple minutes earlier, the Gyrations nightclub defied the otherwise quiet night with its glowing neon signs, thumping bass, flashing strobes and multicolored, rotating spotlights. Dancers circled the dance floor like a human whirlpool, while others attempted lean-in, shouted conversations at the long, curved glass-and-chrome bar with varying degrees of success, and bartenders glided down the length of the bar taking and filling orders with practiced ease. Midnight arrived: one day changed to the next.

Bartenders, drinkers and dancers suddenly dropped en masse. Cocktail glasses and beer bottles crashed to the floor. One unfortunate server, Lettie Gibbs—who had overcome her awkward adolescent years as a self-described "klutz"—pitched forward with a serving tray on which she'd been balancing a champagne bottle and several glasses and sliced her throat open on the glass.

Men and women slipped off barstools, ending conversations mid-sentence, dropping cocktails mid-sip and phones mid-tweet. Dancers fell in whatever direction as inertia carried them into sudden unconsciousness, with an assortment of sprained limbs, broken noses, chipped teeth and one broken jaw.

The pounding music continued to vibrate the walls, the vast array of strobe lights maintained their flashing fervor and the roving spotlights found nothing moving among the jumbled mass of unconscious club-goers—except the shallow pool of blood spreading from the dying body of Lettie Gibbs.

The Finer Diner sat near Moyer's town limits, so it was the first eatery travelers encountered coming off the interstate or their last chance to grab a bite on their way out of town. Though the diner had been in the Finer family for generations, business had peaked decades ago when Moyer's Lake Delsea was a prime tourist attraction. A series of billboards had lured carloads of vacationers partial to boating and camping to Moyer's doorstep and the diner had capitalized on all that traffic throughout the spring and summer seasons. Even autumn once drew a sizable number of folks to the cabins that ringed the lake, those in search of a more introspective and picturesque vacation who preferred to skip the frenzy of summer water sports.

Those halcyon days were long past. The arrival of Pangento Chemical had signaled the end of the town's unemployment woes at the expense of Lake Delsea. Old-timers spoke of accidental spills, toxic runoff and several instances of illegal chemical dumping that poisoned the lake water. Skinny-dipping in the hidden cove of Lake Delsea had long been a teenage rite of passage in Moyer, but ended abruptly when exposure to the water caused rashes, open sores and, if ingested, nausea, diarrhea and vomiting.

With the best burgers in town, The Finer Diner survived the economic downturn through the regular patronage of locals and the steady if unremarkable stream of travelers who ducked off the interstate in search of a quick bite to eat. Most of the latter never saw more of Moyer than the diner itself before resuming their journey to more interesting places.

At 11:58 PM the diner served a dozen Moyer regulars who had either finished work late, missed dinner or preferred the twenty-four-hour breakfast offerings.

Marie Delfino carried a large serving tray to the couple in the back booth, regulars for as long as she'd worked at The Finer Diner. Inveterate night owls, Gabe and Linda stopped by late in the evenings and ordered impressively large meals. That night Gabe ordered the "No Decision" breakfast special with blueberry pancakes, scrambled eggs, bacon, sausage, home fries, wholewheat toast, coffee and a large orange juice. Linda ordered a medium-well "Gut-buster Burger" with extra cheese fries and a large chocolate milkshake. Sometimes Marie wondered if the pair only ate one meal per day so ordered with no regrets.

Pete Papadakis, the diner's overnight short-order cook, had juggled the meals well to avoid either order spending too much time under a heat lamp. Hustling the calorie bombs over to the corner booth, Marie felt her easy smile spread across her face a moment before everything went black. Her consciousness winked out like a snuffed candle.

Along the counter, the rest of the late-night customers slumped, eyes rolled back in their heads. Henry Addison, an elderly man perched on the corner stool, fell sideways and knocked Mabel James in the same direction, which resulted in one person after another tumbling from their stools like dominoes.

Back in the kitchen, Pete was craving a cigarette as he scraped the grill surface clean with a large metal spatula. If he had a free minute or two, he planned to sneak out back and light up long enough to quell the craving. But first he had to—

His thoughts interrupted and no longer in control of his muscles, he pitched forward, bare forearms slamming against the hot grill, eliciting a brief sizzle of burned flesh before his knees buckled and he flopped backward onto the tile floor.

In a display of civic originality, the main thoroughfare of downtown Moyer had been named Central Avenue rather than Main Street. Unfortunately, the contemporary street name seemed at odds with the old-fashioned storefronts that lined both sides of Central Avenue. For more than ten blocks in the commercial district, pastel-colored shops with striped canopies, recessed doorways between twin window displays and occasional sidewalk chalkboard signs adhered to the same aesthetic. Most of the shops were closed, bathed in the amber light of vintage-styled faux gas street lamps.

Close to midnight, only a few storefronts remained open,

mostly restaurants and all-night diners, a few liquor stores
and a tattoo parlor. As a result, pedestrian traffic had become
lighter than usual.

One man, on the downside of middle-aged, in a worn pea
coat, frayed jeans and scuffed boots, tugged on his knit hat
with fingerless gloves as he bumbled along, weaving side to
side as if the individual slabs of sidewalk shifted unexpectedly
underfoot. Muttering to himself as he wandered the
commercial district, Albert occasionally swatted at imaginary
pests buzzing around his head.

Beneath his surface irritation and reaction to these
imagined annoyances, he attempted to focus on people
who crossed his path, hoping the spirit of generosity would
overcome the natural aversion they displayed in his presence.
Years had passed since he'd been able to hold onto a job, so
he panhandled to survive. A buck here, a buck there, with
an occasional fiver or ten-spot keeping him alive, provided
he remembered to make his daily rounds of restaurant
dumpsters. In his clearer moments, he realized he'd never get
ahead again, such was the luck of the draw, but he could get
by, if he put in the effort. For however long he deemed the
effort worthwhile. Some days, he lost that crumb of faith.
Happened most often when he remembered his allotment
of days were numbered, so why bother? Surprisingly, the
question provided its own answer: why not?

Walking along, ready to make his pitch for a modest
handout, a task made more difficult by his tendency to see
people who weren't there. Not really. Like the other products
of his fevered—diseased—imagination. He saw a middle-

aged couple leaving Angelini's, a new Italian restaurant—he'd used the restroom once—and drafted behind them, slowly increasing his forward momentum to intercept them before they ducked into their car a few yards away.

Angelini's. The name had to be a good omen. Angels coming from Angelini's. Charitable angels. Compassionate angels. With a buck or two to spare for their fellow man... helping hand for the downtrodden...

"Eh—excuse me—excuse!"

The woman glanced back at him, startled.

Swatting at yet another dark shape darting around the right side of his face like a bloodthirsty mosquito, Albert grumbled at the unfortunate timing.

"Hurry, Bob!" the woman whispered to her companion, clutching his arm.

"Wait!" Albert called. "I won't hurt—I'm not—could you spare...?" He groaned, shook his head in frustration and decided to start over.

But the man pointed a key fob at a midnight-blue town car and pressed a button, eliciting a chirp as the door locks disengaged, and said, "Some other time, buddy."

"Don't need much," he said quickly, feeling the fish slip the hook. "Just a buck. No skin off—"

Bob shook his head, jaw set. "I said—"

Then he fell, his key fob slipping from his hand as his body struck and rebounded off the left rear quarter panel. Simultaneously, the frightened woman collapsed, snapping one of her high heels as her leg twisted beneath her and she pitched forward, striking the curb with the side of her face.

Standing over the fallen couple, his hands shaking, Albert stared at their unmoving bodies, and focused on the blood trickling from the woman's face to the curb, a steady drip-drip-drip, almost as if it had hypnotized him. Of all the unusual things he had seen and imagined, he couldn't decide how to categorize what had just happened. Too bizarre to have happened, but too mundane for a flight of fancy. Certainly possible the man—or the woman—could have had a heart attack or some kind of brain seizure. But both at the exact same time? It looked real but made no sense.

Then Albert remembered something his mother often told him as a child, *Don't look a gift horse in the mouth.*

He'd asked for assistance and the universe, in its mercy, had provided.

Something else his mother had often said, *God helps those who help themselves.*

He crouched beside the unconscious man—Bob was still breathing—and reached into the chest pocket of his suit jacket, removing a black leather billfold. Ignoring the credit cards—he had no inclination toward identity theft; he merely wanted a handout—Albert plucked out a twenty. "What's that you say, Bob? 'Have another.' Don't mind if I do." Albert took a second twenty, nodding. "Really? All mine? That's very generous of you, Bob." Albert took the rest of the cash, nearly two hundred dollars, mostly tens and twenties, and returned the wallet.

Next, he sidled over to the woman—never caught her name—and probed under her jawline with trembling fingers, searching for a pulse. "You'll be fine... Mrs. Bob. Just a scratch. Your doc can patch that right up. Eh—what's that?

You'd like to donate? Again, very generous. Appreciate it." He searched the designer purse but, aside from credit cards and loose change, only turned up thirty-two dollars. He took the folding money and stuffed it into the pocket with Bob's more substantial contribution.

"Good day—night—to you both," Albert said, nodding with a smile.

He walked past the town car, pleased with how the slow night had turned around for him, taking the shifting ground, literally, in stride. When something darted toward his eyes, he squinted and waved it away, peering further along the sidewalk where he spotted another man, sprawled on the ground as if he'd decided to take a nap on the spur of the moment. The universe continued to smile on him.

A good night indeed.

After a week of vacation spent camping, boating and hiking in the Mark Twain National Forest, Tom Gruber headed home, exhausted but refreshed at the same time. Endless days of small-town law enforcement tended to narrow one's focus to claustrophobic tightness. He'd welcomed the fresh air and plentiful opportunities for physical exertion in the wide-open spaces of the national forest. No computer screens, mind-numbing forms or repetitive citations to consume his time. Instead, he'd spent a fleeting but marvelous week under the big sky, reestablishing his essential connection to nature while the other drones he'd left behind handled the tedious procession of minutiae.

Though disappointed the week of freedom had passed in

a relative blur, he looked forward to familiar surroundings and his own bed. Something to be said for the comforts of home. As he guided his black jeep down the interstate off-ramp at the Moyer exit, he could almost feel himself slipping into auto-pilot mode. Familiar streets and surroundings, roads driven so many times that the individual trips slot into a master memory of the route. Nearing the town limits, he wondered if it was possible to see Moyer with fresh eyes.

This close to midnight, he thought, *maybe not.*

But really, it was a combination of things and exhaustion only played a part. Mostly, he decided he really had adopted a vacation frame of mind and doffed his police officer's hat, so to speak. Officially "off-duty" in mind, body and spirit. And yet, he knew the state of constant wariness swam right below the surface.

His jeep's tires hissed along the blacktop as he passed the "Welcome to Moyer, Missouri" sign, a lulling white noise that could easily tug him from auto-pilot driving to light sleep. He'd encountered more than one motorist who had nodded off behind the wheel. Some had drifted up or down an embankment until their vehicle stopped, harmlessly, but others hadn't been so fortunate. A few had caused multivehicle crashes, slammed into barriers or crashed into homes. Sifting through those memories gave him an espresso jolt, made him sit straighter in his seat, widen his eyes.

As he drove past The Finer Diner, he thought of stopping for a cup of coffee, but mentally vetoed the idea and kept driving along Central Avenue, wondering how long it would take before Officer Gruber rose through his mind fog and asserted himself. Turns out the thought itself was enough to wake the sleeping cop within.

Even though the business district conducted limited business at 12:09 AM, he decided he'd drive through to "check in" on his town. His home was on the other side, so the only time-cost involved sitting through any red traffic lights he could have avoided by taking the roundabout path home. He found himself checking side streets even as he peered ahead to the first string of storefronts.

He thought he might notice furtive movement in a doorway or someone lurking in an alley, or possibly a brief glimpse of a flashlight beam through a dark storefront window. Something subtle to trigger a law enforcement intervention, but he stared agape at what he saw on the road ahead as he came around a bend.

An SUV rumbled in a ditch on the side of the road, headlights piercing the darkness, several toppled mailboxes in its wake. Further ahead, a three-car pileup, a jumble of headlights and taillights glaring in every direction. At least two pedestrians lay unconscious or dead on a nearby sidewalk. In the distance, he saw a house fire and two car fires. After veering to the curb, he slammed the gearshift into park, grabbed a first-aid kit from under his seat and a flashlight from the glove compartment and jumped out of the jeep. He could hear the repetitive whoop of dueling car alarms but no emergency vehicle sirens.

"What the hell—?" he wondered aloud.

Whatever had happened, it was more than he could handle alone.

He tucked the first-aid kit under his arm and hurried toward the nearest fallen pedestrian, reaching for his cell phone to dial 911. As he started to kneel beside the man, and noticed his bleeding forehead in the harsh light of the flashlight beam, the man's eyes flickered open and he sat up, woozy.

Squinting into the light, palm pressed to the flesh wound, the man asked, "What—What happened?"

Gruber exhaled forcefully, taking in another sweeping gaze of the mayhem in Moyer. "I was hoping you could tell me."

TWO

When Dean Winchester tugged on the hose, he bumped the bucket of soapy water with his boot and cursed under his breath. Once he had enough slack, he dropped it, then carried the foamy sloshing bucket along with a rinse bucket across the concrete floor of the bunker's garage to the right rear quarter panel of the Impala. He dipped the microfiber mitt in the soapy water and sloshed it across the panel, determined to remove every bit of road grime. Sure, he could have taken the classic car through a gas station car wash, but those contraptions were hit and miss. Baby deserved better.

Down on one knee, he rubbed vigorously, attempting to erase the abuse of endless miles. Most of the caked-on mud ended up near the tire wells so those areas always needed a little extra elbow grease. Dean dunked the mitt in the rinse bucket to shake off some of the dirt, before plunging it in the wash bucket again to apply a fresh arc of soapy water to the car.

After he was convinced he'd left not a single square inch unwashed, he dropped the mitt in the rinse bucket and picked up the hose. He adjusted the spray nozzle to a thin, powerful stream and cleared the suds and any lingering dirt.

With the car wet and gleaming in the shine of the overhead lights, Dean released the handle of the spray nozzle and flung the hose aside. Then he carried both buckets out of the way. Over one of the half-walls that separated the motorcycle stalls, he'd tossed two fluffy towels and a chamois for detail work. He'd purchased some premium car wax but wanted to make sure Baby was as clean as possible before applying the wax finish.

"Give you that showroom shine."

He'd been talking to the car the whole time. Not surprising since Sam and he weren't exactly seeing eye to eye lately. At least where the British Men of Letters were concerned.

Dean grabbed a towel and began a circuit around the car, wiping off the excess water, taking extra care with the headlights and taillights. He had window cleaner for the windshield. He'd save that for last.

Out of the corner of his eye, he saw Sam rounding the catwalk to come down the stairs. Dean heard his sigh.

"Dean," Sam said. "What are you doing this early?"

"What's it look like?"

"Looks like you're washing the car."

"No," Dean said. "I'm drying the car. Finished washing it."

"Dude," Sam said, shaking his head. "It's the third time this week."

"You're counting?"

"Don't you think it's a bit much?"

"Baby gets dirty out there."

"She hasn't been outside the garage since the last time you washed her."

"Look around, Sam," Dean said, waving his arm for emphasis. "All this dust dulls the finish."

Sam sighed again, crossed his arms and leaned against a support column. "So, that's it? You're gonna wash the car every day now?"

"Not every day," Dean said. Then, hedging, "Unless she needs it."

"Or," Sam said, "you could talk about what's really bothering you."

Dean switched from the plush towel to the chamois. He shook his head, emitted a dry chuckle and said, "What's bothering me? You want the full list or the highlight reel?"

"Your choice."

Dean paused, hand pressing the chamois to the roof of the Impala. "What happened to us, Sam?"

Unsure how to answer the question, Sam's eyebrows rose, creasing his forehead. Then he shook his head. "Dean, what hasn't happened to us?"

"We're hunters, Sam," Dean said. "We hunt. Plain and simple."

"Not always simple."

"Fair enough," Dean said. "But straightforward. We hunt monsters. Track them down. And kill them. At least, we used to. Until the British Men of Letters decided to cross the Atlantic."

"We still hunt."

"We take assignments," Dean said, frowning. "File reports. We're…middle management. Unappreciated middle men.

Worse—we're lackeys. Completely expendable."

"We've always been on the front lines," Sam said. "That hasn't changed. But they can..."

"What?"

"See the big picture," Sam said, pushing himself away from the support column. "You're right. We hunt and hunt and hunt some more. Like a broken record. Always has been. But I feel like we can finally make a difference."

"We've made a difference," Dean said. "More times than I can count. We stopped a frigging apocalypse, Sam."

"I never said we didn't matter, that we don't matter," Sam said. "But this feels more like progress. That we could put an end to this if we work together."

"Never gonna happen."

"I don't believe that," Sam said.

And Dean knew Sam needed that hope, at least a glimmer of the possibility that there would be more to his life, if only in the distant future. Dean hated to spoil the delusion, but he saw no end to it. "Hunters end, Sam. The hunt goes on. We're... links in a chain."

"Doesn't have to be that way."

But Dean could tell by his brother's tone that he was having trouble convincing himself, let alone Dean. And that was fine. Dean had no illusions about the life. Or how it ended. No pension plan. No gold watch. No retirement party. Sudden and brutal. That was a hunter's end.

"We're still hunters, Dean," Sam said. "That hasn't changed."

"Doesn't it bug you?" Dean asked. "Taking orders from them?"

"Common goals, Dean." Sam shrugged. "We've worked with Crowley. More than once. When our interests aligned."

"Well, I trust them about as much as I trust Crowley," Dean said. "Scratch that. I might trust Crowley more. And he's the frigging King of Hell."

"Look, I get it. Mick is a stickler for following their rules—though he may be coming around. And, yes, Ketch is an ass. But ignore the personalities. Focus on the job."

"You get that from their recruitment poster?"

"Makes you feel any better," Sam said, "I'm sure we rub them the wrong way."

"Well, Mom doesn't have a problem with them."

Mary Winchester, murdered by the demon Azazel when Sam was six months old and resurrected thirty-three years later, had decided she'd rather spend her time with the British Men of Letters than with her own sons. She'd partnered with them long before Sam signed on, dragging Dean along for the ride.

"Dean, this has to be weird for her," Sam said. "When she died, I was a baby. You were just a kid. Suddenly it's thirty years later. We moved on. And she hasn't changed. She needs space, some time to adjust."

"Runs off to work with them," Dean grumbled, "and half the time I can't get her to answer a text message."

Sam stepped back and leaned against the support column again. "Give it—Give her time, Dean."

"Then there's Cass," Dean said, shaking his head as he resumed circular motions with the damp chamois. Though aware the roof was already dry, he needed something to occupy his hands. "First, he comes here and steals the Colt to kill Kelly and Lucifer's unborn hell-spawn, which—okay—I can maybe understand. Doubts we'll have the stones to pull the trigger when push comes to shove—or come up with a Plan B. But then he goes on the lam with her. Off the grid. Until he shows up supercharged, torches Dagon and puts us to sleep. Now, instead of killing Evil Junior, he's its protector? No way. Whatever was wearing that Cass suit wasn't Cass."

"He must have some reason—"

"Yeah," Dean said. "Demon seed's bouncing around his angel skull, rearranging the furniture." He shook his head. "And what if Fetus Lucifer turns Super Cass against us? You like our chances?"

"No," Sam said, "but he had his chance and passed. Yeah, he turned off our lights, but here we are, unharmed."

"With more questions than answers."

"True."

Disgusted, Dean balled up the chamois and tossed it in the soapy bucket.

"I don't know, Sam," he said. "This Men of Letters thing feels like a hostile takeover, Mom jumping sides... and now Cass. None of it makes sense."

"So, what do you want to do?"

Dean sighed forcefully and, after a moment, shrugged. If he could answer that question, would he lie awake at night or spend hours in the garage on wash, rinse, repeat? "Don't know, man." He spread his arms. "At least this makes sense. I can't bring back Mom or control Cass—even if I knew where the hell he was. But I can keep Baby clean." He turned his back to Sam and placed his palms along the edge of the car's roof, head lowered. "Everything else…"

He heard Sam approach, felt his brother's hand clamp down on his shoulder. "We'll figure something out, Dean," he said. "We always do. Sometimes it just takes a little longer."

After Sam left, Dean waxed the Impala from front to back, top to bottom, staying in the moment so his mind wouldn't race off in a hundred different directions for answers he'd never find. While those answers remained as elusive as ever, a calm settled over him and he enjoyed the satisfaction of a job well done. Sometimes the simple things were the best cure for unresolved anxiety.

And yet nothing good ever lasts.

Once he'd coiled up the hose, dumped the buckets and put away his cleaning and waxing supplies, his mind began to wander right back into the problem areas of his life, like picking at mental scabs. *So, don't be surprised,* he thought, *when blood wells up to the surface.*

"Stay out of your head," he chided himself. "Stay in the moment."

And, at that moment, his flannel shirt and jeans were damp and uncomfortable.

Before swinging by his bedroom to change into dry clothes, he stopped by the library and saw Sam at one of the wooden tables, staring intently at his laptop screen. Dean smiled. "Hey, if this is a porn moment, I can go."

"What—?" Sam looked up, confused, shook off the

comment with a frown. "No, it's not a—I may have something for us."

"You mean the Men of Letters—"

"No," Sam interrupted. "This is mine. Ours, if you want it."

"Depends," Dean said, although he doubted he'd turn down anything remotely interesting. Staying in the moment was a lot harder when you had nothing to do but wait around for the other evil shoe to drop. "What is it?"

"Moyer, Missouri," Sam said. "Mass blackout."

"Town forgot to pay its electric bill?" Dean asked. "How's that a—?"

"Not a power blackout," Sam explained. "At midnight, everyone in the town blacked out."

"Everyone?"

"Looks like," Sam said, skimming the information on his screen. "Lasted about ten minutes." Sam shook his head, eyebrows raised. "Didn't matter what they were doing. Walking, driving, shopping, eating…"

"Eating?"

"Local all-night diner."

"Insomniacs, people watching late-night TV, raiding the fridge," Sam said. "They all dropped."

"So, at midnight the whole town took a ten-minute nap?"

"Sleep, possibly. Or, I don't know, an altered state of consciousness?"

"You mean, an altered state of *unconsciousness*."

"Seemed to happen instantaneously. No gradual nodding off. More like someone flipped a switch in their brain."

"So, what happened during the group power nap?"

"You can imagine," Sam said. "Anyone driving crashed. Anyone walking, running or dancing fell over. Tons of bruises and sprains, some broken bones and concussions. Several fatalities." He looked up at Dean. "Silver lining. At least it didn't happen at rush hour."

"Hasn't happened again?"

"So far, only one time," Sam said. "Since then... usual police blotter stuff except..."

"Except?"

"Weird," Sam said. "Some vandalism and pranks early in the morning."

"In other words, the usual police blotter stuff."

Sam shook his head. "Dean, it's not the what. It's the who. Fifty-year-old elementary school teacher caught spray-painting her neighbor's garage door. Middle-aged bank manager slashing car tires."

"Not exactly juvenile delinquents, but..."

"They have no memory of the incidents," Sam said. "These two—and here are a few others—experienced lost time."

"Lost time?" Dean asked. "As in UFOs and alien probes?"

"Nobody's mentioned little green—or gray—men."

"Locals have any theories?"

"The press suspects a chemical leak as a potential cause, suggesting Pangento Chemicals, a local manufacturer, might be at fault. And not above a cover-up. Apparently, they have a sketchy environmental track record. Law enforcement making due diligence inquiries but it's still too early to know for sure. If they have a case against Pangento, they aren't saying."

"Makes sense," Dean said. "Anything else?"

"Well, the tinfoil hat society believes it was a field test of some next-gen Black Ops crowd-control weapon." Sam placed his hand on the top of the laptop screen and looked up at Dean as he closed it. "Well?"

"Hey, as long as the Men of Letters are out," Dean said, "count me in."

THREE

As classic rock thumped out of Baby's speakers, Dean tapped his fingers to the beat on the steering wheel. Seeming to mirror his improved mood, late morning sunlight gleamed off the hood of the freshly waxed car as it zoomed along the interstate highway. Sam slouched on the passenger side, shoulder pressed at an angle against the door, discreetly observing his brother through hooded eyes as if he were about to doze off. So far, getting Dean out of the bunker had worked wonders.

Of course, they had yet to cross Moyer's city limits and the case might not amount to anything, but sitting around the bunker directed all thought inward and the anxiety fed on itself. While the bunker served as a haven from supernatural threats, it offered no escape from a restless mind.

They would rather have their resurrected mother stay and hunt with them—if hunting was how she chose to spend her restored life—but they couldn't force the issue. Having his mother—someone he couldn't really remember—reappear thirty-three years into his life was weird for Sam, so he couldn't begin to imagine how strange it must be for her. Strange, yes, as in strangers. A family of strangers. She could probably see the boy Dean had been in his adult face, but Sam must seem like a distant relative she had only met a short time ago. So, yeah, she needed some space and he had no problem with that. At the same time, he could understand how Dean could want her back immediately to catch up on all the lost time.

As far as the British Men of Letters situation went, Sam was willing to roll with it. The Men had, for the most part, a common mission even though they chose to go about that mission in a manner that was, literally, foreign to Sam and Dean and the rest of the American hunters. Sam recognized their efficiency even if he didn't always agree with their methods. He saw a chance to make a real, long-lasting difference, something the domestic hunters rarely achieved. Maybe because they were the equivalent of soldiers on the front line, hip deep in daily battles but never seeing the full scope of the war.

Dean switched lanes and took the off-ramp at the Moyer exit of the interstate. The speed limit dropped significantly but traffic was light. A sign for Moyer directed them to Central Avenue. Pointing to a faded billboard with flaking paint advertising the Delsea Lake Inn, Dean said, "Check in and suit up?"

Sam nodded.

Based on the scant online reporting, Sam doubted much of an investigation was underway, at least regarding the midnight mass blackout. Pangento Chemical denied any involvement and, considering the local corporation employed over half the adult population of Moyer, the police were none too eager to press the issue. Insurance companies on the hook for payouts might grumble, but without a direct cause for sudden mass narcolepsy, they had nobody to blame, no way to recover their losses. A bunch of people fell asleep late at night. Basically, the property damage, injuries and fatalities were the result of multiple accidents. His inner cynic had no doubt the insurance companies would drag their feet before settling any claims.

As they drove along the winding Central Avenue, sun blazing in the blue sky through bucolic surroundings, Sam began to wonder if they'd jumped on this case too soon. Maybe the police had good reason to leave this on the back burner. There had been no recurrence of the mass blackout and no apparent side—

Sam rose from his slouch, leaned forward. "Is that what I think—?"

"A clothing optional 5K?" Dean suggested. "Don't see any racing bibs, but you're not hallucinating."

Along the far shoulder of Central Avenue, with bare backs and some saggy butts to Sam and Dean, seven naked middle-aged men and women raced with careless abandon and a complete lack of modesty.

"Well, that's new," Sam said.

"Welcome to Moyer," Dean said.

The men outnumbered the women, four to three, but the women led the group, except for one, younger man out in front by a few paces, waving his hands overhead as if playing to a cheering crowd. Playing along, the woman closest to him blew kisses to the imagined spectators. One man alternated between running in a zigzag to avoid pretend sniper fire and flapping his arms like a chicken. All ran barefoot, heedless of the rough debris on the side of the road. The last man—about a hundred pounds over his ideal weight, with sweat beading on his bald head—stumbled along in their wake, huffing and puffing and coughing as he slowly lost ground to the others. For no apparent reason, they turned left as a group at the next intersection, heading toward a string of suburban houses and immediately spread out across both sides of the road. Taking advantage of the dearth of traffic, they weaved back and forth, arms waving overhead in apparent celebration, for reasons Sam couldn't guess.

As Dean drove past the side street, Sam glanced back and shook his head. "What was that?"

"Had to guess?" Dean said. "Field trip from the loony bin."

"A bit old for streakers," Sam said. "Is that even a thing anymore?"

"Reliving their youth?"

Seconds later, a police siren whooped behind the group.

Sam leaned back, considering. "The pranks."

"What about them?"

"Unusual behavior," Sam said. "Uncharacteristic behavior."

"Big checkmark in that first box."

"Unless drugs are involved," Sam said. "Same for the second." Middle-aged and unfit adults rarely, if ever, went on cross country runs in the buff. "Lack of sleep might cause odd behavior, but not a few minutes of additional sleep." Sleep wasn't a factor, so… "It fits, Dean."

"Fits what?"

"A pattern of misbehavior," Sam said. "Following the blackout."

"You think they're related?"

"Don't you?"

"Extra sleep?" Dean asked skeptically.

"Not sleep," Sam said. "What if the blackout was something else?"

"Maybe," Dean said. He glanced in the rearview mirror, but Sam doubted he could see the middle-aged streakers or the police rounding them up. They'd traveled too far from the incident. And he and Dean had come too far to turn back. "Let's see where it leads."

"What I have here, Mr. Special Agent Tench, is a big, whopping headache," Chief Reginald Hardigan said, index finger raised for emphasis. "Scratch that. I have a whole heap of little headaches adding up to one mother-suffering doozy of a migraine."

"It's just Special Agent Tench," Dean said. He'd introduced himself and Sam to Moyer's blustering chief of police as Special Agents Tench and Blair. And that's about as far as the introductions had gone before the ruddy-faced and barrel-chested Hardigan launched into his multitude of reasons for not advancing the mass blackout investigation beyond initial inquiries.

"Well, Agent Tench—or whatever the hell it says on your

fancy FBI business cards," Hardigan continued, "there ain't no pill for this head-throbber. Far as I'm concerned, the blackout's old news. I'm down here in the metaphorical basement with the dang house on fire."

"And what, exactly, is the house—?"

Before Dean could fan the flames of the chief's impatience with a sarcastic reply, Sam interjected, "We're here to help."

"Got a woodpecker tapping out love letters in my skull," Hardigan grumbled. "And you two are here to help?"

Sam began to think the man had an actual physical malady rather than an unexplained series of petty crimes. Might explain the perpetually flushed face. "Yes," Sam said. "We'd like to investigate the circumstances of the blackout. If you could tell us anything you discovered at Pangento Chemicals or—"

"Pangento's a dead end," Hardigan said, attempting in vain to hoist his belt up to his waistline. "They denied any involvement."

Dean frowned. "And you believe them?"

"Toured the facilities first thing in the morning. Nothing out of sorts at the site," he said. "And we'll have eggheads in spacesuits testing groundwater and tap water by end of day."

"Biohazard suits?" Sam asked.

"Ain't that a hoot?" Hardigan said, shaking his head in disbelief. "Overkill, in my opinion. Anyway, Pangento's been here for years, employs half the town. We're in this together. Management's just as curious as the rest of us what happened."

They stood in the middle of the squad room ringed by several patrol officers who made a point of avoiding the chief's attention, giving the three of them a wide berth in passing and, when seated at their desks, focusing on computer screens, legal pads and evidence folders. Sam had the impression the chief needed a handy subordinate scapegoat on whom he could unleash some of his building frustration.

Hoping to extract additional information from Hardigan while avoiding collateral damage to the Winchesters' budding independent investigation, Sam proceeded with caution. "Pangento has a checkered history."

"Toxic spills," Dean added bluntly.

But Hardigan took it in his stride. "Ancient history and unconfirmed rumors," he said with a dismissive wave. "Besides, that dog won't hunt."

"Meaning?" Sam asked.

"If they had another spill—and I'm just speculating here— but if they had a spill and contaminated all the water in Moyer, wouldn't somebody have to drink it to be affected?"

Though he had an idea where the chief's argument was headed, Sam said, "Stands to reason."

Hardigan spread his hands. "At the same time?"

"Midnight," Sam said, nodding when Dean looked at him.

A toxic spill would not affect everyone at the same time in the same way. Side effects could be delayed, expressed in different ways to varying degrees of harm. Even if Pangento was responsible for another toxic spill, how could everyone in Moyer lose consciousness at the same time? A toxic cloud seemed more likely as a potential cause, but fumes or evaporating chemicals would spread on wind currents, their toxicity dissipating with time and distance. Everyone could have succumbed, but not everywhere in town at the same moment. Without a highly effective and deliberate delivery system, the simultaneous nature of the mass blackout seemed to exonerate Pangento.

Maybe the tinfoil hat society was onto something.

"Exactly," Hardigan said. "I don't see any way to hang this on Pangento. Meantime, I've got a string of vandalism and disorderly charges backed up like seniors at an all-you-can-eat buffet line. Broken shop windows and graffiti, delivery truck driver who took out a row of fire hydrants before busting an axle, middle school teacher—sweet little old lady—wrote 'Go to Hell' on her chalkboard and walked out on her class, and a dozen more besides. But if you insist on beating the dead horse of the midnight blackout, forget Pangento and look at the train derailment from a few weeks—what fresh hell is this?"

"The streakers," said a cop at the nearest desk.

Sam and Dean followed his gaze to the hallway outside the patrol room where two uniformed cops shepherded the seven middle-aged streakers toward booking and holding. The seven naked men and women huddled together, hunched over in embarrassment, emergency blankets clutched around their torsos. One woman shook her head in disbelief and asked, "What happened? I don't understand…"

Through the open doorway, Sam spotted a bloody footprint on the tile floor. He recalled the group jogging almost obliviously over pebbles, broken glass and litter on the shoulder of Central Avenue.

"Whoa, that's Bart Hodges!" Broder, the seated cop exclaimed. "And… is that Anita Finamore? Used to mow her lawn in middle school…"

Bowman, the cop at the next desk said, "That's the board of directors of the Barclay Homeowners Association."

"I'll be damned," Hardigan said softly. "You're right, Bowman."

Bowman said, "Heard from Sheila in dispatch they all jumped up from a luncheon meeting at Beltram's, ran out to the parking lot, whipped off every last stitch and sprinted down Maple Lane like a nude flash mob."

"Adds a new wrinkle to the association standards," Dean said.

"Quite a few wrinkles," Bowman said, looking away when Hardigan scowled at him.

A third patrol officer carrying a Moyer P.D. duffel bag overstuffed with clothing, leaned through the doorway and called to the chief. "Collected their clothes from Beltram's lot. Short a few wallets and cell phones from the looks of it."

"How liquid was this so-called luncheon?" Hardigan asked.

"According to Peterson, they all passed the breathalyzer. But not one of them remembers a damn thing from the start of lunch until they were zip-tied in the back of the patrol cars."

Hardigan's scowl deepened. "Like the others."

"Others?" Dean asked.

"The perps," Hardigan said. "The vandals, pranksters. Every one of them with a convenient case of temporary amnesia. Next they'll be saying the devil made them do it."

The Winchesters exchanged a look, but Sam doubted demonic involvement. Demons had no qualms about possessing humans as disposable meat suits, but their agenda steered a bit more toward the nefarious rather than broken windows, graffiti tags and streaking.

"You mentioned a train derailment…?" Dean prompted.

"Few weeks back, Hanchett Creek swing bridge—damn near a century old—collapsed under the weight of train cars carrying vinyl chloride to Jefferson City. One of them cars split open, leaked all over. A hundred thousand pounds of the stuff, cloud of gas rolling down the street like something out of one of those creature features—highly flammable. Had to evacuate two dozen homes, put the local school in lockdown, county's Office of Emergency Management issued a 'shelter in place' alert."

"Casualties?" Sam asked.

"Took dozens to the hospital—including emergency workers—with burning eyes and throats, headaches, some had trouble breathing," Hardigan said. "But you know what else that stuff causes?"

Sam glanced at Dean, who gave an almost imperceptible shrug, and cleared his throat. "Not offhand."

"Loss—of—consciousness," Hardigan replied, placing equal emphasis on every word. "And enough of the stuff can kill you. Lucky half the town didn't go up in flames."

"This happened weeks ago," Sam said. "Where's the investigation stand?"

"Who the hell knows," Hardigan said. "NTSB got their hands on it, won't let us move the dang train cars, and the Department of Environmental Protection is buzzing around like flies on a manure pile. All I know is, I want the whole poisonous mess out of my town." He pursed his lips and wagged an index finger at the Winchesters. "Think you boys can help me with that? Put in a good word?"

"Technically, the Hanchett Creek bridge is over the town line," Broder said. "In Bakersburg."

Hardigan stared at Broder so long the younger man nodded his head quickly, as if to silently apologize for the interruption, and turned in his chair to focus all his attention on his computer screen, fingers pecking away at his keyboard.

With a massive sigh, Hardigan returned his attention to the brothers. "What Officer Broder says is *technically* true, but wind don't care a lick about lines on a map. And on the fateful day in question, Moyer was downwind of Bakersburg. Take a guess how many Bakersburg residents were carted to the county hospital, coughing their guts up, after the derailment." He glanced down at the patrol officer. "You got the statistics on that, Officer Broder?"

"Um, none, Chief," Broder said hastily.

"Damn straight," Hardigan said, then turned back to Sam and Dean. "So, you two tell the NTSB I want it all—"

"Hey, Chief," a smiling patrol officer called as he came through the doorway into the squad room. Mid- to late twenties, clean-shaven, with a crewcut and a lean build, he looked like a walking, talking recruitment ad. "Heard you rounded up a bunch of streakers."

Without looking up from his workstation, Bowman said, "Barclay Homeowners Association board."

"I can top that."

"What is it, Gruber?"

"Granted, my guy was still wearing his tighty-whities," Gruber said, unable to contain his smile, "but get this. He was swinging from tree branches in Penninger Park."

"Wannabe king of the jungle?" Dean asked.

"In his dreams!" Gruber laughed. "Of course, he fell."

"Of course," Sam said.

"Damn fool's lucky he only sprained his ankle and dislocated a shoulder." Gruber pulled out a flip notebook. "Anyway, when he's not answering the call of the wild, Mr. Walter Skaggs is a butcher at Moyer Meats."

"Let me guess," Sam said. "He has no memory of climbing the trees."

"How did you—?" He looked quickly between the brothers before focusing on his boss. "Who—?"

Hardigan tucked his thumbs behind his belt, arms akimbo and nodded first to Dean and then Sam. "Agents… Bench and Bear?"

"Tench and Blair," Sam corrected before Dean could grouse. If Hardigan wanted to get under their skin, he was succeeding with Dean, judging by his furrowed brow. Sam took the flubs—intentional or not—in stride, since the Winchesters' fake ID had already passed muster. The less the chief remembered about them the better.

"My mistake," Hardigan said. "Anyway, these FBI agents are investigating the midnight madness."

"Really?"

"Turns out," Hardigan said, turning toward the brothers, "Senior Patrol Officer Tom Gruber here is the man you should be talking to. And I'm not saying that because my plate is full."

"Why's that?" Dean asked.

Gruber answered, "I returned to town while everyone was still out cold."

"What'd I tell you?" Hardigan said with a brisk nod and walked away.

"I could eat," Gruber said. "You up for a burger?"

"Always," Dean said.

FOUR

Less than thirty minutes later, Gruber, Sam and Dean had settled into a corner booth at The Finer Diner where Marie, their server, took their order of two cheeseburgers, a grilled chicken sandwich and three orders of fries.

"Living dangerously?" Dean asked Sam.

"What?"

"No salad?"

"I'll take a pass on diner salad."

"Actually," Gruber said, "it's not bad."

"Maybe next time."

"Fair enough."

Dean took in the diner with a sweeping gaze. Formica booth tables and long countertops, faux leather bench seats and stools, linoleum flooring, broad, clean windows wrapping around three sides of the building, shades at half-mast to blunt the afternoon sun. The place hummed at seventy-five percent of capacity, dozens of conversations blurring together in a comforting white noise, random words bubbling to the surface with clarity but no context. Overall, nothing extraordinary presented itself to casual inspection.

"Why's it Finer?" Dean asked. "The food?"

"What? Oh—the name," Gruber said. "The Finer family's owned the place for generations. But they do make the best burgers in town."

"Hear that, Sam?" Dean said. "You're missing out."

"Won't be the first time," Sam said. He addressed Gruber. "So, Tom, what can you tell us about the midnight blackout?"

Before they could answer, Marie arrived with their food on a large serving tray, smiling as she set the plates before them. "Two Big Cheese Burgers and a Griller Filler chicken sandwich. Fries all around. Sweet tea for Officer Gruber and water for the dapper fellas."

After a quick sip of his iced tea, Gruber said, "Thanks, Marie. Excellent service as always."

"Can I get you anything else?"

Dean grabbed the large cheeseburger before him in both hands, anticipating the first mouthwatering bite. "We're good."

Sam nodded.

"Goes for me too," Gruber said.

Marie nodded, started to turn away then paused. "Couldn't help overhearing you fellas talking about the midnight naps."

With a mouth full of medium-well beef, Dean nodded toward Sam to pass the conversational baton.

"We're investigating the incident," Sam said.

"These men are from the FBI," Gruber told her.

"Do tell," Marie said, impressed. "It was mighty weird. The way all of us swooned at the same time."

"You were awake at midnight?"

Marie nodded. "That's the last time I cover Donnie's shift," she said. "That's for sure!"

"Does that happen often?" Gruber asked.

"Every time he has a hot date," Marie said. "At least that's his excuse. Knows I'm a sucker for true love."

"I think his hot dates are popping up on a phone app," Gruber said. "Doubt true love factors in much."

"You never know what might happen."

"What happened with you?" Sam asked. "At midnight."

Gruber took a flip notebook and pen from the breast pocket of his uniform and began to scribble notes as she spoke. With a mouthful of cheeseburger, Dean cast a meaningful look at Sam, who nodded and took out his own notebook and pen.

"Same as everybody else in here," she said. She glanced around at the booths and along the counter. "Well, nobody here now. Our late-night regulars. One second I was carrying two overflowing plates of food to a booth. Next thing I woke up face down in a pile of food. Good thing Gabe and Linda are big eaters. All the food cushioned my fall. Mostly. Bruised my elbow and nicked my forearm on a broken orange juice glass"—she raised her right forearm to show a bandage affixed there—"but the worst part was my dignity."

"How so?" Sam asked, looking up from his notes.

"Looked like I came out on the wrong end of the world's biggest food fight," she said with a frown of distaste. "In my hair, all over my face and, ugh, my uniform. But I was one of the lucky ones. A few customers had broken bones—those who fell off the stools—and Pete, the night cook, burned his arms on the flat-top grill."

"Did you have any warning?" Dean asked. "Before you blacked out?"

She thought about her response for a few moments then shook her head. "Happened so fast," she said, snapping her fingers to demonstrate. "Kind of like the chicken and the egg, you know?"

"No," Sam said, confused.

"I've rented some bad movies over the years," she said. "Real snoozers. And I'm not afraid to admit I've dozed off during some of those bore-fests. But even the worst ones, I'll feel myself drifting off, nodding out, losing track of what was happening before everything goes dark and I wake up hours later with an aching back."

"Been there," Dean said by way of encouragement.

"Right," she said, nodding to acknowledge a kindred spirit. "But this wasn't like that at all. No in and out of sleep. It's hard to explain but if I was a machine, I would say it felt like somebody yanked my power cord out of the socket."

"And the chicken and egg?" Sam prompted.

"Oh, right," she said, nodding. "I have a vague memory of falling but I was out cold before I hit the floor. It was bang-bang. The falling and the blacking out. Not sure if I started to fall before the lights went out or the other way around."

"Did you experience any pain?"

She let out a dry chuckle and raised her arm. "Only after I woke up." She sighed. "Guess it could have been worse. Could have broken my arm or dislocated my shoulder, like I did way back in high school."

"So, you woke up same as the others?" Sam asked.

"To a chorus of moans and groans, you mean?" She nodded. "True enough. Everyone woke up around the same time." She leaned forward, placing the round serving tray on the edge of the table. "You want to know my theory?"

"Sure," Dean said. He glanced at Sam long enough to know they both expected to hear a tinfoil hat society explanation.

"I told Harry," she began. "But he says I'm crazy."

I'll be the judge of that, Dean thought, but kept silent.

"Harry owns the place," Gruber added for the Winchesters' benefit.

"Well, if you ask me, it was a carbon monoxide leak," Marie said. "I know for a fact he hasn't changed the batteries in those detectors in ages. Aren't they supposed to beep, like smoke detectors, when the batteries are low?"

Not a bad theory, Dean thought, nodding. Carbon monoxide caused loss of consciousness. People offed themselves— sometimes accidentally—by letting their car idle in a closed garage. Slowly suffocated to death. And that was the problem. The people in Moyer lost consciousness suddenly.

"They should," Sam said. "But a leak here wouldn't explain everyone in town losing consciousness."

"Oh, I'm not saying the leak was here," Marie replied. "I wouldn't keep working here if I thought it was dangerous."

"So…?"

"What if the leak was across the whole town," she speculated. "Like… an industrial carbon monoxide leak, from one of those massive factory pipes. Then, of course, the fumes or gas or whatever blew away before everyone died."

Dean said as solemnly as he could manage, "We'll add that to the list of possible causes."

After she walked away, Gruber closed his notebook and set the pen atop it. "Never heard of an industrial carbon monoxide leak. Not sure I want to accuse Pangento—or anyone else—of causing one."

"What can you tell us about the train derailment?" Sam asked.

Dean took another bite of his delicious burger, lamenting that it had cooled considerably since his last bite. Sam had somehow managed to work his way through half of the chicken sandwich during Marie's account of the midnight naps, as she called them. Let Gruber talk, Dean would finish the cheeseburger and nod where appropriate.

Gruber pushed back against the booth, hands clasped over the notebook and pen. "It's Chief's pet peeve. Until they pull those train cars out of Delsea Creek, he won't let it go. Whatever the problem, that's the cause. Inflation, stagnation, bad weather, high school team losing a football game. It's all the same. 'Damn train derailment.'" He sighed, shook his head and ate a couple fries before continuing. "I talked to some of the investigators back when it happened. Short term, it can cause eye and throat irritation, headaches, shortness of breath and dizziness and high levels may cause unconsciousness. Extreme levels can cause death. And it's a known carcinogen. But the affected area was limited. We evacuated homes, locked down the closest school. All the due diligence stuff." After another fry, he added, "I'm not saying some of those people won't have long-term medical issues from the leak, and I'm sure there will be civil lawsuits on top of civil lawsuits for years to come, but I think Chief's off-base on this one. Whatever leaked from those boxcars has long since dissipated."

"Are you suggesting it might not have been vinyl chloride?"

"Sorry," Gruber said around a mouthful of cheeseburger. "Sounded more ominous than I intended. Forgive me if I channeled the chief there for a moment."

"Maybe it's catching," Dean said.

"Possibly," Gruber said, chuckling before taking a sip of sweet tea.

Dean shook his head. "Could use a beer."

"Sorry, hon," Marie said, having glided up to the table at that moment to check on their meals. "No liquor license."

"Doesn't matter," Dean said. "I'm on duty anyway."

"Get you anything else?"

"We're good," Sam said.

"Okay, then," she said with another broad smile. "Holler if that changes."

"Will do," Sam said. As she strode away, he turned his attention back to Gruber. "So, we rule out the derailment."

"Far as I'm concerned."

"Wait a minute," Dean said, momentarily channeling his inner conspiracy-theorist. "Every big pharma drug commercial on TV has a laundry list of possible side effects and they always sound worse than whatever you're taking the drug for."

"Vinyl chloride's a chemical," Sam said. "Not a pharmaceutical."

Dean raised both hands, palms up and simulated a set of

evenly weighted scales, "Chemical, pharmaceutical."

"I checked it out," Gruber said. "It's for making PVC, used in pipes, packing materials, plastic stuff. Toxic, sure, but fairly common."

Sam shot Dean a look, wondering if he wanted to continue the argument. Dean shrugged.

Sam asked Gruber, "So, no blackouts since then?"

"Just that one time," Gruber said. "Weird way to return home, tell you that. But what I wanted to talk about is all the weirdness since midnight."

"The not-so-juvenile delinquents?" Dean asked.

"Exactly," Gruber said. "Taken individually, here and there, you figure it's typical small-town hijinks. Most of it, anyway. But, for the life of me, I can't understand why it's these particular people."

"Bankers, lawyers, accountants," Dean said.

"Nail on the head," Gruber said. "Granted, I haven't been a cop all that long, but you see patterns for this kind of stuff early on. Certain kinds of perps, certain situations. And most of the folks we've brought in have no record. And aside from the random vandalism, there's the—I call them weird acts."

"Such as?" Sam asked.

"One pedestrian punched another in the face for saying 'Good morning.'"

"Before or after coffee?" Dean asked.

Gruber's look seemed to indicate he had his doubts about Dean, but he continued. "Morning commute. Young woman with no apparent history of depression or mental illness tried to commit suicide."

"Hey, it happens," Sam said grimly.

"By climbing the fence on a highway overpass and jumping into oncoming traffic?"

"I'll admit that's unusual. She still alive?"

Gruber nodded. "Broke both legs, an arm, and fractured several ribs. Plan to talk to her when she regains consciousness. Weird, right?"

"Yeah, sure."

"Not that I expect to learn anything from her," Gruber said.

"Because of the amnesia?" Sam asked, picking at his fries.

Gruber wagged a finger at him. "Yes, sir, toss that in the mix. First couple times, you assume it's a convenient excuse. 'I don't know what happened.' Or, 'I don't know why I did that.' Or, 'I've never done anything like this before. Don't know what got into me.' But it's become the party line for all these incidents today. Nobody remembers. Or so they say."

"You have doubts?" Dean asked, lamenting the fact that his cheeseburger was gone, and he was down to his last few fries. He wondered if he should ask about the quality of the diner's pies. "Think they're lying?"

"Maybe not so much lying," he said, "as omitting."

"Omitting what?" Sam asked.

"I'm a cop at heart," Gruber said. "I see weird behavior, my first thought is drugs are involved. Who knows? Maybe some new designer drug the adults are trying. Something that, I don't know, removes your inhibitions and, instead of acid trips or flashbacks, you get a case of temporary amnesia."

"Seems possible," Sam said.

Bored with the prospect of picking up the DEA's slack—

which was not happening—Dean signaled for Marie. If they were about to ditch this case and head back to the bunker, waiting for the next call from the Brits, he'd end their short stint in Moyer with a slice of pie.

"One problem with that theory," Gruber admitted. "If a new designer drug had spread around town to this degree, I would have heard something about it."

"And you haven't?"

"Not a peep," Gruber said. "I'm clutching at straws."

Dean had a thought. "Are all the vandals, perps, whatever, victims of the blackout?"

"They're all from Moyer."

Marie swung by their table. Dean decided to stick with a classic and ordered a slice of apple pie. She promised to be back in two shakes with the pie and Dean said he'd hold her to that.

After she left, Sam said to Gruber, "I think Agent Tench was asking if they were awake at midnight when the blackout happened."

Gruber thought about it for a minute. Dean imagined him silently cataloguing the list of perps and mentally cross referencing it with the known blackout victims. "I'd have to double-check to be sure, but I don't think so. Many of them work nine-to-five, so I can't imagine they were awake at midnight. Of course, the town might be full of insomniacs and I don't know about it."

"Has anything else unusual happened in town?"

"Our plates are pretty damn full as is," Gruber said.

Marie returned with Dean's slice of pie and placed a

fresh fork down beside it. "Enjoy!"

"Well, at least his is," Gruber said, pointing to Dean's pie.

"There's more where that came from," Marie informed them.

"I'm good," Sam said.

"None for me, thanks," Gruber said, patting his waistline.

"Your loss," Dean said around a mouthful. He waved his fork toward Marie appreciatively. "Damn good pie."

Sam leaned back. "So, we have a one-time blackout followed by random acts of weirdness with no apparent connection between them." Gruber nodded. "Unless," Sam added, "there's some equally weird cause and effect we don't understand."

"And if not?" Gruber asked.

"Either way," Dean said as he set his fork down on an empty plate, "whole damn town seems to be losing its mind."

FIVE

As if to underscore Dean's words, a middle-aged businessman sitting across from a woman in a pantsuit two booths away from Gruber and the Winchesters slammed both fists down on his table and started shouting at the woman, "Blah, blah, blah!"

Taken aback by the man's sudden outburst, his dining companion stared at him as if he'd grown a third eye in the middle of his forehead. "Fred, what——?"

From his position in the corner booth, Dean couldn't see the man's face. He watched helpless as the man snatched up his fork, holding it in his fist like an icepick. Dean started to rise, but never could have covered the distance in time. The man raised the fork in the air then brought it down, tines first, into the back of the woman's hand. He struck with enough force to pierce her palm.

The woman screamed, clutching her bleeding hand against her white blouse, heedless of the crimson stain spreading down her torso. Fred slid out of the booth and ran toward the counter, attempting to jump onto a stool but severely overestimating his own athleticism. Instead, he doubled over the counter and scrambled up, legs flailing, as if the diner's floor were riddled with dozens of poisonous snakes.

Dean rushed the man, Gruber on his heels. Before he could warn against it, the woman yanked the fork out of her impaled hand and flung it away in a spray of blood as he passed her booth.

Behind him, Sam told the woman to stay calm and shouted, "Marie! Bring a clean towel!"

Lunch patrons scattered, fleeing booths and stools in equal measure, meals half-eaten, checks unpaid. Fred ran along the countertop, stomping on mounds of uneaten food with reckless abandon. Next, he skipped back along the countertop, kicking empty plates, drinking glasses and coffee mugs off both sides of the counter, huffing and puffing as he spun in tight circles, face flushed and eyes wild as he danced his demented tarantella.

Running alongside the counter, Dean had to duck and dodge the plates, saucers and mugs Fred launched his way. He swiped out a hand and nearly caught one of Fred's ankles. Beside him, Gruber grunted as a broken soup bowl clipped his ear.

"Fred, stop it!" Gruber yelled. "Right now!"

The countertop ended with a curve near the front door. Fred would have to stop, jump down, or reverse course. No other choices. Dean had him cornered.

The overhead fluorescent lights flickered, casting sudden shadows and pockets of darkness, as if a series of power surges had come down the electrical lines.

Fred's eyes seemed to roll back in his head as he pitched forward, tumbling over the edge of the counter and crashing to the floor. A moment later, Fred groaned and convulsed, in obvious pain from his awkward fall.

Dean kneeled beside him, looking for anything unusual in the flickering light. A moment later the fluorescents resumed their normal faint buzzing and steady illumination. And Fred looked like any ordinary middle-aged businessman who had taken an awkward fall. Except his lower pant legs and shoes were covered in grease and bits of food, and smelled of strong coffee. Moaning, he clutched his elbow. "What happened? It hurts?"

Gruber squeezed the transmit button on his shoulder mic and called for an ambulance. Then he knelt beside Fred and said, "You're under arrest for aggravated assault." As he pulled Fred's arm back to cuff him, Fred yelped in pain.

Fred continued to grimace. "What—are you talking about?"

"You stabbed that woman with a fork," Gruber said, tightening the cuffs. "Little pain's no more than instant karma."

"Who? What—?"

"Let me guess," Dean said. "You don't remember anything."

"I—I was eating lunch," Fred said. "I had a little bit of heartburn and I…"

"What?"

"I—I woke up here, on the floor? Did somebody push me?" Fred said. "I'm the victim here. I'm—hurt!"

Dean heard a rhythmic thumping from behind him. Twisting around, he cast about for the source of the sound.

As he rose from a crouch, he saw a man outside the diner, banging his head against the plate glass.

"Hey!" Dean called, but the man couldn't hear him.

While Gruber hoisted fork-wielding Fred to his feet, Dean moved toward the door, waving at the man outside who continued to pound his forehead against the plate glass. The next thump ended with a squishy sound as the man's brow split open. Blood streaked the glass, but the man didn't stop.

The next blow cracked the glass.

After staggering backward from the force of the impact, the man lunged forward and whipped his face toward the dripping smear of blood. Fearing the next impact would force the man's head through the window and potentially slice his throat open, Dean rushed through the door, swerved around an A-frame chalkboard sign and hurled himself against the man. He wrapped both arms around the man's torso, driving a shoulder into his ribs to tackle him. They fell together, the man's right shoulder and back slamming into the unforgiving sidewalk before Dean rolled clear.

For a fleeting moment, Dean blacked out, or seemed to, because he had no sense of lost time. If he'd lost consciousness from the jarring impact, it had happened in the space between heartbeats. Crouched by the curb, he examined the man's bloody forehead. Pulped and bruised flesh but, fortunately, no exposed bone. Nevertheless, the man could have fractured his forehead—or given himself a concussion—and needed prompt medical attention.

"Stay with him," Gruber called as he hustled Fred to his patrol car, shoving him unceremoniously into the back seat.

"Ambulance should be here any minute."

Beside Dean, the man with the bloody forehead groaned and placed his palm against the mess of flesh above his blood-matted eyebrows. He cursed in pain, his hand jerking back reflexively before approaching the wounded area with trembling fingers.

"Dude, what were you thinking?" Dean asked, shaking his head.

"I don't—what happened?"

Here we go again, Dean thought. "You don't remember?"

"No, I—I stopped outside the diner," the man said, struggling to recall the events leading up to his head-banging incident. "I was reading the lunch specials on the outdoor sign—that one, over there—and then I—I…"

"What?"

"I had trouble focusing on the words…"

"Blurred vision?"

"No, mentally," he said. "Like they were a bunch of jumbled symbols and I had no idea what they meant. But that lasted only a moment or two and then I…"

"What?" Dean asked, encouraged that he hadn't been struck with a complete case of temporary amnesia.

"I don't know how to explain it," he said. "I felt like the sign was falling away from me or I was falling away. Like when you look through the wrong end of a telescope. But mostly, the darkness blotted everything out. Sight, sound." He shook his head, then winced at the pain engendered by the sudden motion. "That's all I remember until I—woke up, lying on the sidewalk. Did I fall?"

Dean cleared his throat. "You—had help."

The man glanced up, noticed the bloodied plate glass window. "Is that—did I...?"

"Yeah," Dean said. "You tried to enter the diner head first."

"Why would I do that?"

"I don't know," Dean said. "Maybe you weren't happy with the specials."

"That's—I don't understand."

"Makes two of us," Dean said. "But we'll have a doctor check you out."

Sam sat facing Kelly Burke, in a corner booth by the cash register, far from the table she'd recently shared with Fred Harris until he snapped. After shoving the plates and glasses aside, Sam had wrapped her injured hand in a clean dish towel and had her apply pressure to both sides with her other hand. Lying on the Formica tabletop between them, like a proverbial smoking gun, lay the bloody fork, tines up, a bead of crimson slowly tracing a path down one twisted tine to pool with other drops below. To keep it out of view from her, Sam draped a paper napkin over it.

Most of the diner's patrons had cleared out after Fred's violent outburst, jumped in their cars and driven away. A few hardy—or hungry—souls returned to finish their half-eaten meals, occasionally glancing toward Kelly and Sam, possibly wondering if Sam would also channel his inner Mr. Hyde at a moment's notice.

Kelly stared at the fork, shaking her head. "I don't understand it," she said, her voice a bit raw. "Why would

Fred do something like this?" She raised her wrapped hand and shuddered when she noticed blood seeping through the folded layers of cloth.

"Keep pressure on it," Sam reminded her. He glanced toward the kitchen, where Marie was searching for the diner's first-aid kit. Apparently, Pete—the short-order cook during the blackout—had applied most of the bandages to his burnt forearms but she hoped a few might remain, if she could figure out where he'd stashed the kit. Though Kelly had lost a fair amount of blood, Sam hoped a good surgeon could minimize any permanent damage to the hand. Until she had a professional assessment, he wanted to keep her mind from dwelling on worst-case scenarios.

"So, are you two close?"

"No, not really," Kelly said. "I've only met him a couple times."

"You were dating?"

"No!" she said. "It was completely professional. I'm the office manager at Holzworth Heating and Cooling. We hired Fred's company to keep our office supplies stocked. Everything's available online, but sometimes you can't wait overnight or two days or whatever. Fred's local, so we can have anything we need in a couple hours. His prices are competitive. We keep a smaller inventory and I have fewer headaches. He offered to take me out to lunch on his expense account to celebrate his winning the contract. But, really, it was a win-win situation. I offered to pick up the tab, but he insisted."

"You think he was expecting something more than a business lunch?"

"We took several bids," she said, shaking her head. "His was the lowest. No favoritism. Besides, it was lunch in a diner, not dinner or cocktails in the evening."

"But more than coffee."

"Wait—are you implying I led him on or something?" she asked. "Because we're both married, and everything was strictly business, even boring. I mean, we're talking about paper clips and toner cartridges here."

"Of course," Sam said. "So, you have no idea why he might have snapped?"

"No," she said. "Everything was fine... until it wasn't."

"No triggers? Anger?"

"His reaction was... immature," she said. "I mean, he was doing most of the talking, asking about inventory levels for this and that, when would be the best time for him to stop by and check or if he wanted me to call first. He seemed excited to get rolling, establish a routine. And then he's screaming, 'Blah, blah, blah.' Who does that?"

"What changed?"

"Fred's a fast talker," Kelly said. "Maybe because the office supply business is, frankly, not that exciting. So, he talks fast rather than bore you to death. Probably a good strategy." Sam nodded. "But it was his eyes that seemed to glaze over."

"Like he was boring himself?"

"Exactly," she said. "I mostly nodded, gave an occasional suggestion about how much toner or paper we might go through in a month, which is stuff we talked about before, so maybe he wanted confirmation, whatever. Anyway, he's talking a mile a minute, in between gulps of food, and then he stops. For a second I thought he was choking, but I guess he just lost his train of thought. Stopped talking mid-sentence and looked around. Embarrassed for him, I reminded him what he was saying before he… faded out. But he was different."

"Different how?"

"All the excitement about the new business was gone. Like that," she said, raising her uninjured hand to snap her fingers. "I said, 'Fred, are you okay?'"

"And that's when he started shouting?"

She nodded. "I had this insane thought that I'd offended him somehow, but before I could even ask, he grabbed the fork and…" She squeezed her eyes shut at the brutal memory, her voice trailing off. "Well, you know the rest." She stared down at the dish towel, stippled with red.

"Completely unprovoked," Sam said, more of a statement than a question. Before escorting her to the corner booth, Sam had stood near the table where Fred attacked her, sniffing for a hint of sulfur, but detected none.

Again, she nodded. "Like I said, I don't know him that well. Maybe he has a history of mental illness and he's off his meds. But, he gave us references and we followed up with them. Nobody had a bad word to say about him."

Marie came out of the kitchen carrying a small, white plastic case with a red cross on the lid. She frowned as she approached them. "I'm sorry," she said. "Pete really cleaned it out. There's only two small bandages left, a bit of gauze, and maybe a little bit of antibiotic cream—if you squeeze the tube hard enough."

"Thanks," Sam said, taking the kit from her. "We'll make do."

Fortunately, as soon as he opened the depleted medical kit, he heard the siren of an approaching ambulance.

Six

Officer Gruber stood with the Winchesters while the paramedics treated Kelly Burke's impaled hand, replacing the dish towel with antibiotics and proper bandages. Hesitantly, she asked them if her hand would suffer permanent damage. Victor, the senior paramedic, said, "That's above my pay grade, ma'am. We'll take you to county hospital, have the doc there evaluate your injury."

"I can drive," she said, almost as hesitantly.

"Wouldn't advise that, ma'am," said Charlene, the other paramedic. "Might aggravate that injury."

"You're right, of course," Kelly said, nodding. "I should call my husband, let him know… I don't even know where to begin."

Victor helped her into the back of the ambulance. She sat next to the gurney upon which they'd earlier secured the bloodied head-banger, Tim Powell, who continued to moan softly, his eyes closed.

While Charlene closed the doors of the ambulance, Victor

approached Gruber and the Winchesters, "Guess we're lucky it was only two." He glanced toward the back seat of the patrol car. "He should have that elbow looked at by a doctor."

"You looked at it," Gruber said. "Said it was just a bruise."

"I'm no doctor."

"Noted."

"If it swells or the pain gets worse…"

"Got it, Vic," Gruber said.

"I'm serious, Tom."

"So am I," Gruber said. "After what he did, he goes to the back of the line."

A minute later, the ambulance left, no siren.

Gruber turned to Sam. "Nothing from the woman? Burke?"

Sam shook his head. "No warning," he said. "No trigger. He drove the conversation. Business as usual one minute, senseless rage the next."

"Followed by another case of temporary amnesia," Dean added.

Gruber glanced through the side window of his cruiser at Fred Harris, who sat hunched forward, head hanging, staring forlornly down at his feet. "Probably a member of the damn chamber of commerce," Gruber said. "At this rate, wouldn't surprise me if he sings in the church choir."

"Powell, the head-banger, didn't remember hammering his skull against the window," Dean said. "But he did remember something. Not sure how helpful it is." He explained how Powell suddenly had trouble reading the sidewalk sign specials before falling away into darkness.

"Never made it inside the diner," Sam said. "So, we can't blame the bottomless cup of coffee."

"All kidding aside," Gruber said. "If we rule out food, drink, chemical spills and toxic gases, are we back to my designer drug theory?"

"Even though you've heard nothing through the cop grapevine about such a drug?" Sam asked.

"There's that," Gruber admitted. "But I'm far from an all-knowing, all-seeing oracle." He sighed. "If I was in the dark, I wouldn't... Wait a minute. What if that's it? A visual trigger. Like one of those subliminal ads you used to hear about."

"Like the word 'sex' hidden in ice cubes in a vodka ad?" Dean asked.

"Something like that," Gruber said. "But instead of suggesting sex, what if it could trigger violence or other uncharacteristic behavior?"

"Sounds more plausible than a massive carbon monoxide leak," Sam said charitably, but Dean saw right through it.

Gruber scratched his chin, thoughtful. "Wouldn't explain the simultaneous blackouts, though. How could everyone awake in town see the same image at the same time?"

"You believe the blackouts are related to the vandalism and violence?" asked Sam.

"Know my town well enough to know it only got this weird after the midnight weirdness," Gruber said. "One night the entire town does a group faint and the next day a bunch of people start acting weird." He looked to Dean. "Like you said, Special Agent Tench, the blackout might not have been caused by a drug, per se, but there's been a whole laundry list of side effects."

Dean nodded. "Hard to argue with that."

Gruber climbed into his patrol car and drove Fred to the police station. A few moments after the cruiser pulled out of the lot, a dinged red pickup truck with patches of primer and a chassis that looked as if it had seen a quarter-million miles since its car lot debut rolled up the driveway in squeaky shocks and pulled into the vacated parking space.

"Good, you're still here," Marie said as she exited the diner and approached them. "When I called Pete to ask where the hell he stashed the first-aid kit, I mentioned the FBI was here, asking about the blackout and he volunteered to come in."

A burly, olive-skinned man with a full head of wavy black hair and a pronounced five o'clock shadow climbed out of the pickup truck. He wore a gray sweatshirt over jeans, both sleeves pushed up past the elbows, revealing white bandages across the underside of his forearms down to the base of his palms.

"Pete," Marie said. "Special Agents…?"

"Tench and Blair," Dean said, not bothering to flash his phony credentials.

"Pete Papadakis," he said, shaking their hands in turn. "That was one crazy night, am I right? And not in a good way." He chuckled. "But how can I help?"

"What do you remember?" Sam asked.

"Craving a cigarette."

"Excuse me?"

Pete chuckled again. "It's true," he said. "That's about the last thing I remember before the lights went out. Not the real lights." He rapped his skull with his right fist. "These lights. Marie was there, busy night, mostly regulars. I was trying to clear out the orders and all I could think about was sneaking out back for a puff or two." He leaned back against the rust-colored pickup, eyes staring off into space as he spoke. "I had just scraped the flat top clean with a spatula. Basket of onion rings in the deep fryer, but I thought I could slip out for a minute. Then—boom!" He struck his palms together for emphasis.

"What?" Dean asked. "Something exploded?"

"No, the darkness came," he said. "Almost like somebody flipped a switch inside my brain, 'Goodnight, Pete!'" He chuckled again. "No, not a real voice. Just that sudden. Like falling asleep soon as your head hits the pillow. But, in this case, I fell forward and slapped my arms on the flat top. For a moment, I almost shook it off and woke up. You burn yourself, that pain is quick, yes sir. Faster than the sleep. But whatever was dragging me down was too strong to fight. I'm lucky I fell back onto the floor, or the burns could have been much worse. Mostly first degree. Not bad. Second degree closer to my elbows."

"Did you see or hear anything unusual before you lost consciousness?"

One eyebrow arched, Pete asked, "Other than a whiff of my own flesh cooking?"

"Yes," Dean said. "Other than that."

He thought it over. "Not really. Craving a cigarette. I could almost smell it, taste it. Other than that, nothing unusual. Of course, if I hadn't fallen on the floor…" He glanced down at his bandaged forearms. "But, hey, could have been worse, right?"

"Yeah. Sure," Sam said.

"Lots of people got hurt. Bumps and bruises mostly." Pete looked toward Marie. "I heard Nellie Quick lost a few teeth when she fell! Right in front!"

"Oh, no!" Marie said. "I recall some blood on her mouth. Thought she bit her lip."

"Heard she looks like a hockey player," Pete said, chuckling. "Could play for the Blues."

Marie laughed, then caught herself, mortified. "Sorry. That's awful, Pete." She looked around to make sure nobody was in earshot. "But that woman is very particular about her appearance."

Pete turned back to the Winchesters. "So, got any theories? Terrorists? UFOs?"

"We're investigating possibilities," Sam said noncommittally.

As the Winchesters walked toward the Impala, Dean overheard Marie chatting with Pete.

"At breakfast this morning, Clyde Barksdale told me his bomb shelter is stocked for any emergency. Convinced it's the end times."

"If it is," Pete said, "what good is a damn bomb shelter?"

Marie laughed. "You try talking sense to that man."

Dean drove off the lot. A glance in the rearview mirror showed Marie heading back inside the diner while Pete fired up his battered pickup, a puff of smoke belching from the rusted exhaust pipe. Dean wondered if those two kept the Moyer grapevine thriving. Pete had come to the diner hours before his scheduled shift time to tell what little he knew about the midnight incident in what was more likely a fishing expedition. Harmless small-town gossip, maybe, but they were no closer to the cause of the mass blackout or the weird behavior.

"Possibilities?" Dean asked. "Got anything in mind?"

"Assuming terrorists, UFOs and carbon monoxide are far down the list," Sam said, "could be any number of things. Demonic possession. Angel possession. Psychics. Witches."

"Hex bags," Dean said, latching onto the last suggestion. "What if it's not random? What if somebody in Moyer has a hit list?"

"Wouldn't explain the midnight incident."

"No," Dean agreed. "If they're related. Maybe they're not."

"I don't know, Dean," Sam said. "Gruber had a good point."

"Could be coincidence."

"What are you suggesting?"

"Let's rule out demons," Dean said. "Because we know demons. And some of these incidents, pranks or whatever, well, not their style."

"I checked the diner for sulfur."

"And?"

"Not a whiff," Sam admitted.

"There you go," Dean said. "And this oddball stuff doesn't fit angel possession either."

"But that's also why a hit list doesn't makes any sense," Sam said. "It's a mixed bag. Juvenile pranks. Things that might tarnish a reputation? Sure. But then you have extreme violence and attempted suicides."

"So, what kind of list would cover that range of targets?" Dean asked.

Sam took a moment to consider possibilities. "Maybe it's not one person with a list."

"Multiple lists?"

"Or a coven, maybe a group of psychics working together," Sam speculated. "Everyone brings their own list."

"Meaning, what, a revenge club?"

"Or," Sam continued, "a smokescreen."

"Thought we ruled out a toxic gas emission."

"Funny," Sam said. "But we're not talking about the blackouts."

"We're not?"

"Let's ignore them right now," Sam said. "Focus on the pranks and violence. What if the person with the hit list had a short list of real targets, but sticking to that list would point the finger right back at them?"

"So, all the rest are random?"

"More or less."

Dean considered this for a minute or so. "That's a big smokescreen."

"If it's needed to hide the real victims," Sam said, "then, yeah."

"Like a sniper shooting up a crowd to disguise his main target."

"General idea," Sam said, nodding, "but our sniper isn't using bullets."

"So, we start looking for hex bags."

"Or we start talking to the victims," Sam said. "Figure out who'd put them on a hit list."

"Which victims?"

"Said it yourself," Sam replied. "Ignore the smokescreen and talk to the serious victims."

"Is Kelly Burke on that list?" Dean asked.

"Maybe," Sam said. "But I never asked her about enemies since she was eating lunch with her attacker. Think bigger."

"You mean—?"

Sam nodded. "County hospital," he said. "But we'll need a name."

Her name was Nancy Vickers, a twenty-four-year-old graphic designer at Thornbury Printing, a company founded by her great uncle almost fifty years ago but struggling to compete in the Internet age with multiple online DIY options. "But there's no craftsmanship and everything starts to have a sameness about it. Know what I mean? A blandness." She shrugged and winced in pain. "That's what happens when you start with a cookie-cutter foundation."

She sighed, adjusted her casted left arm, grimacing as she bumped her damaged ribs. "So, yeah, business is slow, but that's not news. And it's no reason to try to kill myself. I would never do that!"

"Okay," Sam said in a soothing tone. "Why don't you start at the beginning?"

When Dean and Sam had arrived on her floor, introduced themselves and asked to see Nancy, the charge nurse—Beth, per her name tag—seemed startled to see them. She stood within the C-shaped nursing station, telephone receiver in her left hand, the fingers of her right poised over the keypad.

"How did you know?" she asked. "I haven't even finished dialing Officer Gruber yet."

"Know what?" Sam asked.

"That Miss Vickers is awake."

"We didn't," Dean said. "Okay if we talk to her?"

"She woke up less than thirty minutes ago."

"We won't be long," Sam said. "Promise."

"And she'll need to go under psychiatric evaluation before she's released."

"Understood," Sam said.

"But I'm calling Gruber!"

"Good," Dean said. "He knows we're here."

Inside Nancy's private room, she took a few calming breaths before speaking again. "Okay, I'm ready," she said, "but there's not much to tell."

"Because you don't remember?" Sam guessed.

She looked between them. "How—How did you know?"

"Lot of that going around," Dean said.

"I don't understand."

"Tell us what you do remember," Sam said.

"Right, okay, well, I was driving to work, my morning commute," she said. "It's not far, but I live across town. Sometimes I'll stop for a coffee at the Gas-N-Sip. I prefer Bigelow's Bistro, but it's a bit out of my way and the wait's longer. Mostly it's the same routine. Know it like the back of my hand. And you know how you kind of zone out when you drive the same route all the time. Your brain goes on auto-pilot."

Dean nodded. While he had no regular commute, he'd

done enough driving to know what she meant by auto-pilot. Same thing happened on long, open roads.

Nancy reached for the control to raise her bed higher than the current forty-five-degree elevation, managed a steeper incline, then attempted to adjust her position and yelped in pain as she strained her ribs. She bit down on a knuckle while she rode a wave of pain.

"You okay?" Sam asked.

"It's hard to move at all without pain," she said. "Even breathing hurts, but I'll be fine… eventually. Besides, the pain helps me focus."

"It does?"

"Yes. No. Not really," she said. "But at least I'm alive."

"So, you were zoning out on your morning commute," Dean prompted.

"Right," she said. "The drive was mostly a blur and then nothing until I was falling…" She furrowed her brow and shook her head. "No, that's not right."

"What is it?" Sam asked.

"I remember—I remember what happened next!"

SEVEN

"That's great," Sam said. "What can you tell us?"

"At some point during the drive, I remember looking through the windshield and having no idea where I was. Nothing looked familiar. When I took my foot off the accelerator, I tried to get my bearings, to see a landmark…"

She stared across the room, focused on the surfacing memory rather than anything in front of her. "But it was random curiosity, like I didn't really care one way or the other. And then I…"

"What?" Sam asked. "What happened?"

"I… I pulled over to the shoulder, parked and got out of my car…"

"Why?"

She shook her head. "I have no idea."

"Where were you?"

"Halfway up the overpass incline," she said, almost trancelike as she relived the memory. "Jefferson Avenue. Must have been somewhere between Second and Fourth."

"What happened after you left your car?"

"I walked up to the overpass," she said, almost in disbelief as the words came out of her mouth. "There's a chain-link safety fence there and the top is slanted inward. Sometimes people attach flags to the fence and you can see them when you drive by below. Political signs too. And never one. Always in bunches. So annoying."

Knuckles rapped on the doorjamb.

Startled, Dean looked to his right and saw Nurse Beth standing there, a question on her face. "Everything okay in here?"

"We're fine," Sam said. "She's fine."

"My legs itch," Nancy said, back in the moment, free of the reverie. "And my arm. These casts are driving me nuts."

"I'll see what we can do," Beth said in a soothing tone.

As the nurse withdrew, Nancy called after her. "I'm really not suicidal!" She listened for a moment. Silence. "Damn it," she said to the Winchesters. "They think I'm crazy, don't they? Or terminally depressed?" She sighed. "This is nuts. Not me! The situation is nuts. All of it." She looked from Sam to Dean and back again. "You believe me, don't you?"

"We want to understand what happened on the overpass," Sam said, his calm and measured voice almost parroting the charge nurse's.

A safe approach, if they were assuming Nancy had attempted suicide of her own volition, but Dean had his doubts about that. If some external supernatural force was responsible for the odd, violent and suicidal behavior in Moyer, whether it was hex bags or something else, the victims would be as baffled as the police and the Winchesters at this point.

"You and me both," Nancy said. "So, where was I? Oh, right, walking up the overpass. There were no flags or signs. Just the fence. And the traffic rushing below. Everyone drives too fast on Jefferson. Act like it's the interstate or something."

"You climbed the fence," Dean said, attempting to get her back on track.

"I guess I did," she said softly.

"You don't remember?" Sam asked, disappointed.

"I… It's hard to explain," she said, her gaze beginning to lose its focus again. "I watched myself park the car and walk up to the overpass. Kicked off my heels and climbed the fence in my stockinged feet. And I struggled around that slanted top section of the fence, like a kid on a jungle gym. But I was watching myself from the inside."

"Help me understand."

"I had no thought, no control over my—what do the doctors call it—motor functions? I felt… removed. Like a passenger in my own body. I witnessed it happening. Yes"—she nodded—"that's the right word. I witnessed it—but I had no say in what I was doing in each individual moment or what happened next. I could see the details, but I couldn't feel—I couldn't feel *anything*."

"No sense of touch?"

"Emotions," she said. "I had no control over my actions, but I had no emotional response to them either. When I witnessed my body climbing over the safety fence, I guessed what was coming—I was about to fall or jump into oncoming traffic—but I had no sense of fear or dread."

"Could someone have drugged you?" Sam asked.

"Spiked your coffee?" Dean suggested.

"No," she said. "I was running late. Skipped the coffee pit stop. Figured I'd gulp down the bitter metallic crap Stewart brews in the office. But…"

"What?" Sam asked.

"Now that I think about it, you're right."

"Which part?"

"The sense of touch thing," she said. "The memory I have… it's visual only. I can't remember the feel of the chain-link fence or the smell of car exhaust or the sounds of traffic. And even my vision, the visual memory, it's like I was looking…"

"Through the wrong end of a telescope?" Dean asked.

She nodded. "Yes! I was numb. And everything seemed distant, even though it was happening to my body." Absently, the fingers of her right hand scratched beneath the edge of the cast that rose to her left elbow. "I clung to the other side of the fence for a moment. The drivers had only a few moments to notice me up there before they passed beneath. I could see some of them waving frantically, pounding on their horns, but I couldn't hear anything. Some swerved out of the lane right beneath me, others braked, some sped up to get by before I could—I jumped. No hesitation. Almost flung myself away from the fence. The fall lasted a split-second. I saw the cars rushing toward me in complete silence, the startled, horrified faces of the drivers convinced they were about to run over—kill me and then… darkness…"

"You blacked out," Sam said, nodding. "That's understandable—"

"No, the darkness rippled and flashed away, and everything rushed back into me, the suffocating smell of exhaust, the hiss and screech of tires, blaring horns, voices yelling and"— she closed her eyes for a moment and her body shuddered as if an electric charge blasted every nerve in her body simultaneously—"the pain! Oh, my God, I had been so numb to everything and in that one moment I felt my legs break, the sound and the give inside." Sweat began to bead on her brow. "A motorcyclist swerved away, narrowly missing me but the car behind him, squealing tires, the metal grill rushing toward—I flung out my forearm, in front of my face, squeezed my eyes shut, gritted my teeth—a blast of pain in my elbow, shooting up to my shoulder and collarbone and I could feel myself spinning, almost flipping aside and then... that's all I remember until I woke up briefly as paramedics strapped me to the ambulance gurney, hysterical, completely confused. I couldn't remember any of it. The last thing I recalled was leaving my home that morning, driving to work. I thought I'd been in a car accident, that it must have been bad and then everything faded away. I think I woke up a couple times here, but not for very long until about a half-hour ago."

"Wow," Sam said.

"Crazy, huh," she said with a lopsided grin. "The story, not me. I'm checking the 'Not Crazy' box on any forms they have me sign."

"No," Sam said. "When you started, you said there wasn't much to tell."

She smiled. "When I started, there wasn't... I mean, I

couldn't remember anything but driving to work and the few moments after I fell."

"You strained your ribs," Dean said. "When you started talking to us."

"You're right," Nancy said. "That pain, I guess it triggered the memories I couldn't recall. Maybe I was blocking it out, or didn't want to believe I could do something like that."

"Maybe," Sam said, thoughtful.

"But it's not like I'm secretly depressed or anything," she said. "I've applied for some design jobs in Jefferson City and Columbia. I have a few interviews scheduled…" She frowned, looked down at her arm and leg casts. "Interviews I'll never make it to now. If I'm not careful, I'll talk myself into a state of depression!"

"They're tech companies, right?" Sam asked.

"Yeah, why?"

"Maybe you can interview with video chat," he suggested. "Telecommute if you get a job."

"Maybe," she said, looking down at her broken and casted body doubtfully. "Eventually."

"This is gonna sound weird," Sam said before she could spiral into actual depression. "But, do you have any enemies?"

"Enemies?"

"Someone who might be glad you got hurt," Dean said. "Almost died."

"Someone who wanted one of those jobs," Sam suggested.

"God, no," she said. "The job market's bad but not that cutthroat."

"So, no enemies?"

"I design signs, marketing campaigns for businesses," she said. "I show them comps and they approve or ask for revisions. Even if the campaigns failed, I doubt they'd be coming after me."

"Relationship problems?" Dean asked. "Jealous exes?"

"First, that's kind of personal," she said. "And second, no, nothing like that. Wait, is this because you think someone drugged me?"

"We're investigating all possibilities," Sam said. "Someone with a personal grudge, business deal gone wrong, that sort of thing."

"Even if any of that happened, if I had a mortal enemy, how could that person make me jump off an overpass?"

Dean looked at Sam. Neither of them had an answer.

In the heart of Moyer's business district, Alice Tippin, a retired bookkeeper, left the Sweet Town Bakery and walked along the westbound side of Central Avenue, carrying a box of cupcakes for her niece's birthday party in her left hand, keys in her right. Since her retirement, she walked at least five miles a day, often with no destination in mind. Sometimes, however, she'd walk along the main strip of businesses for a little retail therapy. Mostly, she window-shopped. Because she lived less than a mile from the stores, she left her car at home. This day was no different. Out of habit and warnings from self-defense classes for women, she held her keys in her hand, apartment key clutched between her thumb and index finger. As she passed in front of a hair salon, she turned toward the window and stumbled when she saw only blackness.

Alice regained her balance and her head turned toward the curb. She veered toward the row of cars parked in all the metered spaces and her white-knuckled hand stretched out, key poking from her hand like a metal claw. One by one, she walked by the cars, minivans and SUVs and pressed the tip of the key into their paint, scraping a continuous line interrupted only by the spaces between the front and rear bumpers of each vehicle.

At the intersection, she paused beside a trashcan and dropped her keys to the sidewalk. She reached into the bakery bag and removed the box of cupcakes, untied the string wrapped around the box and proceeded to eat the cupcakes. She shoved the first one in her mouth, as if to eat the whole thing in one bite, smearing swirled icing on her lips and the tip of her nose. She tossed aside the liner and ate the next one in the same manner.

People walking past her on Central Avenue stared first in curiosity, then in apprehension, giving her a wide berth as she ate a half-dozen cupcakes with increasing messiness. Bored—or simply full—she dropped the uneaten cupcakes to the ground and heedlessly stepped on them as she made her way to the trashcan.

She looked down into the jumbled mound of debris for a moment, then reached into it, pushing aside fast food wrappers and cartons, empty soda cans and plastic bottles until her fingers curled around the neck of a whiskey bottle with a red "Paid" sticker from the Moyer Liquor Shoppe. Only a few amber drops remained. Nevertheless, she upended the bottle over her icing-coated lips and waited for them to drip onto her tongue.

When nothing remained of the liquor, she raised the bottle over her head again, but this time hurled it toward the windshield of the nearest car, a midnight-blue hatchback. The bottle shattered, leaving a starburst and one long crack in the windshield.

"Hey!" a man shouted behind her. "What the hell, lady!"

Alice staggered, suddenly aware that a gray-haired man had shoved her and was about to do so again. "Stop it!" she yelled at the man. "What are you—?"

She became aware of the cake and icing smeared all over her face, the crushed box of cupcakes at her feet near her discarded keys, and a slight feeling of nausea.

"What happened?"

Across the street, a few blocks away, one teenaged boy chased another, leaping from one parked car to the next. Each would land on the trunk of a car, bound over the roof across the hood and jump to the next car in a variation of the-floor-is-lava game. Hatchbacks and SUVs presented more of a challenge. If the pursued failed to make a jump or fell to the street, the roles and direction of the game reversed. Both teens laughed breathlessly, seemingly oblivious to cuts, scrapes and bruises.

After two reversals and extensive damage to two dozen cars, including a cracked windshield and several busted headlights and taillights, a good Samaritan rushed between two cars and tackled the lead teen in mid-air. They both collapsed in the street. One moment the teen was tense as a board, then he sagged, grumbling in pain.

The chasing teen, who had suffered a lacerated scalp during a previous fall, stopped on the hood of an old station wagon, kicked at the hood ornament, missed and fell on his rear with a metallic thump. Disappointed, he shook his head, flinging droplets of blood to either side. Then he too seemed to deflate, falling onto his side, moaning as he clutched the gash on his brow.

Miles away, Hal Greener, a Moyer mail carrier for almost ten years, drove his truck along the route he knew like the back of his hand. Minute by minute, he made stuttered progress, stopping at each mailbox along the sun-dappled streets to drop off letters and mailers, shifting into park when he had a box to run up to a welcome mat. Except for Christmastime, when the number of boxes increased significantly, requiring longer stops, he made his rounds like clockwork, starting and finishing within a few minutes of the same time every day.

Hal was less than thirty minutes into the day's route, in the shade of a maple tree, when his hand paused next to the slot of the Gallaghers' mailbox. Between his fingers he held several bills, a postcard advertisement and what looked like a birthday card for Susan, the Gallaghers' youngest child. They had five kids. Susan was the only girl.

The shade seemed darker than usual, obscuring Hal's vision. He tried to blink it away. His body trembled briefly and, convulsively, his hand crimped the letters and card. Then, instead of stuffing them in the mail slot, he tossed them high in the air. They fluttered to the ground like crude confetti.

The mail truck jerked forward, as if Hal had forgotten how to drive it. He weaved back and forth across the quiet street, never coming quite close enough to put any mail in a single mailbox. Instead, he grabbed each packet of mail in the tote on the front seat, yanked off the rubber band that bundled them, and flung them out the window, laughing hysterically as he left a scattered trail of undelivered bills, catalogs, magazines and advertisements. After a while, he started to toss the boxes, big and small, out the driver side window, making wide U-turns up driveways and onto lawns as he steered the wheels of his truck over each package.

When the last package had been delivered—somewhere on some street—he drove onto the state road, steered the mail truck into a drainage ditch and slumped over the wheel.

A moment later, with the truck listing at a forty-five-degree angle, he pushed himself back and fell sideways against the opposite door, wondering what trick gravity was playing on him. Nobody heard him mutter, "Where am I?"

The lunch crowd had thinned at Giogini's Ristorante by the time the Scheidecker party of six pushed back their chairs, gathered their belongings and left. They had run their server, Savannah Barnes, ragged with all their sides, add-on orders, drink refills and desserts, pushing their check well north of two hundred bucks, but she had smiled and stayed pleasant throughout, despite the rush and numerous distractions, especially after Jordan had called in sick at the last minute, nearly doubling the number of tables she had to cover. They'd hurried out while she'd been preoccupied. And she discovered why when she swung by their table with a serving tray under her arm and opened the check presenter. Above George Scheidecker's crimped signature, he'd brought down the total as-is, with a line drawn through the tip section of the check. Then she noticed some loose change by the candle holder, totaling $1.13 if she subtracted for the Canadian dime, not to mention the roach-sized blob of pocket lint he'd left behind for her.

By design, Giogini's ambient lighting was dim, even in the morning, but Savannah felt a darkness blot out her vision. She squeezed her eyes shut, frozen where she stood for a moment. The serving tray slipped from under her arm and crashed to the floor, startling the remaining diners.

Turning on her heels, she stormed over to a nearby table and grabbed a plate of spaghetti and meatballs as an elderly woman was about to sprinkle parmesan cheese on the mound of pasta. As she left with the plate, knocking a fork on the floor in the process, the woman called out to her.

"Miss, why are you taking my lunch?"

By the time the woman struggled her way out of the booth to follow her or flag down the manager, Savannah had shoved open the doors to the waiting area and exited the restaurant.

Savannah crossed the parking lot, the steaming plate of spaghetti and meatballs held aloft, and spotted the elder Scheidecker behind the wheel of a white SUV that looked as if it hadn't been washed in months. When he saw her, his eyes opened wide and he gunned the engine, rumbling toward the exit. She darted in front of him and hurled the plate at his windshield.

Pasta and marinara sauce splattered and clung to the

glass, blocking the driver's side. Meatballs slid down to the hood, rolling along the windshield wipers until Scheidecker flicked them on to clear the mess from his field of vision. But he never slowed, and Savannah jumped back to avoid a collision. The SUV surged into traffic, eliciting a barrage of horns and squealing brakes, before jumping the median and the opposite curb, clipping a bench and bowling over a trashcan.

Savannah waited for Scheidecker to come back, either to berate her, threaten to sue or lodge a complaint with her boss. She stood there waiting, a steak knife taken from his table clutched in her right fist, but he continued to put distance between his damaged SUV and Giogini's parking lot, driving well over the posted speed limit.

She blinked at a flash of light, looked down at the knife in her hand and followed the trail of spaghetti and meatballs leading out to Queen's Lane. Behind her, she heard her manager, barking her name repeatedly.

Finally, exasperated, she called, "Savannah! What's gotten into you?"

Savannah turned to face her. "Dina... what just happened?"

Gabe Longley, local barber, turned into the produce aisle of Moyer Market holding a plastic basket by the wire handle as he made his way to the organic section, stopping first at the peaches. A contingent of appreciative gnats hovering over the display elicited a frown of distaste while Gabe decided whether to move on to other offerings.

The overhead lights buzzed and flickered suddenly.

Gabe blinked at the sudden darkness.

He cast aside his empty wire basket, leaned forward and gathered as many peaches as he could within the embrace of both arms and pulled them all down to the floor. It looked as if someone had overturned a ball pit in a children's restaurant but, unlike balls, the peaches didn't bounce.

Unperturbed, Gabe whistled an improvised tune and skipped along the produce aisle, pausing to topple mounds of apples, oranges, cantaloupes and anything else round with the potential to roll.

Half a mile away, Chuck Wakely, a retired plumber, dropped the leash of his bulldog, Digby, and stared at the half open window of an old van with a faded mural on the side depicting a dragon or possibly a sea serpent.

Sensing something different about his owner, Digby whined and shuffled backward.

Unlocking the door, Chuck climbed into the van and proceeded to hotwire it, a criminal skill he'd neither acquired nor perpetrated in his entire life. He drove away, leaving a confused Digby behind. For the next five minutes, he veered into parked cars on both sides of the street with the apparent goal of ripping off as many sideview mirrors as possible, bonus points for every car alarm he tripped.

His earlier misgivings gone, Digby padded along the sidewalk, attempting to keep the receding van in his line of sight. When the van turned a corner, Digby barked nervously. Trailing his leash, the bulldog faithfully jogged through the carnage.

EIGHT

Sam and Dean stepped off the elevator at the ground floor of the county hospital and proceeded toward the exit. Dean had been quiet since they left Nancy's room. Probably trying to decide if her experience invalidated his hex bag theory. On the one hand, she seemed to have had no control over her actions from the time she parked her car until after she jumped off the overpass. Of course, Sam had to allow for the possibility she was in denial about a suicide attempt. He never claimed to be a psychiatrist, but his gut told him she hadn't tried to end her life. On the other hand, she had no apparent enemies, nobody in her life personally or professionally who might wish her harm let alone a brutal death. And of all the people who claimed to have no memory or control of their uncharacteristic actions, Nancy's incident had been severe enough to suggest she would have been a clear—and perhaps primary—target on any sort of hit list which employed the other pranks, indiscretions and acts of vandalism as a culpability smokescreen.

Of interest to Sam was the apparent ability of pain to pierce the veil of amnesia affecting all the victims. Dean had noticed that with the diner head-banger. And now the same thing had happened with Nancy. Initially, she had a complete gap in her memory, but a flare-up of pain from her cracked ribs unlocked a visual record of what happened.

Nancy had also told them she experienced no sensory or emotional connection to the event, from the time she parked her car on the shoulder until she leapt from the overpass fence. As if someone or something had hijacked the experience from her, leaving her with only the suppressed visual memory, like a subconscious record. She had referenced the common phenomenon of zoning out on the expected, ordinary details of a daily commute. The brain must register the details, even when someone can't recall passing a building or intersection they drive past each day. Visual white noise, cast aside as nonessential.

The memory suppression could be deliberate, Sam thought. *Or the natural result of having the immediacy of the peculiar actions blocked from our consciousness.*

"Dean, what if these people can't remember committing these acts because they weren't the ones committing them?"

"What?" Dean stopped and looked at him. "Somebody took their place? Body doubles? Or is angel possession back on the table?"

"That's not what I'm saying."

"Good, because last time I checked, angels need permission to take over," Dean said. "And, according to Cass, it's not easy for an angel to find a vessel strong enough to survive.

They break down fast or die immediately. That's a lot of time and effort for a bunch of angels to pull off some pranks."

"You're right, Dean," Sam said. "I don't get an angel vibe from any of this."

"So, what are you saying?"

"A different kind of possession," Sam replied. "What if something hijacked the experience from each, well, host. So, that in their minds—"

"The hosts' minds?" Dean asked, resuming his path to the exit.

Sam heard the wail of approaching sirens.

"Yes," he said. "The hosts don't have access to the memory because it wasn't their memory in the first place."

"So, something took their body for a psychic joyride?"

"I don't know," Sam said. "Maybe."

"Are we missing something?" Dean wondered. "Could it be demons?"

Sam shook his head. "Still not getting that vibe either. Streakers? Graffiti? Pranks? Demons have a much darker agenda. And when they grab a meat suit, they tend to be squatters. In it for the long haul. Besides, they're all about stealth, not drawing attention to themselves."

The automatic doors slid open with a *whoosh*.

"Doesn't rule out the possibility of a hit list."

"No."

The sirens were getting louder.

"Because, as far as experiences go—"

Two ambulances, red lights flashing, turned into the parking lot and followed the curved driveway up to the emergency room entrance. Several cars, minivans and SUVs followed in their wake, roaring up the ramp into the parking lot, front and rear bumpers perilously close to one another. Before they reached the parked ambulances, they split up in search of the nearest parking spaces.

Dean frowned. "This can't be good."

"Could be us," Sam said. "More weirdness."

Dean sighed. "I'm never getting out of this suit."

Paramedics had pulled open the double doors on both ambulances. Within moments, they helped several blood-spattered high-school-aged girls in team uniforms out of the back before unloading the gurneys carrying the more seriously injured. A few of the walking girls clung to lacrosse sticks, but most pressed bandages to bleeding foreheads, noses and ears, while others cradled injured shoulders and elbows. Tears streamed down some of their faces. One girl with a broken nose and a bludgeoned ear quietly sobbed as emergency room nurses and the paramedics guided them inside.

Sam and Dean hurried toward the ambulances.

Close behind them, the passengers from the cars that had followed the ambulances to the hospital made a beeline for the same entrance. Sam scanned the group. More injured lacrosse players, with less severe injuries, accompanied by concerned teachers and anxious parents.

Sam caught the shoulder of the last EMT out of the ambulance as he helped guide a gurney through the automatic doors. His patient writhed in pain with what looked like an orbital fracture of her right eye, a broken nose and a split lip.

"What happened?" Sam asked.

Without slowing, the paramedic appraised them in the blink of an eye. The Fed suits probably saved them from a cursory dismissal. "Who are you?"

"FBI," Sam said, not bothering to dig out his fake ID.

"FBI?" he asked. "What's the—Never mind. All I know is, team's coach grabbed one of their lacrosse sticks and started beating them with it."

Dean scanned the area. "Where's the coach?"

"Bus driver and the assistant coach held her down until the police came and took her away."

As the late arrivals flowed past the Winchesters, Sam heard a girl with a bleeding ear tell her mother, "Coach McDermitt said we weren't practicing hard enough. Called us losers."

Another girl, cupping her left elbow with her right hand, said, "She, like, literally had fire in her eyes."

Sam and Dean followed them into the crowded emergency room, now made more claustrophobic with the influx of new patients. Benches and chairs were scattered around the long U-shaped room, all occupied. A short hallway led back to curtained enclosures on either side, with a row of private offices at the far end.

The paramedics took the girls on the gurneys back to the curtained section. Other girls and their guardians lined up at four clerical stations and were rewarded with clipboards, pens and pages of forms to complete before their treatment. Emergency, the uninitiated soon discovered, was a relative term.

Some held bandages or icepacks to faces, limbs or other body parts. Others panted, short of breath, or moaned quietly. A young boy sobbed into his mother's shoulder.

A red-faced toddler, probably feverish, cried inconsolably as her grandmother rocked her and hummed a soothing song. A heavy man with a thinning pate and a ragged ponytail held a bucket between his knees, shoulders trembling as his stomach rumbled alarmingly. Along the far wall, which had a cutout for a long fish tank, a middle-aged man paced, clutching his side as he mumbled to himself.

Sam could count the number of suffering patients taking the long wait in their stride on the fingers of one hand. The overwhelming majority grumbled about the level of care and perceived incompetence on display.

Catching the attention of one of the nurses behind one of the clerical stations, Sam glanced at her nametag and asked, "Is this normal, Lindsay?"

"And you are?"

"Special Agents Blair and Tench," Sam said, indicating Dean with a tilt of his head toward the doorway. "FBI."

"Are you here to arrest someone?"

"No, not yet, anyway," Sam said. "Ongoing investigation."

"Well, to answer your question, nothing is ever normal here," she said bluntly. "But it's been better. This is definitely… not ideal."

"How long?"

"How long has it been like this?" she asked. "All day."

"Since the midnight blackouts?"

"Now that you mention it," she said, nodding. "Feels like we barely recovered from all those emergency calls. But these accidents and incidents are unrelated to whatever happened at midnight, obviously. Just seems like nothing's been right—

or, as you say, normal—since then. Lot of clumsy and angry people out there."

"Real nasty string of bad luck," said another nurse, who overheard their conversation as she passed by, clipboard in hand.

"Can't last, right?"

She stopped and stared at Sam. Her nametag read *Alexis*. "What makes you say that?"

Sam shrugged, almost taken aback by her negativity. "Law of averages."

"From your lips to God's ears."

The fluorescent lights above buzzed and winked out for a moment, casting a sudden shadow before flickering back on.

"That's all we need," Alexis said with a weary sigh. "Power outage in the middle of this mess."

"That's what backup generators are for," Lindsay said evenly.

"I'm sure they *never* fail," Alexis scoffed, and continued along the row of desks to pass through the counter gate and flap out into the waiting area.

Sam returned to where Dean waited by the doors. "Got their hands full."

"You think?"

"They've been swamped since the mass blackout."

"Maybe Gruber's right," Dean said. "About the connection."

"Makes sense."

Alexis escorted a lacrosse girl with a bleeding ear and scalp back to a treatment area.

As Sam and Dean walked toward the exit, Dean said, "Doesn't make it any easier to understand."

The pacing man paused mid-turn and shouted, "Hey, I was here before her!"

The nauseated man cradling the bucket looked up. "I've been here an hour."

"I've been here ninety-two minutes," an old woman said, in the middle of crocheting a scarf. "And I'm not getting any younger."

Dean walked through the exit when the automated doors opened, but Sam held back. The room had felt combustible after the arrival of the injured lacrosse players and now sparks were flying.

Around the crowded room, other patients voiced their frustration, a chorus of suffering.

"My son has a fever!"

"Half the people here have a fever, buddy!"

"This is bullshit!" yelled the pacing man. "My stomach is killing me."

"Your stomach?" said the nauseated man. "Here! Borrow my spew bucket!"

"Shove that bucket up your ass, pal!"

Another man, with a bruised cheek and puffy eye, approached the pacer and said, "Calm down, buddy. It's an emergency room, not a deli. You can't take a number—"

"Who asked you?" the pacer said, shoving the other man away from him.

"Tough guy, huh?" nauseated man said as he climbed to his feet and lumbered toward the formerly pacing man.

"Oh, no, Mr. Ponytail is gonna vomit on me."

"Don't worry," the other man said. "When I'm done, those

nurses will take you right back. No waiting!"

The former pacer picked up a potted fern and hurled it at him, aiming for his scalp. Nauseated man, swatted the projectile aside with his bucket, inadvertently flinging the container's contents on a large man in a leather jacket who had been dozing fitfully a minute ago.

"What the hell!" leather jacket shouted, flinging a strand of the other man's bile from his fingertips. "You son of a bitch!"

"Dean!" Sam called.

Leather jacket charged bucket man, driving him against the wall with a crash that cracked the glass of the long fish tank.

Dean returned, taking in the scene. "That escalated fast."

"Everyone, calm down!" Sam called.

"Bite me!" someone shouted.

"We're FBI," Dean shouted, flashing his ID and badge.

The pacer, who had jumped out of the way at the last minute, spun around and tripped over another man's outstretched leg. That man jumped up and shoved him. After climbing to his feet, the pacer bent over and bull-rushed him.

With all the shouting, hooting and fighting, Sam wasn't surprised nobody paid attention to him and Dean. The fight had a weird inevitability to it, spreading like a contact virus. Kicking feet and flying fists often missed their mark. Chairs fell over, people collided, offense taken at every turn. Each time someone slammed up against a wall or hurled a chair across the room, the fluorescent lights blinked on and off, shifting light and darkness across a sea of outraged faces. Existing injuries became more pronounced and serious contusions blossomed like flowers in time-lapse photography.

The fight reminded Sam of countless barroom brawls in classic Hollywood Westerns. It seemed oddly appropriate that the mass frustration of endless waiting would result in each patient requiring more immediate medical assistance. In that context, a group riot was almost logical.

Sam and Dean mutually concluded that the participants would not listen to reason—or threats of incarceration—and that the only way to stop the fighting before it became deadly was to physically intervene. They pulled combatants apart, stoically taking the odd punch or kick without retaliating. Even so, they were completely outnumbered.

Nurse Lindsay called for the orderlies, while Alexis dialed 911. An emergency room doctor surveyed the melee, hung back and grabbed the phone from Alexis.

Sam was holding leather jacket man back when he caught sight of an object hurtling toward him. By the time he realized it was the base of a table lamp, it struck his jaw and he felt his knees buckle.

NINE

As Sam fell to one knee, stunned, leather jacket man disengaged and moved to pick a fight with someone else nearby. But Sam swung his forearm, clubbing the man behind his closest knee, causing him to stumble. In a moment, Sam grabbed him and put him in a sleeper hold, retreating to a wall so nobody could attack him from behind.

From this new vantage point, Sam surveyed the emergency room. Since most of the people there had preexisting illnesses or injuries, the scattered brawls had a short half-life. Dean landed a solid punch in nauseated man's gut, which stopped the big man in his tracks. Collapsing to all fours, he vomited between his splayed hands, removing him from the fray he had helped instigate.

A few continued to wrestle and struggle half-heartedly, gagging, coughing or having re-opened clotted wounds. Several cowered behind overturned tables and chairs while others had retreated to the hallway between the curtained treatment areas. The toddler continued to wail back there.

One white-clad orderly stood between two contentious men, holding them apart at arm's length like a referee in a chippy boxing match. Another orderly, a man big enough to have played left tackle for an SEC contender, had pacing man in a headlock but he continued to struggle, despite a bloody and possibly broken nose, pulling ineffectually on the orderly's meaty forearm while simultaneously attempting to back-kick his shins.

"Listen, Mr….?"

"Davick," pacing man croaked, "Archie Davick."

"Luther Broady," the orderly said. "Pleased to meet you."

"Nothing pleasant about any of this!"

"Be that as it may, Mr. Davick," the orderly said, effectively oblivious to Archie's attempts to break free, "you need to settle down before I have Nurse Alexis over there stick you with some sleepy juice."

"I will not settle down," Davick croaked. "I demand immediate treatment."

"Everyone will get treatment."

"Not good enough," Davick said, continuing to struggle. "I plan to sue this hospital for every dime."

"You're free to take that up with your lawyer," Broady said. "But right now, I need you to be civil. Can you do that?"

"Right after I sue you for assault and battery!"

Sam lowered leather jacket man to the floor and stepped over his unconscious body. Out of the corner of his eye, he saw Gruber stride into the emergency room. With professional efficiency, the Moyer cop took in the situation with a sweeping gaze, pausing a moment to register Sam and

Dean before shifting his attention to Luther, the orderly, and Archie Davick.

"What the hell happened here?"

"Patients behaving oddly," Dean said. "The new normal."

"God, I hope not," Gruber said, his right hand dropping to his duty belt. "Luther? Everything under control here?"

"Far as I'm concerned, Officer Gruber," Luther said. "Mr. Davick here might have other ideas. Promised him some sleepy juice if he doesn't behave."

"Or I cuff him and give him a ride in the back of my patrol car."

"Works for me," Luther said. "What's it gonna be, Mr. Davick?"

"Let me go!"

Above them, an acrylic fluorescent light cover, which had been loose and dangling at one corner, slipped out of its track and fell to the carpet, while the light it had muted crackled and blinked rapidly. Startled, Luther momentarily lost his hold on Davick as shadows jumped and shifted across his face. Before Davick could pull away, Luther reached out and grabbed him by his shoulder. "Not so fa—"

Luther's eyes seemed to lose focus, as if he were stunned, then red light flickered in them for a moment, like embers in prodded coals. The transition happened so fast, Sam almost doubted what he'd seen.

He recalled the words of the wounded lacrosse player describing her enraged coach. *"Fire in her eyes."*

Is that what she saw?

Luther's big hands clamped down on Davick's shoulders,

painfully, judging by the way the smaller man winced.

When Luther spoke again, his voice was preternaturally deep, as if some otherworldly force was speaking through his towering body rather than Luther himself. *"Some need to fall in line. But some won't listen."*

"Please!" Davick gasped, his face ashen. "You're—hurting me!"

Sensing the sudden change in Luther's demeanor, Gruber stepped forward, a taser held in his outstretched hand. "Luther, that's enough," he said in a calm but firm tone. The taser's laser sights darted across Davick's body up to Luther's shoulder and neck area, but the shot was far from ideal. "Let him go. I'll take it from here."

"Let this set an example for all of you," Luther said, releasing Davick's shoulders long enough to grab his jaw in his right hand, the back of his head in his left and twist violently, snapping Davick's spine.

In the hallway, a woman screamed.

"Jesus, Luther!"

Luther released Davick's head. The man's limp body collapsed on the linoleum floor with a muffled thump. Reaching into his back pocket, the large orderly withdrew a folded hunting knife with a carbon fiber handle.

As he flipped open the steel blade, Gruber fired the taser. The cartridge popped. Electricity crackled as the probes struck Luther's abdomen and delivered five-thousand paralyzing volts. Luther's hand convulsed on the knife handle. He staggered forward without muscular control and collapsed, his body convulsing.

When his body struck the floor, the overhead lights flickered off and on several times. Luther's shadow jittered around his large body as if it too had been electrified. Then, as the light normalized, the shadow seemed to detach from Luther's prone form and dart away.

Noticing the odd movement of the shadow, Sam cast a concerned look at Dean, who nodded. He'd seen it too. Compared to a demon vacating a meat suit in a column of black smoke vomiting up from the host's mouth, the departing shadow was subtle enough to miss if you weren't looking for something odd. While Sam's brain wanted to chalk it up to a trick of the light or an optical illusion, something to dismiss as having no consequence, his hunter's instincts warned him to ignore it at his own peril.

After five seconds, the taser's electrical assault ceased and Luther lay still. Gruber wasted no time kneeling on the back of the orderly's legs and slipping a zip tie over his wrists. He released the expended taser cartridge and holstered the device.

"On your feet," Gruber ordered, hooking his hand inside Luther's right elbow to help him stand.

The emergency room doctor, who had hung back during the outbreak of violence, rushed forward to check on Davick, but it was too late for medical intervention. Davick's fate was sealed before his body struck the floor.

Wounded and scared patients climbed to their feet and came out from behind overturned tables and chairs, talking softly among themselves. Davick's death had shaken all of them, even those who had been active participants in the free-for-all battle. The worst offenders stood with hunched shoulders and downcast faces, hoping to avoid opprobrium and possible arrest. A few muttered, "What happened?" or "Do you remember?"

Sam moved beside Dean and whispered, "You notice his eyes?"

"Before the voice change?"

Sam nodded. "Something the girl said about her coach."

"'Fire in her eyes,'" Dean said. "I remember."

"Like the flash in a shifter's eyes," Sam said. The retinal flare in shapeshifter eyes was a bright gold rather than red, and their eyes appeared white on surveillance camera footage.

The doctor called Alexis to his side, where they conferred and adjusted the triage hierarchy based upon the additional wounds suffered during the fighting. He asked Stan, the other orderly, to grab a gurney and take Davick to the morgue immediately. Then, he told Lindsay to call the medical examiner. Before retreating to the treatment area, the doctor looked around the room. "For those who don't know me, I'm Dr. Machett, and I'm truly sorry all of you had to witness this horrifying incident." He looked toward Luther, who seemed confused more than anything else, as if he were caught in some dream of unwarranted persecution. "And I apologize for the circumstances that led to this... But I promise you, Mr. Broady will face the full wrath of the law for what he's done."

Frowning, Broady looked at Gruber and spoke softly. "Tom? What's he talking about? I tried to stop the fight before..."

"Quiet, Luther," Gruber said. "I plan to take your

statement—after I read you your rights. But we have dozens of eyewitnesses."

"To what?" Luther asked, perplexed. "What happened?"

"If you choose to stay," the doctor continued, "I will treat you. If you prefer to leave and seek care elsewhere, I understand."

As the doctor walked back to the treatment area, Gruber raised his hand to command everyone's attention. "Before you leave, I need to get contact information and take statements from all of you."

Some people groaned or muttered complaints, but a man had been murdered and numerous others had been assaulted, potentially resulting in numerous criminal charges and civil lawsuits. Considering they were in a room with a dead man and some of those present might be uncomfortable or traumatized by the incident, Lindsay suggested they use one of the hospital's conference rooms.

Gruber thanked her for the recommendation and turned to the Winchesters. "I'll call for backup, but I need to get Broady processed. And there's likely to be additional arrests. So, I'd like to get your statements first since you witnessed a good bit of this. That all right with you?"

Playing his role as an FBI agent, Sam nodded with an "of course" attitude, while Dean almost grimaced as he gave a half-hearted, "Yeah."

Not that Sam blamed his brother. By this point, they were certain something other than free will was responsible for Moyer's pranks, vandalism, assaults and, now, murder. Until they discovered and stopped the true cause of the disturbances, they had to follow the law enforcement playbook.

They backed away from the clusters of patients, seated and milling around, so they could talk in private. "We've come a long way from middle-aged streakers," Dean said grimly. "We need to figure out what this is."

"So far, we know it's something. But is it one something," Sam asked, "or many somethings?"

"Don't kid yourself, Sam," Dean said. "We're outnumbered."

"Yeah."

TEN

As darkness fell across Moyer, shadows cast by the surrendering sun stretched like taffy across pavement and blacktop, scaling walls and spanning fences. Everything solid and certain was tethered to a funhouse-mirror world, without weight or substance or continuity. Streetlights flickered to life, spawning temporary shadows riven by headlights. Security lights blazed, casting stark shadows unseen in daylight hours, while motion detectors presented temporary performances of light and shade when anyone crossed their path.

But in Moyer, not all shadows were beholden to substance and light.

They glided along streets, hiding in deeper darkness to avoid detection. Their outlines resembled humans rather than amorphous shapes, though the edges of most of them lacked definition and had the nebulous, ill-defined quality of a faded memory. Unlike their light-cast cousins, they existed in three dimensions, taking up physical space when their will was strong enough or when agitated, but their substance was as thready as the edges of their outlines, one of several states available to them.

Some followed people taking evening walks. The cover of night gave them the courage to venture throughout the neighborhood. What was one more shadow in a world of shadows and encompassing darkness? Barking dogs were ignored or chided for a false alarm. Some sensitive people experienced the feeling of being watched, the hairs on the nape of their neck rising.

At night, the free shadows of Moyer roamed along streets and alleys, seeking hosts. Though they had substance, they were adept at slipping through cracks and crevices and keyholes, like a persistent winter wind.

For them, houses and stores with locked windows and doors posed no real barrier. State-of-the-art security systems had no defense against the sliding darkness that moved like a stain across hardwood floors and carpets, walls and stairs. And the minds of those inside the locked and secured buildings were just as permeable, just as susceptible to invasion as the structures that sheltered them.

On the west side of Moyer, fronting long-neglected farmland, stood a sprawling clapboard farmhouse generously described as a fixer-upper. And though recently purchased, the fixing process had not proceeded sufficiently for any of the townspeople to notice improvements. The neglected house attracted a significant contingent of the free shadows. Viewed from far above, the activity around the house resembled a disturbed ant hill, with free shadows circling the house, slipping in and out of its many cracks and crevices.

By this time of night, all but one of the home's four residents were asleep. On the second floor, in the south corner bedroom, nine-year-old Ethan Yates sat cross-legged in the middle of his bed, the darkness of the room leavened only by a Scooby-Doo nightlight. Ever since Ethan woke up, Scooby's head had flickered off and on every few seconds. He hoped he'd remember in the morning to ask his mother to change the bulb.

For now, in the fluttery darkness, he was afraid to leave his bed, the only safe place in his room. With each wink of Scooby's light, he noticed them moving around his room. Large ink-spot ripples of blackness blotting out sections of his walls in passing, some floating to spill through gaps in the windowsill, others slipping across the ceiling, deeper than the darkness and layers of shadows that defined his bedroom at night.

He was not afraid of the dark; he was afraid of what overwhelmed the dark.

Whatever they were, they didn't speak to him. They reminded him of the mice that lived inside the walls of the last house. They also reminded him of a movie he saw, one that gave him nightmares, about people lost on a boat in the ocean, surrounded by sharks. Their dark, menacing shapes coursed silently through the water, always ready to attack, to feed on the people.

Because the dark shapes had the outlines of people but were not human, Ethan called them boogeymen. But not aloud, not to them. Instinctively, he sensed they were dangerous.

Something about the way they invaded his home, caring nothing for borders or boundaries. If strangers crept into a home, the owners called the police.

The boogeymen tolerated him but, as his father might say, they showed him no sign of respect. Yet they were aware of him. Occasionally, one would glide across the hardwood floor and come within inches of his face, studying him like he might examine a weird insect he'd trapped in an overturned jar. And each time one of them came within reach, Ethan fought the urge to squeeze his eyes shut and pray for it to leave. He made himself look back at the darkness, to try to understand it.

When they turned or circled him, he could see a thickness to them. They weren't simply dark spots. They took up space in the world, but it almost hurt to stare at them too long. Human eyes—his eyes, anyway—had trouble understanding how these things existed in the world. The edges of most of them, especially the hands and feet, blurred or became wispy, like smoke from an ashtray. On some, the edges almost seemed to vibrate in and out of focus. It made him think that they struggled to maintain their shapes, that if they relaxed too long, they would fade away, possibly unable to return.

He wondered if they could be aliens come to Earth to examine human beings. But how could they fly a spaceship? And they didn't look like any aliens he'd ever seen on TV or in the movies. No, they were boogeymen and they took the shape of people to hide themselves in the shadows of people. Not for the first time, Ethan wondered if only children could see their true form. Maybe adults only ever saw normal shadows where the boogeymen hid.

If Addie saw them, Ethan figured she would scream and wake their parents. And the boogeymen might hurt all of them. Ethan could be brave because he had a new friend, Barry. His friend had warned him they would come, so Ethan wouldn't scream for help. Ethan had protested, saying he would holler not scream. Screaming was for babies and girls in scary movies. Barry prepared Ethan, but that wasn't always enough. The boogeymen made Ethan nervous when they invaded his house. They appeared in his room, but he saw them leave through his door, slip through the gap between the bottom of the door and the floor, or flow through the keyhole. Ethan read once that rats could get through any hole, if it was big enough for their head to pass through. The widest bone in their body was their skull. The boogeymen had no bones. They could slip through the smallest crack.

So, Barry stayed close.

"Barry, you promise, right?"

He waited for Barry's answer, a whisper he could hear—but not with his ears.

"I know, but promise again," Ethan said. "Good. But you're here to protect me. Nobody's staying with Addie or Mom and Dad."

He waited again, listening to Barry.

"Yeah, but I feel bad. They're asleep and—"

Barry interrupted.

"I know they're supposed to stay asleep, but if one of the boogey—if one of them decides to—"

Ethan sighed at the response.

"'A promise is a promise,'" Ethan said, repeating what Barry had told him several times before. "But you're here and you can't control them. You told me so."

Ethan listened.

"For now, but that could change, couldn't it?"

Ethan nodded. He'd heard Barry's assurances before, but things had changed, hadn't they?

"What about the other people?" Ethan asked. "I saw it on the news. Mom and Dad talked about it at dinner. Is that… Is that because of them?"

Ethan waited through a long pause before Barry finally answered.

"I know you're not like them," Ethan said. "But they—they scare me…"

Ethan flinched as his doorknob turned.

He'd never seen the boogeymen move anything in his room. Other than Barry's assurances, that was the one thing that had calmed him during their nightly invasions. If they couldn't really move anything, maybe they couldn't hurt him.

The door swung inward and he sighed in relief when he saw his mother's face in the pale light. She wore a gauzy white nightgown and, if not for the pink ribbon decorating the neckline, she'd look like a ghost. "Ethan why are you still—?" She glanced at Scooby's flickering face. "What's wrong with your nightlight?"

"That's what woke me," Ethan said, making a show of rubbing his knuckles in the corner of his right eye. "It's dying."

As quick as the door had opened, the boogeymen sank back into the shadows, in the layered darkness, invisible to her. But Ethan thought he could find them. After a moment, his eyes located a few unmoving dark spots, black stains clinging to the floor, walls and ceiling.

He shuddered, as if he'd caught a chill or the flu. Utterly motionless, the boogeymen scared him now most of all. Somehow, he sensed how dangerous the moment was, with his mother awake, inches from some of them. Despite his earlier protests, what his mother did next almost made him scream.

She flipped up the wall light switch.

When the overhead light blazed to life, Ethan thought for sure they would kill his mother, and then him so there would be no witnesses. And then Addie and finally his dad. The police would come in a few days and find them all murdered. He squeezed his eyes shut, half to shield his eyes from the sudden burst of light, but also in fear of what would happen in the next few seconds.

Slowly, he squinted his eyes open. The darkness and the shadows were mostly gone, some clinging behind the door, on the far side of the bed, near the windows. No longer were the boogeymen evident. They'd somehow made their dark shapes disappear or blend in with the lighter shadows.

"I'll look for a new bulb in the morning," she said. "But you need to get to sleep, young man."

"Okay, Mom," he said, trying to suppress the quaver in his voice.

She started to close the door, then paused. "I thought I heard you talking to someone in here."

He spread his hands and chuckled nervously. "I'm all alone."

"Yes, you are."

"Talking to myself, I guess," he said. "Had trouble falling asleep."

"Well, keep your eyes closed and you won't notice the blinking light so much."

"Okay, Mom."

"Goodnight," she said. "Love you."

"Love you, Mom." After she turned off the overhead light and pulled the door closed, he called out, "Be careful, Mom!"

He waited a moment, listening to her footfalls as she returned to his parents' bedroom. Once he was sure she was gone, he whispered, "Barry? Are you still here?"

He listened. "Good, I thought she might have scared you off."

Glancing around his room, he saw only normal shadows and darkness. Across the room, Scooby continued to flicker, but much less often. Ethan flopped onto his stomach and pushed himself to the edge of the bed, hanging over it far enough to lower his head and look under the box spring.

When Barry visited, he preferred to stay under the bed. Even when they talked, Barry never came out in the open. He told Ethan when they first met that he looked different and didn't want to scare him. Under the bed, Barry had the cover of darkness. The glow from the nightlight reached only the edge of the bed, not all the way under.

Looking at Barry upside down, Ethan couldn't see details of his face or make out too many details about his body. He was a darkness in the shadows. Ethan sometimes caught glimpses of his friend, the slope of a nose, the curl of fingers, the hump of a knee as Barry shifted around under the bed but no more than that.

"They won't hurt Mom, will they?" Ethan asked. "It's my fault she woke up. Promise me they won't take it out on her?" He waited for Barry's answer. "Good. Thanks, Barry."

Ethan had decided Barry was related to the boogeymen in some way. He had to be familiar to them if he talked to them and asked them not to bother Ethan or his family. But unlike the boogeymen, Ethan trusted Barry and enjoyed his company. After all, dogs were a lot like wolves, but Ethan wasn't scared of dogs. Most dogs were friendly. Wolves were dangerous.

"Okay, I guess I should go to sleep before Mom comes back."

Ethan righted himself on the bed, laid back and rested his head on his pillow. After a moment, he closed his eyes and waited. He counted silently to ten, then opened his eyes just a bit, to get a peek.

Barry rose from beneath the bed, shaped like a normal person, but made of darkness. Definitely taller than Ethan if they stood side by side. He'd had the feeling Barry was older than him. Like an older brother. As Ethan waited, squinting into the darkness and at Barry's deeper darkness, Barry didn't move. Ethan thought he might say something more, but he only seemed to turn away and glide toward the window, his leg shapes flowing in a crude animation of human legs, pretending to support weight as he crossed the room. But unlike any human, Barry slipped through a gap in the windowsill and disappeared into the night.

ELEVEN

Weary from a long day investigating and witnessing the confusing and destructive behavior permeating the town, and after over an hour of questioning from one of Moyer's finest, Dean and Sam checked into the imaginatively named Moyer Motor Lodge. Without heading back to the interstate and driving to the nearest rest stop or—God forbid—booking a bed and breakfast, there weren't a lot of rooming options. The Delsea Lake Inn was cheaper with a much better view, but Gruber mentioned a recent bedbug infestation that management claimed to have eradicated. Nevertheless, he advised them to "proceed with caution."

So, the Moyer Motor Lodge it was.

Dean couldn't wait to finally ditch the Fed suit. He'd whipped off his tie, folded it and tucked it in a jacket pocket while waiting for the room key. Standing there, he'd noticed that instead of paintings, the lobby had enlarged decades-old photos of people vacationing by a scenic lake. The prints had faded, the colors almost entirely bleached away.

In a way, the framed photos mirrored the general state of the motel. Small areas of disrepair had gone untended. A quick perusal revealed marks on the walls, scuffs on the floors, worn carpet, chips in wood surfaces. If Dean had to guess, the motel had fallen on hard times a while ago and continued to teeter on the brink of insolvency. But it was, thankfully, free of bedbugs.

The brass plaques on the frames of the bigger prints mentioned Lake Delsea and the month and year of the photo. Not much after the mid-Seventies. Out of idle curiosity, Dean asked, "Nothing recent?"

"My mother took those back in the day," the balding clerk said. "Besides, the lake's been closed to tourism for decades."

Dean recalled that Pangento chemical spills—or possible toxic dumping—had soured everyone on the lake. The spill may or may not have been intentional, but the chamber of commerce had been unable to salvage Moyer's tourism reputation. Instead, Moyer became a chemical factory town.

"Reclaimed wilderness now."

"What?" Dean asked.

"Lake Delsea," the clerk said. "Overgrown. Main pier's still there. And some of the summer shops and shacks. Mostly, it's a teenager hangout."

"Oh?"

"Yes, sir," he said. "They go there to drink, do drugs. The cops found paraphernalia there. Busted a few kids. 'Bout a year ago, one of them got drunk, took a swim on a dare and drowned. Lot of people say the lake's cursed."

"Is that so?"

"If you believe that kind of thing," the clerk said with a shrug. "Personally, I won't swim in the lake."

"You think it's cursed?" Dean asked, intrigued. Could Lake Delsea have some connection to the weird behavior plaguing the town? "Haunted?"

"No," he replied. "I think it's polluted. And I'd rather not swim in toxic sewage, thank you very much."

"Well, that's understandable."

"Oh, Pangento say they cleaned it up but I don't trust them."

Dean smiled. "Not a company man?"

"Hell no," he said vehemently. "They broke this town once. And if they ever pull up stakes, Moyer would become nothing but a ghost town. That bunch! No regard for anything but their bottom line." He shook his head for emphasis. "I'd leave sooner than work for them."

"A man of principle."

"You know it," he said and slid a key fob across the counter. "Room 142. Two doubles."

"Make a friend?" Sam asked as they carried their overnight bags down the walkway to their room. "You were in there a while."

"Hearing lore of the haunted Lake Delsea."

"Really?"

"Not unless pollution attracts more ghosts than juvenile delinquents."

"You know, Dean, we could call Mick," Sam suggested. "Maybe the Brits have seen something like this before."

"No way, Sam," Dean said. "This one's you and me. No

interference. Whatever this is, we'll figure it out on our own."

Dean unlocked the door, unsurprised to find the walls hung with more photos from Lake Delsea's glory days. At least one duplicate of a lobby photo, but the colors had lasted longer in the room's print. Less sun exposure. And yet, just as depressing. Almost felt as if the motel itself was haunted, that they had stepped back in time to a bygone Moyer when the whole world waited impatiently for the death of disco.

Lacking the energy to ditch the Fed suit, Dean picked up the TV remote and plopped onto the nearest lumpy bed, flicking through a limited selection of channels with the sound on mute. Sam filled a glass with water from the faucet, took a sip and frowned.

"No good?"

"Well water, maybe."

"Or a Pangento cocktail."

"Remind me to pick up some bottled water," Sam said as he held the glass up to the lamplight.

Dean had no idea what his brother expected to see in the water, but if it was that bad, Dean planned to survive on beer, either canned or bottled.

Sam pulled out a chair from a utilitarian desk and sat with his arms crossed over the back. "So, what do we think?"

"If I hadn't seen Orderly Red-eyes," Dean said, "I'd put money on a toxic mutant."

"The weird shadow movement," Sam said. "The flicker of red in the eyes right before the orderly's voice changed, before *he* changed."

"Same as the lacrosse coach," Dean said. "If we believe random lacrosse girl."

"No reason not to," Sam said. "From the beginning, people here have been acting out of character."

"After the midnight blackouts."

"Right," Sam said. "My gut told me we were dealing with something that stripped away people's inhibitions."

"And their clothing," Dean said, referencing the streakers.

"Acting without filters, no restraint," Sam said. During their debrief in the hospital conference room, Gruber mentioned incidents that hadn't yet made the news, including the restaurant server tossing a plate of spaghetti and meatballs at the windshield of a bad tipper, and the mail carrier who decided delivering mail to mailboxes was less satisfying than tossing it in the street and driving over it. "Even giving into their baser impulses. Worst case, something is unleashing their ids. Everyone has a dark thought now and then, but some of these people are acting out their worst impulses."

"'Told' you?" Dean asked. "Past tense. What changed your mind—or gut?"

"Talking to Nancy about the attempted suicide. I don't think that was a suppressed impulse brought to the fore."

"The psychic joyride," Dean said, nodding. "And the hidden hit list."

"But she had no enemies."

"That she knew of," Dean said. "Revenge is a dish best served cold."

"Today, in the emergency room, was totally random," Sam

replied. "That orderly did not act on a dark impulse. And how could the so-called hit list maker know that Davick would get frustrated with the wait, pick a fight, and make himself a target for that orderly?" Sam shook his head. "For those few moments after Luther's eyes flashed red, something else was at the wheel."

"We've already agreed the streaking, pranks and vandalism incidents don't fit the demon MO," Dean said. "What about a trickster? They love mischief, pranks. And murder's not a deal-breaker."

"Not their style," Sam said. "What did Bobby say? They target the high and mighty to bring them down."

"Nothing high and mighty about a graphic designer or an orderly," Dean agreed.

"And that trickster sense of humor is lacking," Sam said. "Even a gallows sense of humor." Dean opened his mouth to interrupt, but Sam cut him off. "Other than the streakers."

"So, where's that leave us?"

Sam spread his arms wide. "Back to the lore. Follow the possession angle. Something that takes control of human hosts."

"What if time is a factor?"

"How so?" Sam asked, finally pulling off his own necktie.

"The possessions have been short," Dean said. "A few seconds up to an hour tops. Maybe they can only maintain control for a limited amount of time."

"Streakers may have lasted the longest," Sam said. "Maybe extreme behavior causes them to lose control faster. If they tap into what the host secretly would like to say or do, they stay in the driver's seat longer. But if they try to kill the host or have the host murder someone, the host rebels enough to force them out."

"Like having a pleasant dream versus a nightmare," Dean said. "You want the dream to last, but the nightmare can't end fast enough."

"Speaking of nightmares," Sam said, sniffing the sleeve of his jacket. "I still smell that puke bucket."

"Gift that keeps on giving."

"Mind if I take the shower first?"

"Be my guest," Dean said.

While Sam changed and showered, Dean hung up his own suit jacket and pulled out the laptop. He'd leave the lore-sifting to his brother. While they talked, he'd had an idea on how to prove the mass blackouts were connected to the bouts of mischief and mayhem that followed. Television news had the attention span of a toddler, always focusing on the shiny new thing. A fire here, a car crash there, hazy security footage of a convenience store robbery after the break. Local papers, if they were still in business, were short-staffed and had to make coverage choices wisely. But the Internet, the great accumulator, could fill in the gaps. Any stories he'd missed or that had been covered well after the fact would have an online home. Even blog posts sometimes served a purpose. Once you weeded out the flat-earthers and tinfoil hat society.

First, he examined any article or blog post covering the short period between the mass blackout and the initial reports of odd behavior, combing through the online police blotter for Moyer. Anything that didn't raise an eyebrow, he skipped. He examined human interest stories, came across an article about a nearby 5K race to raise money for a local boy who needed surgery. Judging by the finish-line pictures, it was not a clothing optional run. And, of course, the usual fires, car accidents and shoplifting sprees. Nothing meriting a raised eyebrow until the weirdness began. And much of what he'd heard about from Gruber hadn't been covered anywhere yet, either formally or in social media posts.

If nothing had happened to trigger the mischief after the blackout, maybe it happened before the blackout. Skipping back a week, with the benefit of foresight, he looked for any stories leading up to the blackout that might have been a harbinger of what was to come. He moved forward, day by day, skimming articles, seeking anything related to fainting, loss of consciousness or random bouts of narcolepsy. Whoever or whatever was responsible for knocking out the whole town at once may have had a trial run beforehand to work out any kinks.

He examined the police blotter again, checked their social media presence on the off chance any locals reported anything odd there. Seemed like a lot of people lived most of their waking lives on social media, so reporting something there rather than calling 911 might seem perfectly natural to them.

As he came closer to blackout day, he despaired of finding any connection between the blackout and the dirty deeds that followed. But not establishing that connection felt like ignoring the elephant in the room. They all agreed the events were connected and they were staring right at them, but the explanation remained elusive.

Social media finally arched his eyebrow when he read of an explosion in the hours of the afternoon before the blackout. Something big enough and loud enough to be heard by multiple people, though some didn't realize it at the time. Police investigated and discovered the explosion had been caused by old, unstable dynamite stored in the rotted loft of a barn on a long-abandoned farm. Apparently, a lightning strike during an afternoon storm dislodged one of the crates, setting off the explosion. Only those in homes nearest the blast distinguished the explosion as a separate event from the storm. Everyone else assumed lightning blew a transformer. Nobody had been present or injured at the barn. And the police disposed of the rest of the dynamite with a controlled explosion.

Disappointed, Dean shoved the laptop away. "Frigging dead end."

Sam emerged from the bathroom in street clothes, his hair wet. "What is?"

Dean explained his fruitless search for a connection.

"Lore?"

Passing the digital baton to his brother, Dean said, "All yours."

Sam settled down at the narrow desk with the laptop. From open browser tabs, he saw that Dean had been looking into possible causes for the midnight blackouts, including an article about an explosion of unstable dynamite on an abandoned farm the afternoon before the incident. Curious, Sam checked the address against county records. The owner, Martin Warhurst Jr., had died last year, and the property was currently tied up in probate court. Martin had inherited the farm and land over forty years ago, when his father died, but he'd stayed in New York and never worked there himself. The explosion was due, in part, to the long-term neglect of an absentee owner who lived most of his life a thousand miles from Moyer—an owner who had died the better part of a year ago. Hard to see any connection to the blackouts eight hours later. No wonder Dean considered the lead a dead end.

Rather than waste any more time down that rabbit hole, Sam decided to course-correct with research relevant to the shadows. Wading through the mass of supernatural lore could take months for the uninitiated. Hunters had an advantage. Experience. And the Winchester family had decades of experience. You saved a lot of time when you knew what was irrelevant.

Focusing on the jittery shadows and the red eye flares, Sam searched his bookmarked sites. Only a couple minutes into his search, his phone rang, breaking his concentration. "Yeah," he said, distracted, then recovered, remembering his cover identity. "Go for Agent Blair."

Gruber's voice. "It's official," he said, sounding weary. "I'm never leaving this hospital."

"Job offer?" Sam asked.

"Funny," Gruber said, a smile coming through the line. "But no. I'm still a cop, unfortunately."

"What happened?"

"Patient decided to perform liposuction on himself."

"I assume the patient was not a doctor."

"Truck driver," Gruber replied.

"Not ideal."

"With kidney stones," Gruber added. "Liposuction wasn't scheduled."

"Is he okay?"

"Passed out from shock and blood loss. Or both," Gruber said. "Point is: I couldn't question him."

"That's not why you called."

"No," Gruber admitted. "I found some security footage I'd like to run by you and your partner."

"What is it?"

"I think it's better if you see it yourself."

"Be there in fifteen minutes," Sam said. "Thirty, tops."

"Who's got two thumbs to twiddle?"

"Funny," Sam said and disconnected.

The shower cut off as Sam rapped on the bathroom door.

"Dude, you had your turn," Dean called. "Find something?"

"No," Sam said, "but Gruber wants our opinion on something."

Dean opened the door, a towel wrapped around his waist. "Something?"

"Security footage."

"Couldn't wait?"

"Apparently not."

"I'll drop you off," Dean said and closed the door again.

"Not interested?"

"It's not that," Dean called through the door. "I want to interview more blackout victims."

"Any particular reason?" Sam asked as he closed the laptop and slipped it into its case.

"We're missing something," Dean said. "Out there

somewhere, somebody saw it or heard or experienced it—and remembers. And anyone working that shift is probably working now—or soon will be."

"Makes sense."

Dean stepped out of the bathroom and grabbed the car keys.

The long day continued into night, but at least Sam had rid himself of the bucket odor. As they climbed into the Impala to go their separate ways, Sam made a mental note to have their suits dry-cleaned.

TWELVE

Gruber met Sam in the hospital lobby and walked with him to the security office.

To pass the time, Sam asked, "So, how did the truck driver get his hands on a scalpel?"

"Not a scalpel," Gruber said. "Pocket knife from his jeans. And, obviously, he didn't bother to sterilize the damn thing. Or his hands, which he used to reach inside his gut and... Never mind, you probably don't want to know the details. Doctor says if the wound doesn't kill him, the inevitable staph infection will. They're pumping him full of antibiotics."

After a moment, a security guard let them in, then excused himself to grab a cup of coffee. Gruber sat at a desk facing a computer with security footage frozen on it. Grabbing the nearest chair, Sam positioned himself to Gruber's left.

"Show me," he said.

"We have recorded footage from two cameras in the emergency room," Gruber said. He switched to a split-screen view and played the recording from the two cameras side by side. One camera had a view from the fish tank wall toward the restrooms and the hallway leading back to the curtained treatment areas; the other camera faced the front of the emergency room from behind the clerical station. The time stamps on both playbacks matched and they picked up moments before the fighting began. Both cameras recorded in black and white. Neither recorded sound, but it was evident that an argument had begun even before the ponytailed man with the vomit bucket climbed out of his seat and turned to face Archie Davick.

"That's Cal Bonkowski with the bucket."

As Sam remembered, the fighting escalated quickly from the moment Cal's bucket splashed leather jacket man.

"Biker-chic there is Augie Mills."

The fighting spread like a brushfire after a long drought. The slightest contact set people off, shoving, punching, kicking. Nobody turned the other cheek. And it soon overwhelmed the room. Sam watched the digital recording of himself and Dean, attempting to break up combatants, stop squabbles before they turned violent and bloody. But no sooner had they pried apart two fighters than another pair squared off. In spots, whole groups clawed and punched and kicked each other, in what looked like an ultraviolent rugby scrum.

"What am I looking for?"

"Focus on the fighters who never give up," Gruber said. "Some never stop until they are unconscious, cuffed or zip-tied. The others seem to get swept up in the madness but—"

"They bail at the first opportunity."

"All it takes is one good punch, a solid kick, a bloody

nose," Gruber said, "and they decide enough is enough. That's what I'd call normal behavior. Everyone's tough until they get punched in the mouth. They're willing to see reason at that point."

"The ones cowering behind overturned chairs and tables."

"You and Tench are in the middle of the worst of it," Gruber said. "By choice. You put yourselves in harm's way. But I think you were too close to the action to see what was happening with the others."

"So, some had the stomach for it," Sam reasoned, "to keep fighting, while others called it quits. Makes sense. They were already hurt or sick."

"Normally, I'd agree with you," Gruber said. "But some who kept fighting were in worse shape than some who tagged out. Bonkowski could barely keep himself from heaving in his bucket until the fight started."

Sam thought it possible that whatever possessed the Moyer residents had control of those who refused to quit, but he couldn't really make that point with Gruber. If he started talking about possession, he had a good idea where the conversation would lead. Instead, he asked, "You see a pattern?"

"I made a list of the fighters and the quitters," Gruber said. "I know a bunch of them—Moyer's a relatively small town and I make a point to know the residents—and the ones I don't know, I looked up while I was waiting to talk to Mr. DIY Liposuction."

"This is a county hospital," Sam said. "Are we outside the city limits?"

"Yes, we are," Gruber said.

"They're all from Moyer," Sam guessed. "The fighters?"

"Every single one," Gruber said, nodding. "A few of the quitters are from Moyer, but most are not. Majority are from here, Bakersburg."

"Was anyone outside Moyer affected by the blackout?" Sam asked.

"Been asking around," Gruber said. "So far, nobody outside Moyer lost consciousness at midnight."

"So, whatever it was, it specifically targeted Moyer residents."

"How is that even possible?" Gruber asked. "If you draw an outline around the town's borders, it's not a perfect circle, not even a square. Looks more like a long rectangle on end, tilting east. You can't release a chemical agent or anything else dead center and limit the effects to the border but not beyond."

Sam thought he'd noticed something during the playback of the security footage, but needed confirmation. "Can you replay that?"

"The whole thing?"

Sam nodded. Gruber zipped backward to the first argument, then hit play.

Sam watched as the bickering and threats between Davick and Bonkowski turned into an emergency room riot. But this time, he kept his eyes attuned to the Moyer fighters, the ones who wouldn't quit until unconscious or forcibly restrained.

Gruber leaned toward the screen. "What do you see?"

"Look at their faces," Sam said, pointing. "Whenever they take a hit to the face, punch to a kidney, or a kick to a shin."

Nodding, Gruber said, "Their faces never seem to change."

"They were sick or injured before this began," Sam said.

"But you'd never know it. While they fought, they didn't feel pain."

"Huh."

"But later, after the fighting ends, they seem to feel the new wounds, wincing, clutching their sides, rubbing bruises, hands pressed to facial lacerations."

Sam wondered if whatever possessed the Moyer residents could switch off pain receptors. Maybe they could live the experience à la carte. Emotions switched on, pain awareness nullified. That might be a way to make the experience— the joyride—last longer. Unfortunately, once the intruder vacated the body, the human host suffered the consequences of the ordeal. Legal, physical… and mental.

THIRTEEN

Dean stopped at the diner first. Pete, the short-order cook, worked his normal shift, but had nothing new to add. No additional memories unlocked beyond the momentary recovery when he burned his forearms before sinking back into unconsciousness. True to her word, Marie had refused to cover Donnie's shift. Whether the young man had another case of true love or a hot date lined up for the night, he was stuck doling out late-night meals. Before the blackout, he and his date had too much to drink and fell asleep watching a streaming horror movie before the clock struck midnight.

"Wouldn't have taken much to knock me out even if I'd been awake," he said as he filled a serving tray. "We'd planned to go to Gyrations later, zone out to some EDM, but never made it."

Not a fan of electronic dance music, Dean figured the kid was lucky but declined to tell him so. Instead Dean asked him to point out any regulars who might have been in the diner the previous night. A few, sporting fresh bandages, were easy to spot. Dean made a circuit of the diner.

Gabe and Linda, a couple who looked like they had ordered one of everything from the menu, made it through the witching hour relatively unscathed. They'd been sitting in the same booth waiting for their order. Both had merely slumped unconscious in the booth, unlike their unlucky server, Marie.

Henry Addison, who napped throughout the day but could never seem to sleep through the night, sipped from a bowl of tomato soup and told Dean he'd simply toppled off his stool. "Sad to say, I knocked Mabel James off her stool as well," he said. "I'm afraid it's my fault she's laid up with a sprained ankle."

None of them experienced the brief wakefulness Pete had. None had any warning before the event. Wherever they had stood or sat, they all went down hard. And they all awoke within seconds of each other.

Taking another tack, Dean asked them if they recalled anything usual happening in the days leading up to the midnight event. A few mentioned the afternoon thunderstorms, but nothing stood out.

Dean ordered a slice of blueberry pie, had it boxed and took it to go. He recalled the last time he'd had blueberry pie. Sam had been kidnapped and tortured for information by Lady Bevell—an early black mark against the British Men of Letters. After they rescued Sam and returned to the bunker, their mother bought Dean a delicious blueberry pie. He smiled, and wondered what she was doing now.

He stopped next at Placko Products and talked to the front desk security guard, asking about the reports of casualties after the blackout. Beyond the guard station, Dean heard the rumble of conveyor belts and the continual beeping of forklift horns. If he stayed much longer, he thought the sound might drive him crazy. But maybe it became one more layer of white noise in the factory.

Ed Brunson, a site manager instructed the guard to "give Agent Tench a visitor badge" and then he took Dean on a tour of the facility. The Placko employees experienced a series of minor injuries and one deadly one. A night shift supervisor had died during the incident, falling down a metal staircase that gave access to a catwalk that overlooked the forty-foot high warehouse.

"Horrible accident," Ed said as they stopped near the stairway. "Larry was a great guy. Been here since day one. The way it happened…" He looked up the stairs and Dean thought he detected a slight shiver of dread. "Could have been any one of us working that shift."

"Where were you when it happened?"

"In my office," he said. "One second, I'm checking our numbers on the computer. Next thing I know my face is mashed on the keyboard."

Dean talked to a few of the employees, several who had suffered some bumps and bruises and heard more of the same. No warning, no recall. He turned in his visitor badge and returned to the Impala.

"Frigging wild goose chase," he muttered softly as he shoved the key in the ignition. The motor turned over, rumbling reassuringly. He could always count on Baby.

Glancing at the empty seat beside him, he wondered if

Sam had had better luck reviewing security footage with Gruber. If he had, he probably would have checked in with Dean. Before deciding on his next move, he glanced at the box from the diner and decided a slice of pie might provide some investigative inspiration.

With the car idling, he wolfed down the pie and tossed the plastic fork in the box. "Thanks, Donnie," he said, finally deciding to return to the motel and wait for Sam's call. If his brother had been staring at security footage all night with nothing to show for it, Dean doubted a second pair of tired eyes would unlock Moyer's mysteries.

He flicked on the radio, which he'd already tuned to the local classic rock station, and shuddered at Donnie's taste in music. But, that gave him an idea. Donnie had mentioned scrapped plans to go to Gyrations last night. He wondered what happened when everyone on a crowded dance floor took a dive in the middle of an EDM set. With rapid movement, the potential for injury probably increased. And if some of those dancers had been drinking alcohol or using illicit drugs, or a combination, their experiences with the blackout might have been altered in a way that would give some clue how the whole thing went down.

Of course, if repeatedly beeping forklifts had rubbed his nerves raw, he had no idea how long he could tolerate EDM purgatory. *Oh, well. Nobody ever said hunting was easy.*

A neon sign spelled out the dance club name on its widest wall. To the right of the word Gyrations, blue and pink outlines of neon dancers—not much more than stick figures—shifted back and forth. Rather than a passable demonstrating of gyrating, the binary motion of the stick figures looked more like the hokey pokey. As Dean pulled into the parking lot, the music blasting from inside the club overwhelmed a Clapton guitar solo coming from his car speakers as several people stepped outside to smoke a cigarette. Reluctantly, Dean switched off the ignition and the stereo.

"No turning back now," he muttered as he crossed the parking lot to enter the black-and-silver building.

In the lobby, a perky hostess in a glittery silver dress requested a cover charge in exchange for a wristband entitling him to two free drinks. Instead, Dean flashed his FBI credentials and said, "Official business."

"Oh," she said, surprised, her smile faltering. "Can I help?"

The building vibrated with repetitive, pulsing electronic music. He could feel it through the soles of his boots. Though tempted to say neighbors had filed a noise complaint, he asked if she'd worked the previous night during the blackouts. But that had been her regular night off, and she'd been home all night, in Bakersburg. He noticed a small black ribbon pinned to her dress and inquired about it.

"In memory of Lettie Gibbs," she said. "One of our servers. She died last night."

"What happened?"

"It was awful," she said, momentarily covering her mouth. "They said she fell and—and she sliced her throat on a broken champagne bottle. By the time everyone woke up…"

"You know her?"

"Of course."

"I'm sorry for your loss," Dean said. "I'd like to talk to

anyone who was here when it happened."

"Sure," she said, and waved him down a short hallway decorated with flashing, multicolored, multidirectional neon piping that ended at two smoky glass doors, each in the shape of a half circle. As he approached, both doors swung open toward him, greeting him with an undiluted blast of EDM.

Inside the main room a long, curving glass-and-chrome bar overlooked a large dance floor surrounded by recessed spaces with intimate tables in a similar style, each a step to three steps up from the dancers. More multicolored neon piping decorated black walls scattered throughout an abundance of floor-to-ceiling mirrors. Rotating spotlights and an impressive assortment of strobe lights created flares on the chrome and, combined with the mirrors, made the interior space a dizzying spectacle.

Along with the two free drinks, Dean thought the cover charge should include a handful of aspirin. Even allowing for the soul-crushing music, Dean found the size of the crowd—including those on the dance floor, sitting at tables or clustered along the bar—a bit underwhelming. On the other hand, only a day had passed since a cocktail server had had her throat severed by a broken bottle, so he was surprised anyone had showed up at all. And now that he looked around, he realized the dancers were a bit subdued in their movements. Pairs and groups conversing evinced serious expressions more often than smiling, animated chatter.

Dean flashed his ID at the nearest bartender and ordered a bottle of beer. Might help the music go down. But he doubted it.

With a deft movement, the bartender flipped the cap off the beer bottle and pushed it toward Dean along with a frosted mug. Dean ignored the mug and took a swig right from the bottle. "Investigating the blackout."

"Awful night," the bartender said.

"You were here?"

He nodded. "Real shame about Lettie," he said. "Manager decided to close the place in the morning, out of respect, but some of her friends wanted to take up a collection for her family. Lot of the regulars knew her." He nodded toward a collection jar a few stools down the counter with a photo of a smiling young woman taped to the front above her name in large print with details about the collection in smaller print below.

Dean asked him what he experienced around the blackout event. Within a few minutes, word spread, and other servers stopped by to relay their accounts. Even some of the regular customers added their pieces to the puzzle. The physical toll of the blackout, beyond Lettie's death, included sprains, contusions, a few broken noses, chipped teeth and one broken jaw. Most of those injured the previous night hadn't come back, but many others had returned to discuss the shared experience with each other.

Gareth, a Gyrations server with an assortment of sterling silver facial piercings, was convinced aliens had abducted the residents of Moyer the previous night. "For experimentation," he said. "Explains the lost time."

"That's a lot of people to probe," Dean said. "In a short amount of time."

"Okay, maybe not all of us," he said, adapting his theory

on the fly. "But with everyone out cold, they could pick and choose who they wanted—and maybe those are the ones acting crazy now."

"Interesting theory."

"Don't laugh."

"I'm not laughing," Dean said, suppressing a chuckle.

"Aliens smart enough to travel across the galaxy would have tech good enough to hide themselves from us."

"That's enough, Gareth," said Erin, another server, as she stepped away with a drink order. "Want that FBI man to toss you in the loony bin?"

"Hey," Gareth called after her. "For all we know, they could be standing here right now watching us!"

Not if they have any taste in music, Dean thought.

Dean tried to determine if any of them had resisted the initial blackout, as had Pete the short-order cook, or if any of them had woken up before the others. But his questioning revealed nothing beyond the expected responses. Neither alcohol nor illicit substances had any mitigating effect on the loss of consciousness.

He looked around the dance club again. Saw a couple stuff some bills in the Lettie fund jar. The woman squeezed the man's hand and he wrapped his arm around her shoulder.

Hard to believe less than twenty-four hours have passed—

Dean glanced at his phone display.

11:58 PM.

"Standing here right now watching us…"

Sam and he had been treating the blackout as a one-time event and the weird behavior that followed as an ongoing problem to investigate. The police were so busy putting out fires, they had no time to deal with the blackout that preceded them. And the residents of Moyer treated the blackout like a localized natural disaster, even so far as to collect funds to help the survivors. But what if everything was based on a faulty assumption? They had no idea how or why the blackout happened, which meant they had no reason to believe it couldn't happen again.

11:59 PM.

Pushing his beer bottle away, Dean stood up, turned toward the dance floor and cupped his hands around his mouth so everyone would hear him over the synthesized dance track, "Listen! Everybody down! On the floor—now!"

Those who heard him turned toward him, confused frowns on their faces. But most of them couldn't hear him above the music.

Confused, the bartender caught Dean's arm. "What's going on?"

Dean spotted Erin, a few stools away, filling her serving tray with several cocktail glasses. He sprang toward her, slapped his hand on the tray as she started to lift it off the bar, rattling the glasses. "Everyone—down!"

More quizzical looks from those around him.

"It's almost midnight!"

Erin's eyes opened wide in understanding.

Nodding, Dean turned to the bartender. "This could happen ag—!"

FOURTEEN

Disoriented, Dean woke up and took stock. Lying on his side. Elbow and chin sore. Felt as if he'd taken a punch.

EDM blasted from recessed speakers, all around him, helping him recall where he'd been when he'd lost consciousness. Gyrations, right before midnight. It had happened to him. A blackout. A second blackout, possibly across the entire town again. Patting his pockets, he searched for his phone, then remembered he'd left it on the bar. He climbed to his feet, raised the phone and read the display.

12:02 AM.

Behind and in front of the bar and across the dance floor, people groaned and stumbled as they stood up, almost swaying in unison as they recovered from the simultaneous collapse and unconsciousness.

Not as long this time.

Like an aftershock…?

Dean struggled to recall his last few moments, basically interviewing himself in the immediate aftermath, before his memory faded. But what memory? Trying to warn the others. Unable to finish a sentence. The sensory shutdown and the process of falling happened so close together, he only had a sensation of collapsing without feeling any of the physical effects—until he awoke.

Even though he'd seen it coming, and tried to warn everyone, he'd been unable to fight it off. Before his elbow or chin struck the floor, he was out cold. And he had to agree with the description others had given. It had happened as suddenly as if he had a power switch on the back of his head and a random passerby had flicked it off. There hadn't been anything *to* fight off. One moment he'd been completely alert and aware, even adrenalized by what he feared was about to happen, and the next moment… nothing.

Once Dean got his bearings, he examined his surroundings. The music continued to play, the roving spotlights followed their automated pattern, and the strobe lights pulsing above the dance floor continued to induce headaches. Next, he checked for any serious injuries. Erin rubbed her own elbow, hobbling around on a broken high heel. Frustrated, she pulled off the undamaged shoe and snapped off that heel, so she could walk without the forced limp of a wardrobe malfunction.

One of the dancers had fallen near a table, sweeping glasses to the floor and landing on top of some broken shards, lacerating her forearm. She held the bleeding arm away from her dress as she walked gingerly toward the bar.

The bartender Dean tried to warn before the second blackout declared himself a trained EMT and left the bar to treat her. Almost everyone else had pulled through with bumps and bruises. Though most hadn't understood Dean's warning, they had stopped in their tracks to listen, so had simply collapsed where they stood. While he had their attention, he asked if anyone remembered anything unusual—other than his shouted warning—before they fell, or if anyone had awakened before 12:02. Again, no outliers. A uniform event for all of them.

More lost time. A lot could happen in two minutes when you lay unresponsive, completely helpless. Dean wondered if the whole town of Moyer had fallen into a state of unconsciousness again. This event had been shorter than the first, possibly not as widespread. Too soon to tell.

He picked up his phone to call Sam, but noticed movement on the other side of the smoked-glass half-circle doors a moment before they automatically swung open. A man in jeans and boots strode through the doorway as if he belonged there. He seemed dressed for a barstool rather than a dance floor, but he made a beeline toward the mass of people below.

Dean tried to recall if he'd seen the man earlier, if he'd possibly stepped outside for a cigarette when the blackout happened and was now rejoining a group of friends or a date. Nothing about the man's face seemed familiar. He neither called nor signaled to anyone present, and nobody acknowledged his approach. If he had arrived right before the blackout and taken a sudden plunge, Dean might have expected him to order a shot of whiskey before busting a move.

Maybe he's not a drinker.

Nevertheless, something was *off* about the guy. At first,

Dean couldn't decide what bothered him. Then it came to him. The man never looked to his left or right. No doubt, no hesitation, no curiosity, as if he didn't care what happened or what happened to him. On the other hand, it had been a weird couple of nights in Moyer. Maybe the guy finally decided to dance like nobody was watching.

Dean turned back toward the bar, about to place his call, when a woman screamed, "He's got a knife!"

Shoving the phone in his pocket, Dean sprinted toward the dance floor, mentally kicking himself for not trusting his instincts. He veered left from the man's right side, saw the raised hunting knife. At the edge of the strobe lights, the man froze mid-step a split-second before Dean drove a shoulder into his ribs. During the man's brief pause, Dean noticed dark streaks on the gleaming blade—*blood*—and recalled the perky hostess from Bakersburg who had tried to collect a cover charge.

The man never braced for impact, never turned to fend off Dean's attack. As a result, Dean drove him sideways several yards before they crashed into four tall-legged chairs around a small circular glass table. Everything fell over with a thundering crash, including the table and the cocktail glasses and beer bottles previously atop it, momentarily drowning out the pulsing rhythm of the endless EDM mix.

Dean sprang to his feet and reached for the man's knife hand—but found it empty. The knife had spun out of his grip, sliding across the floor to stop against the wall, trailing a few drops of blood. Expecting the man to lunge for the blade, Dean moved between him and the wall, but he sat there, dazed and motionless, leaning back on his elbows.

They faced each other in the relatively sheltered conversational nook where the table and chairs had been positioned. Beyond the glare of the roving spotlights and the intense flicker-flash of the strobe lights, the music was slightly quieter.

"Who—What are you?" Dean asked.

Red light flickered in the man's eyes, like static on an old television set.

Lost signal?

The man's arms gave out and his body went limp. He flopped onto his back, the back of his head striking the floor hard enough to elicit a sympathetic wince.

Unsure what to expect, Dean approached cautiously.

"Hey! Anybody home?"

Suddenly, the man's body convulsed, caught in the throes of a seizure.

After a quick step back, Dean paused, startled as the man sagged again. But this time, a darkness deeper than the surrounding shadows around them emerged from the man's body, as if he'd excreted it from his pores. To Dean's amazement, the darker shadow flowed upright in the middle of the nook, without being cast against a wall or against a piece of toppled furniture. A man-shaped silhouette of darkness, it seemed to exist in space, right before him.

A shadow without a source.

Cautiously, hoping he wouldn't regret it, Dean extended an arm, but not in greeting. In exploration. His mind fought the logic of what his eyes saw, producing a headache more confounding than the one from the EDM mixes. Impossibly, something insubstantial appeared to have a degree of substance. Throwing caution out the window, he took a tentative step forward—

And it shifted toward him in the blink of an eye, an aggressive move. Instinctively, Dean backed away, aware that he might be leading—or luring—it back toward the dance floor. What little substance it had must be unaffected by inertia. And Dean had no desire to become its new host.

It edged closer, inches from Dean, who took another quick step backward. Reflexively, he held his palms up, a defensive posture which had zero chance of preventing the shadow from slipping through his pores. Any square inch of exposed flesh could be vulnerable, but he was fresh out of hazmat suits.

The roving spotlight fell across Dean's shoulders, slicing through the shadows at the perimeter of the conversational nook, but revealing nothing of the inkblot silhouette hovering before him. Unlike a normal shadow, light couldn't dispel it. Instead, it obstructed light.

Come a little closer, he thought. *Maybe the light will reveal a weakness.*

With that in mind, Dean slipped a little further into the light, inch by inch. And the dark shape came with him, as if pulled along in his wake. Maybe curious. Possibly hungry. But a moment later, the automated spotlight whipped away from them and the flashing strobe lights dominated.

The cat-and-mouse spell broken, the dark shape skittered away, retreating from the dance floor, heading toward the bar—and the exit.

"Wait!"

Dean sensed a missed opportunity, that he'd been about to learn something important if he managed to avoid possession followed by a potential murder spree and guaranteed amnesia. The shadow slipped through the crack between the doors with no more trouble than a puff of air.

"Did you see that?" someone on the dance floor asked. "What was that?"

But the questions went unanswered. Apparently, nobody else had noticed the shape.

Groggy, the man whose body had played host to the parasitic shadow, sat up and rubbed his ribs. Dean had hit him hard enough to crack a few of them but obviously the man would not remember that.

Dazed, he looked around, brow furrowed, finally settling on Dean's face. "Where—how did I get here?" Then he noticed the bloody knife and examined his own hand, arms and legs. "What happened?"

"It's okay, man," Dean said. "You weren't yourself."

"Did somebody drug me?"

"It's more complicated than that," Dean said. "What's your name?"

"Jasper James," he said. "But how—?"

"Stay here."

With a quick nod, he raced toward the lobby.

"Wait! I don't..." the man called after Dean, his voice trailing off.

Jasper might technically be innocent—if not in the eyes of the unknowing law—but he'd used that knife before heading to the Gyrations dance floor and Dean had a bad feeling he'd find a dead body at the hostess station.

He breathed a sigh of relief when he saw her. Alive. Sitting against a wall near her black hostess cart, legs splayed, holding her right hand by its wrist, staring as blood flowed from a gash in her palm to spatter her silver dress.

"He—He—He…" Tears streaming down her face, she looked up at Dean, as if seeking help with the words that eluded her.

Dean went down on one knee beside her, gently took her hand and examined the wound. The cut ran diagonally from the gap between her index and middle fingers down to the corner of her palm, deep enough to require stitches. "It's okay," he said. "You'll be fine."

"I'll be fine?"

Dean nodded.

"That's good," she said softly.

"Hold on."

Rising, he examined the shelf in the back of the hostess cart. Cash box, wrist bands, tablet with an attachment to swipe credit or debit cards for those who chose to pay digitally.

"I must have passed out," she said. "I woke up here, against the wall. Think I hit my head. I was woozy, tried to stand and fell again."

Possible concussion, Dean thought as he opened a bottom compartment on the cart and—bingo! Rolled cloth napkins.

"Then this man came in. I raised my arm, asked him to help me up, but he—he slashed me with a knife! Why would he…?"

Dean knelt beside her again and flattened the napkin.

"Hold out your hand." As he wrapped it, she winced in pain. "Never got your name," Dean said.

"Mia," she said.

"Okay, Mia," he said. "I need you to apply pressure here. That should stop the bleeding."

"It burns," she said.

"I'll call for help," Dean said. "Get you something for the pain."

The doors opened behind Dean. The bartender approached. Dean rose to meet him. "Call 911," he said. "She's been cut."

"Bad?" he asked softly.

"She'll need stitches."

The bartender removed a cell phone from his vest pocket and promised to return with the first-aid kit he'd retrieved from the office. "There's antibiotic cream and some gauze left."

"Thanks," Dean said. "And have somebody turn off the damn music."

To call Sam, Dean stepped outside—and into a world gone mad.

Car alarms whooped, and people shouted, calling for help. Over a block away, a family stood silently outside a house fire raging out of control while their dog barked at the flames. He heard the rapid *thwupping* sound of an approaching helicopter, probably a news station's "eye in the sky" chopper. Press moths to the flame.

Looking left to right, Dean spotted several car crashes with at least one car's engine block aflame. About what he'd expected, but it could've been worse. Shaking his head, he called Sam's cell.

After two rings, Sam picked up, his voice calm. "Dean?"

"Sam? You're okay?"

"Yeah," Sam said. "You sound surprised."

"After the blackout…" Dean began. "Wait—Where are you?"

"County hospital," Sam said. "Reviewing security footage with Gruber."

"And the hospital—Where is it, exactly?"

"You don't remember?" Sam asked, puzzled. "Dean, you dropped me off here."

"You're not in Moyer, are you?"

"Not technically," Sam said. "Hospital's over the town line, in Bakersburg."

"So, you don't know yet."

"Know what? Dean, you're not making any sense."

"I was in Moyer at midnight," Dean said. "I'm in Moyer right now."

"Okay."

"Sam, it happened again," he said. "Another blackout. Only two minutes this time."

Dean waited a moment while Sam relayed the news to Gruber. "And you?" Sam asked, concerned. "Dean, did you—?"

"Hit the floor like a sack of potatoes."

In the distance, Dean finally heard the wail of approaching sirens. By now, emergency dispatch would be flooded with calls.

"Before you ask, I'm fine. Couple bruises. But you might want to warn the emergency room staff. They're about to have their hands full. Again."

FIFTEEN

According to Sam, Gruber offered to drop him off at the Moyer Motor Lodge to save Dean the trouble of circling back to the hospital. Dean guessed that Sam worried about him driving more than necessary after having the consciousness rug pulled out from under him. When Sam stepped through the door, the concerned look on his face confirmed Dean's suspicions.

"Sam, I'm fine," Dean said. "No side effects."

"So far."

"Anything changes," Dean said, "you'll be the first to know."

"No matter how small?"

"Sure," Dean said. "But what about Gruber? Running on fumes."

"On his way to buy a case of energy drinks," Sam said. "He may have had a one-hour power nap in the last twenty-four hours. Feels guilty for taking vacation."

"Why? All he missed was the blackout."

"Both times," Sam said.

"Well, I don't recommend it."

"Dean?"

"It's okay, Sam," Dean said. "I'm okay."

"So, let's do this."

"What?"

"Tell me about it."

"Really?"

"Humor me," Sam said. "A minor detail could—"

"Okay," Dean said to skip the sales pitch. "Well, it's the same as everyone else. Not much to tell. Except, I thought it might happen again."

"After?" Sam asked. "I don't understand."

"Before," Dean said. "I saw the time. Two minutes before midnight. And I had the thought, what if it happens again?"

"Like a premonition?"

"No. Nothing like that," Dean said. "Coincidence."

"What if it wasn't coincidence?"

"Tomato, tamale."

"That's not—Never mind," Sam said. "Go on."

"I tried to warn everyone at the dance club," Dean said, "to get down. In case it happened again. Which it did."

"How did it feel to you?"

"Same as the others. Like somebody flipped a frigging switch in my brain," Dean said. "As fast as a room goes dark when you switch off the light."

"So, no dizziness, headache or nausea before the lights went out?"

"Nothing. No warning," Dean said. "Down and out. Or out and then down. Then, two minutes later, I woke up on the floor. Same as everyone else in the club."

"I thought, maybe, with your experience…"

"I know," Dean said, frustrated that he could add nothing to the investigation even after falling victim to the second blackout. "One odd thing…"

"What?"

"We all took a while to come to our senses," Dean said. "Like waking up suddenly from a deep sleep. But Jasper, the possessed guy with the knife"—Dean had described the knife attacks to Sam over the phone—"walked into Gyrations as if nothing had happened to him."

"So, anyone already hijacked is immune to the blackout event."

"Unless he recovered much faster than the rest of us."

"What about his shadow?"

"Came from inside him," Dean said. "But it wasn't his shadow."

"Was it like the shadow movement we saw after Luther killed Davick?"

"No," Dean said. "Something about its exit from his body—it struggled and forced itself out. Nothing graceful about it."

"And it hung around?"

"For a minute," Dean said. "Couldn't decide between attacking me or cutting its losses."

"You think it could have possessed you?"

"Who the hell knows, Sam? Maybe whatever causes the blackout unlocks something in the brain," Dean said.

"So, what if the blackout is just a side effect of that?"

"Again, who knows?" Dean said. "But something was off. Whatever it is, it showed itself, unintentionally."

"What makes you say that?"

"After Gruber tasered Luther, the shadow darted away from him, almost like a trick of the light. Hardly anyone noticed."

"Unless you were looking for something odd," Sam agreed.

"Think about it," Dean said. "How they look, whatever they are, I bet they hide in the shadows, an invisible enemy."

"Natural camouflage."

"But the one at the club, not so much," Dean said. "Maybe it was sick or stunned. Acted like I felt after the blackout. As if it needed to get its bearings. But why?"

"Maybe resisting the blackout took a toll."

"Maybe," Dean allowed, but he thought there was something more there he was missing. "What about Gruber's security footage? Anything useful?"

Sam told him about the incongruities in the fighting between Moyer residents and those from outside of the town. Bakersburg residents were immune to possession, while the possessed from Moyer were impervious to pain. At least until the fighting—and the possible possessions—ended.

"Mia, the hostess, blacked out along with the rest of us," Dean said. "She's from Bakersburg. So, no blackout immunity for... Bakersburgers?" Dean frowned. "Damn. Now I'm hungry."

"You and Mia," Sam said. "Let's assume no immunity for anyone within Moyer's borders during either midnight event. Anyone in town is fair game. And, officially, they're Bakersburgans."

"Still hungry," Dean said. "That stuff we grabbed from the hospital cafeteria was a failed chemistry experiment. Not food." *Should've ordered two slices of that blueberry pie.*

"Want me to drive you somewhere?"

"Not happening."

"I could check the front desk for menus."

"Didn't see any when I checked in."

"I could ask."

"Forget it," Dean said, covering a yawn as he rubbed a kink in his neck he hadn't noticed before. *Might have pulled something when I collapsed—or when I tackled Jasper.* "I'm wiped out."

"Side effect?"

"Long day," Dean countered. He climbed on the bed, lying on his back, right forearm across his eyes. "Catch a few hours' sleep, I'll be good as new."

"Sure, Dean," Sam said as he sat at the narrow desk and flipped open the laptop. "Got something I want to check out."

"What?" Dean yawned again, the feeling of lethargy swamping him. *Maybe it is a side effect.*

"Traffic cam coverage," Sam said, his voice already fading to Dean's ears. "Had an idea."

"That's…" Another yawn. "Good."

Dean closed his eyes, hearing only faint keyboard clicks as Sam hacked the traffic cams.

"Bakersburgans?" he murmured. "How could you know that?"

"Town's website," Sam said. "Old article. Saw it earlier. Apparently, they had a debate about what to call…"

* * *

Sam looked over his shoulder. "Dean?"

No answer.

Out like a light, Sam thought. It had been a long day. And having your consciousness forcefully switched off had to take a toll on your mind, regardless of Dean's protests that he was fine, no side effects.

Turning back to the traffic cam live feeds, Sam skipped his way around town, mostly through the business districts, commercial centers and public transit stops. The camera views were black-and-white, dark and grainy. If he'd been seeking a human suspect, the cameras would have provided little detail beyond the subject's general height and shape and possibly what type of clothes he or she wore, a face obscured by a cap, hood or ski mask. But Sam was not looking for a human suspect. He wasn't looking for humans at all.

Within a few minutes, he began to spot them, dark shapes sliding through the shadows. Streetlights couldn't penetrate their darkness. While normal shadows faded to gray, they remained black as obsidian. Yet when people walked within range of the cameras, Sam had trouble spotting any unusual darkness sifting through the shadows. They hid within the surrounding darkness or remained preternaturally still in the presence of humans.

Some displayed a complete, distinctive human silhouette— head, torso, two arms and two legs—while others were malformed or blurry at their extremities. On some he could distinguish individual fingers. Others had fuzzy stumps or smoky mist beyond forearms and wrists.

Sometimes they seemed to ride the currents of air, like plastic bags caught in a breeze, displaying no sentience. But they often switched direction, darted from place to place, slipped into real shadows when a human approached.

Sam wondered about the human form mimicry. Clearly, they were not human and would never pass for human, so why make the attempt? A creature of darkness hiding in the shadows made sense. Many animals had natural camouflage to disguise themselves from prey. Or maybe it was as simple as assuming the shape of a human shadow, a second layer of camouflage allowing proximity to humans. And yet Sam had no idea how a human could hurt or kill one of these shadow creatures.

On a hunch, Sam called Gruber, who agreed to meet him at the police station, even though he was officially off-duty. Apparently, the police department frowned on their senior patrol officers working more than twenty-four consecutive hours.

"Some nonsense about impaired reflexes and risks to public safety," Gruber joked. "So, what's this about?"

"We can do this in the morning."

"C'mon," Gruber said, "I doubt I'll be able to sleep. Besides, tonight's blackout cluster bomb was bad, but not nearly as bad as the first one."

"Why?"

"We got lucky," Gruber said. "Shorter duration, fewer car accidents, bleeders had less unattended bleeding time, same for accident victims and, frankly, I think a lot of people who were up and about at midnight stopped to reflect on what had happened to themselves or others the night before."

"Mindfulness saves lives."

"In this case," Gruber said. "Now tell me what you need."

"Security footage."

"Thought you'd have had your fill of that at the hospital."

Tempted to tell Gruber what he had witnessed through the hacked traffic cams, Sam decided to wait. Sometimes, seeing is believing. And, sometimes, denial was eternal. Instead, Sam told him what footage he wanted to see.

Before leaving for the police station, Sam approached Dean and almost called his name, but his brother was sound asleep. After the blackout, he probably needed the rest. If Sam woke Dean to tell him he was leaving, he'd insist on accompanying him. Besides, Sam was following a hunch, not responding to an emergency. Dean could sit this one out. So, Sam left a note on the bedside table.

Crossing the room, he reached for the door handle, paused and returned to Dean's bedside. Following another hunch, he removed an EMF detector from his bag, switched it on and placed it beside the note.

As Sam left the room and closed the door quietly behind him, the detector's lights glowed in the dark room, the device reassuringly silent.

Sixteen

By the time Sam arrived at the police station, the post-blackout emergency calls had dwindled to a few. Holding and booking would stay busy into the early morning hours, but the extra dispatch personnel had left and the overnight pair that remained flipped a coin to see who would take first break. From the squad room, Gruber had collected three extra computers and lined them up in the conference room, which was located across from the chief's office, currently vacant, to the senior patrol officer's relief.

"Said he'd better not see me till morning," Gruber explained.

"And yet you're here," Sam said.

"What can I say? Off-duty calls," Gruber replied. "Anyway, I've queued up all the stored feeds I could find. Some live cams don't save footage, and some overwrite the disks after so many hours unless they're backed up. Generally, it's a whole lot of nothing, so no reason to save it. If a crime is reported, then pertinent footage is offloaded as evidence."

"So, let's see what we've got," Sam said, taking the chair next to Gruber.

"Some of this footage I started to review last night—early yesterday morning, I guess," Gruber said. He connected the monitors to the computers and powered everything up. "Before half the town decided to go crazy. It's all a blur. But car accidents, for example. With the blackout, interviews were a waste of time since everyone was unconscious at the time of the accidents. Is either party at fault? Both? Neither? I have no idea how the insurance companies will sort this out, but they'll certainly have something interesting to study." Gruber logged into three computers, one keyboard at a time. "Same for the accidents, especially the fatal ones, though I imagine they'll be classified as accidental deaths. I mean, how could they not?"

"Unless we prove somebody caused the blackouts."

"Who could have done this? A mad scientist? A Bond villain?" Gruber asked, smiling. "Maybe a secret government agency conducting unsanctioned scientific experiments on US citizens?"

"Option C," Sam said. "Not that far-fetched." Incidents of governments experimenting on their citizens were rare, but Sam was leaning toward something even more unbelievable, at least to the layman. *Or the lawman.*

"Are you sure you're with the FBI?"

"According to my ID," Sam said, deadpan.

"I don't normally wear a conspiracy hat," Gruber said, rubbing his stubbled jaw. "Maybe an oversight on my part."

"Let's agree we can rule out a Bond villain as a suspect,"

Sam said. "Show me what you've got."

Gruber called up recorded footage from a few minutes before midnight from the day before on all three computers, and each computer had a four-square grid of camera views from locations around Moyer. One by one, he clicked the play icons to start the queued playback on all grids and screens. Some of the views matched what Sam had hacked into live at the motel. But everything he watched on these screens had happened over twenty-four hours previously.

Sam watched casually as the time stamps switched from 11:57 PM to 11:58 PM and nothing seemed unusual. Traffic remained light, as expected at that hour. Only a few people walked the streets. In the commercial district, a few late diners walked from restaurants to parked cars.

The time stamp jumped to 11:59 PM. Sam leaned in close enough to block out the rest of the room, his gaze flickering from one screen to the next, zigzagging across the grids, and he thought he saw a dark shape ripple across the shadows in one shot. And again, in another grid view. Something obvious if you were looking for it, but easily overlooked if you were accustomed to scanning for people or motor vehicles. He could have pointed the shapes out to Gruber, but they would be meaningless shifting of light and shadow to him, with no context. Sam had to wait for something more definitive to clue him in to the real enemy.

Meanwhile, Sam waited for the fateful moment when everyone… stopped.

12:00 AM.

Everything happened at once and lasted seconds.

Cars drifted out of their lanes or made sudden turns as drivers slumped in their seats. A camera above a storefront showed a car burst into the frame and smash the display window. One traffic camera with a long view of a busy highway showed a pileup of several cars as one after the other descended an embankment above a storm drain. Along downtown streets, people walking alone or in pairs captured on multiple cameras, fell in unison, as if heeding a silent command.

Before a minute had passed, Moyer became a ghost town. Nothing moved. Cars either slowed to a halt in the middle of the roads as drivers no longer pressed on accelerators, or they crashed into buildings, mailboxes or parked cars. Steam rose from some. Fire from a couple. People lay in the streets, unmoving, or sat slumped over steering wheels or deflated airbags. One camera, however, showed a feral cat trotting down an alley, checking out the collection of dumpsters behind an outdoor shopping center.

On a few screens, Sam noticed darker shapes, sliding through shadows. Their appearances were so infrequent, their movements so subtle, Sam began to wonder if he was imagining them, the way the brain sees faces in random blotches or in patterns on wallpaper.

Focusing on the humans, as still as fallen mannequins, Sam said, "Eerie. They don't move at all. Not even a twitch."

"Like watching a preview of the end of the world," Gruber added. "By the time I reached town, people were starting to wake up. I never saw everyone like this."

"If you'd returned a few minutes sooner," Sam said. "You'd be lying right beside them."

"Strange to think that not a single person in Moyer was—"

"Hold on," Sam said, pointing at the monitor on the far right, bottom left square in the grid of four. "Check the time stamp on that one."

Gruber looked. "12:01… Wait, 12:02 now."

"So, why is that man walking around when everyone else is out cold?"

Adjusting the monitor so they could both see it better, Gruber switched to full screen. The man wore a knit hat, an old pea coat, threadbare jeans and old boots, his hands covered with fingerless gloves. He walked with a stumbling gait, as if completely exhausted or moderately inebriated. And he appeared to be muttering to himself, a running, animated monologue which included an array of hand gestures.

"Could be a simple explanation," Gruber said.

"Such as?"

"Incorrect time stamp," Gruber said. "Most of this footage is never viewed. It could have been off by an hour if someone forgot to fall back or spring ahead."

"Look," Sam said. "Top right of the frame. Guy lying next to a car."

As they watched, the raggedy man crouched beside the unconscious man and snatched his wallet, plucked out the cash and returned the empty billfold before moving on, out of frame.

"Damn," Sam said. "Do you know where that is?"

Gruber rewound the footage, examined details in the frame. "Definitely downtown."

"Is this all there is?" Sam asked.

"What are you looking for?"

"Something that shows us where he was right at midnight."

"I have a few more cam views I planned to queue after these."

Gruber opened a file they hadn't viewed yet. "This is also from Central Avenue, a few blocks back, depending on how fast he walked…"

The view showed an extreme angle of a row of shops and restaurants and the sidewalks in front of them without much coverage of the street, a security camera view rather than a traffic cam. To the left of the frame, a middle-aged couple emerged from a restaurant, the man in a two-piece suit, the woman wearing a cocktail dress.

The timestamp read 11:59 PM.

Gruber provided commentary. "That's Angelini's, a new Italian restaurant in town. Can't ID the couple, especially not from this angle. But no sign of—"

"Spoke too soon," Sam said, as the raggedy man entered the frame behind the couple, closing the distance between them. He swung his hand next to his head as if he was swatting at a flying pest by his ear.

Leaning forward, Sam spotted a dark shape flow between the camera and the man's pea coat. It slipped into and out of frame so fast, if he hadn't been paying close attention he might have missed it. Then Sam noticed another dark shape ripple past the side panel of an SUV. Sam wondered if the raggedy man noticed the shapes but thought he was imagining them.

He raised his hand again and must have called out to the couple, as the woman glanced back. The man swatted at something near his head again. Sam detected no dark shape movement, but it could have occurred out of camera range.

The woman clutched the arm of her companion and whispered something to him. He pointed his key fob at a nearby SUV and disengaged the locks. Raggedy man continued to plead his case, but SUV man shook his head.

A moment later, he fell over, dropping the key fob as his body rebounded off the side of his car. Right beside him, his dining companion collapsed, her leg twisting awkwardly underneath her before her face slammed into the curb. Man and woman fell simultaneously.

Raggedy man stared down at them, his hands shaking, obviously confused.

After a few seconds, he shook off his disbelief, and crouched beside the man, reached into the chest pocket of his suit and removed a billfold. After a moment or two, he seemed to return the wallet to the suit pocket, while stuffing his pocket with the cash he'd lifted. Then he turned his attention to the woman.

Gruber leaned forward. "What's he doing?"

"Checking for a pulse," Sam said. "She's bleeding."

Raggedy man removed more folding money from the woman's purse, then left it lying beside her.

"We had some reports of missing cash after the blackout," Gruber said. "But nothing else was taken, not credit cards or cell phones, so I chalked it up to memory lapses or a pickpocket. Obviously never considered the possibility the thefts happened while everyone was unconscious."

12:02 AM.

As raggedy man stood up, he wavered before catching his

balance. He nodded politely toward the unconscious man and woman, then continued walking along Central Avenue. But before he walked out of the camera frame, he glanced back over his shoulder, a brief, grainy flash of his face beneath the knit hat. Sam doubted he heard anything, as he was—as far as they knew—the only conscious person in the whole town. The more likely explanation was that he was tracking one of the dark shapes moving past him. Or he simply couldn't believe his good fortune and, belatedly, felt a pang of guilt.

Then he was gone.

Gruber reversed the recording and paused on the side view of raggedy man's face. He clicked on the digital zoom button to increase the size of the face. But it was mostly light blur and shadows, no distinguishing features.

"Know him?" Sam asked.

Gruber sighed. "Can't tell from this image," he said. "But I have an idea."

Sam leaned back in his chair, fingers interlaced behind his head. One person in the entire town had immunity from the blackouts. And what did they know about him? From his apparel, Sam guessed he was homeless. Judging by his behavior, he was either an opportunistic thief or a man with a faulty moral compass. Based on his reactions, he had some awareness of the shadow creatures. Maybe he only sensed their presence without seeing them. Even if that was true, he was several steps ahead of his fellow townspeople.

Gruber continued to stare at the blurry face.

"Hoping you can get a conviction from that?" Sam asked.

"Would be nice," Gruber said, smiling. "Looking for any detail to confirm my suspicions."

Sam leaned forward. "We need another view."

"We've looked at all the coverage for that area of town."

"What about tonight?" Sam said. "The second blackout."

"If he stayed awake again…"

"Easy to spot in a motionless town."

"I'll need time to gather fresh footage."

"I'll brew fresh coffee," Sam said.

"Sounds like a plan."

Thirty minutes later, they returned to their seats before the multiple monitor setup with piping hot coffee and a new batch of security and traffic cam footage to review. With a shorter blackout window, they found their shot in less than ten minutes.

Wearing his pea coat, raggedy man sat hunched over on a wrought iron bench near a bronze plaque denoting the entrance to Penninger Park as the timestamp changed to 12:00 AM. As if hearing sounds nearby—probably somebody collapsing though no one else was in the shot—he looked up startled, glanced from left to right and a smile lit up his face.

"He just realized it happened again," Sam said. "And Blackout Bank is open for business."

"And I just realized my hunch was right," Gruber said, momentarily pausing the image when raggedy man looked straight toward the camera. "I do know him."

"He lives here? In Moyer?"

"In a manner of speaking."

SEVENTEEN

Around town, as night rolled into the early morning hours, and the emergency vehicles retreated, the shadows with substance roamed freely along the deserted streets. They avoided the commercial district for two reasons. Closed stores were vacant, so held little appeal for them, while bars and all-night businesses presented an exposure risk.

Instinctually, they escaped detection by moving in and with shadows. Their interaction with humans remained on the periphery of human affairs, the stuff of campfire tales and urban legend. While they remained unknown and undetected, they had free rein of the living world, invisible observers, unthreatened by mankind.

But something had changed in their nature. Observation alone became insufficient. No longer trapped on the sidelines, they now had the ability to participate, to experience again. So far, the humans had no answer for their invasions and remained clueless of their existence.

With a new sense of abandon, the dark shapes sailed down

suburban streets, hovering above sidewalks, sliding up walls, down roofs and chimneys, through gaps in windowsills, under doorways, through keyholes. Like moths to flames, they were drawn to sleeping humans. Their human shapes overlaid human bodies, stretching their extremities to reach the human extremities, morphing and mapping their shapes until the human was coated head to toe in inkblot darkness like a second layer of skin, which then eased down through the pores, settling into the host—

—and taking control.

Once they had taken up residence inside a human, they suppressed the human's consciousness, shoving it below any sensory connection to the world, deeper than sleep. As soon as they took over, they made the human body rise and took it for a test drive.

One made a husband climb out of bed, walk down the hall and throw himself down the stairs, just to experience what the moment felt like. Before the man's wife awoke, the free shadow took control of her and made her leap out the second-story window.

Another went into a crowded house, jumped from one family member to the next, had each rise and walk to another room and dropped them there to sleep it off. When they awoke, every one of them would think they had been sleepwalking. One of the younger ones liked to take the humans out in the street for short bouts of mischief. Throwing rocks at neighboring houses or striking a baseball bat against car windshields.

Another, whose natural shape jittered uncontrollably,

enjoyed suicide scenarios. It had a difficult time taking and maintaining control of humans, and faced failure more often than success, which created a buzzing rage inside it. Despite having control of the humans, its attempts to make them commit suicide triggered their basic instinct of self-preservation. It had made the girl climb the fence and jump down into oncoming traffic, but it had felt her fighting back, struggling to stop what was happening.

Now it slipped inside an old man and had him get into his car—barefoot and wearing pajamas—and drive to one of the busier roads. Older minds were weaker, more accepting of their own mortality even if they didn't acknowledge it. That helped it retain control when it had the old man swerve in front of an oncoming tractor-trailer. The trucker managed to avoid a head-on collision but sideswiped the old man's car, crumpling the right rear wheel well, which began to rub against the back tire.

Losing speed, it had the old man swerve again, this time into a tree. The crash was jarring even as the airbag deployed and it let itself be thrown up and out of the host body, unsure if it had been successful.

But the night was young.

The shadow shape hovered before the motel room door, its head-shape level with the room number, 142. After a moment of consideration, it moved forward, its edge pushing through the thin gap between door and doorjamb, emerging inside the room without having to distort its shape. The room held two twin beds, the one on the right occupied by a sleeping man, not a Moyer native. But touched by darkness nonetheless.

Receptive.

It glided forward, closing the distance between them.

On a small table next to the man, a blocky device with lights and a meter activated, lights flashing, emitting a squealing sound, almost in protest.

The sleeping man rolled over in his sleep, arm extended, swatting at the table…

Dean rose from the depths of a troubling dream of a shadow army marching on a city of humans, when the scared man next to him opened his mouth and began to squeal, an almost robotic sound that startled Dean. He grabbed the man's shoulders and shook him. *Not human,* Dean thought in the dream. *What is he?*

A spy, hidden among the humans, to warn the shadow army.

He demanded the man stop squealing but…

Groggy, Dean rolled over and reached out to shut off the alarm clock he couldn't remember setting. He had no idea how long he'd been asleep, but he felt wiped out, as if he'd run a marathon. Sleep had not refreshed him and now the stupid alarm—

His hands closed over the EMF detector.

He swung his legs to the floor and stared at the device, which had suddenly become silent. Before the mental fog lifted, he wondered how Sam had programmed an EMF detector to function as an alarm clock, but stopped himself mid-speculation.

He looked around the dark room. No sign of Sam.

"Sam?" he called. "Sammy, you here?"

An EMF detector.

Beside the bed.

Sam had left it behind. He'd left it powered on for some reason. What did Sam know? Or suspect? Then Dean saw the note, read it quickly. Sam had gone to the police station to review traffic cam footage from the night of the first blackout. Nothing in the note about the EMF detector.

No surprise he'd dreamed of a shadow army and an invasion, considering the case they were working, and that Dean had seen a shadow shape up close after it possessed a man long enough to assault someone with a knife and threaten others. And while he had incorporated the sound of the EMF in his dream, something had triggered the alarm right inside his motel room.

Dean looked around the motel room, cloaked in darkness and shadows.

It could be hiding anywhere in here.

Attempting to appear unhurried and unconcerned, Dean stood up and walked over to his bag, slipping one hand inside, searching for a familiar cylindrical shape. When his hand clamped down on the flashlight, he turned to face the darkened room. Then he flicked on the power switch and pulled it from the bag, piercing the darkness with a powerful beam of light. He swung the flashlight in wide sweeping arcs, sequentially obliterating darkness and shadows in every corner of the room, hoping direct light could weaken or even banish it. Catch it on the move, expose every patch of darkness, including areas the room lights couldn't reach. Whatever the shadows were, they couldn't outrun light. If one was hiding in his room, he'd find and reveal it. What he'd do if he found one was a bridge he'd cross later. Would a few shotgun salt rounds get its attention—or simply put a hole in the wall?

Finding a shadow among shadows presented its own challenge. From what he'd learned by observing one at the club, they could go anywhere, hide anywhere, even—

—the ceiling.

He pointed the flashlight straight up and swept the ceiling from corner to corner, front to back, zigzagging the beam as fast as his eyes could track. Nothing.

Next, he dropped to his knees and swept the beam under both beds. Then he checked behind the desk and television, inside the closet and bathroom. Again, nothing.

With a relieved sigh, he turned on all the lights in the room, banishing the darkness and minimizing shadows. At least if one entered—returned—to his room, he'd see it. He dropped the flashlight back in his bag and placed the EMF detector close to the door.

Once again, he examined the room and his eyes settled on the framed photos of lake life hanging over each bed. A third hung over the television. The shadow creature was thin enough to hide behind any of them. A darkness the flashlight would not have exposed. One by one, he checked the frames, but each one was bolted to the wall. Though who would steal the antiquated photos, he couldn't guess. Maybe the frames themselves had some aftermarket value, but he doubted it.

He had a small crowbar in his duffel. For a few moments, he considered ripping the frames off the wall, but he had an easier way to check. If one of the shadows set off the EMF meter before, it would do so again if he brought it within proximity of the hidden intruder.

A few moments later, the EMF remained silent.

"Gone," he whispered.

EIGHTEEN

Maurice Hogarth lounged in a worn executive chair he'd picked up at a local yard sale, feet crossed at the ankles on the corner of his small desk while he talked into his laptop's webcam. Instead of wallpaper, various hard rock posters plastered his bedroom walls. Even the ceiling and the back of his door paid homage to some of his favorite bands. Only the windows—at his mother's insistence—had been spared. Months ago, he considered ripping up the carpeting to cover the floor, but he couldn't disrespect his bands by walking on them.

His bedroom was L-shaped, with his desk located in the short side of the L, what his parents called a study nook. When he wasn't live-streaming his album reviews, he called it his privacy station. Presently, his broadcast booth was on air, the posters in the nook bathed in black light for dramatic effect.

But he'd long since stopped reviewing *Skull Town*, the latest album by Morpheus Adrift. The vinyl disk continued to play on repeat on his turntable, the volume on the stereo as low as it had ever been since the day he brought home his first subwoofer. He'd begun his broadcast review before midnight and had been halfway through his analysis of the thirteen tracks, pulling heartily on a joint, when everything went dark.

After the two-minute blackout, he extinguished the smoldering spliff. It had burnt his rug, but fortunately hadn't set the house on fire while he was oblivious to the world. Instead of returning to the album review, he'd stayed online with his limited audience to discuss what had happened. His parents had slept through it all, completely unaware, even though the crash he must have made when he fell out of his chair should have been enough to wake them. Which begged the question…

"Is it possible to black out when you're already asleep?"

His laptop screen showed his image up top, with a row of viewers in thumbnail images below. Six guys, all friends from Moyer, and Sally Jennings, a cute girl his age from Bakersburg. His regulars. His attempts to broaden his viewer base had, so far, been unsuccessful, despite posting his recording online for general consumption. He needed to ramp up his marketing game. For now, the broadcasts had an air of exclusivity he kind of enjoyed. Like how his favorite bands had gotten started playing in small venues before performing for stadium crowds. His motto: start small and build a core following.

"Sure, man," said Cory Henderson, the self-professed philosopher of the bunch, "if you sink to a deeper state of unconsciousness."

"Somewhere between sleep," Sally said, "and a coma."

"Exactly," Cory said, nodding. "Bitch gets it."

"What did you just call me?"

"Not cool, bro," Reggie Coleman said.

Maurice clicked on Cory's thumbnail and hovered his finger over the delete key. "Have to boot you, Cory."

Cory waved his palms in front of the screen before Maurice could disconnect him. "Sorry, Mo!"

"Not me you should be apologizing to."

"No disrespect, Sally," Cory said quickly.

"That don't sound like an apology," Frank Newton said, giving Cory a thumbs-down.

"C'mon, Fig," Cory said. "You know what I meant."

"She don't," said Eddie Alvarez. "Spell it out, dude."

"You guys are busting my balls here," Cory whined.

"Boot in three, two…"

"All right, okay," Cory said. "Sorry, Sally. I'm not like that."

"Then don't act like that," Sally said.

"Did that hurt?" Reggie asked Cory.

"Little bit," Cory said, holding his index finger and thumb an inch apart.

"Not the time to be measuring your manhood, Cory," Gary Geiger said.

"Screw you, Gary."

"Where were we?" Maurice said.

"Somewhere between dazed and confused," Gary Geiger replied.

Stevie Foulkes rolled his eyes. "That doesn't even make sense, nimrod!"

"You guys scared the crap out of me," Sally said. "I didn't

know what the hell was going on. Thought you were pranking me or something."

"Pranking?" Maurice asked. "How?"

"You were talking about track seven, Mo, and then you all collapsed at once. Your chair fell over, Reggie faceplanted on his keyboard. Cory—you drool, by the way—and everyone else looked like they decided to take instant naps."

"Another blackout," Fig said. "Like midnight yesterday."

"But not as long," Maurice said. "Only a couple minutes this time."

"I heard people were acting weird in Moyer all day," Sally said. "I thought you guys were goofing around, scare the out-of-town girl."

"We weren't goofing," Stevie said.

"Figured that out after the first minute," Sally said. "Started yelling at you guys to wake up. I was about to call 911 when you started to come around."

"Wonder why Bakersburg doesn't black out," Fig said.

"It's like a human EMP," Reggie said.

"What's that?" Gary asked. "Email program?"

"Electromagnetic pulse, dimwit," Stevie said.

"Hey! It was a fair question."

"Anyway, this EMP knocks out human brains," Reggie suggested. "And Bakersburg is beyond the blast radius."

Gary frowned. "Knocks out human brains?"

"Yeah," Reggie said, warming to his own theory. "The human brain runs on chemical and electrical signals. After the blast, our brains need time to reboot."

"Okay, genius," Fig said. "Who's knocking out our brains?"

"Aliens, obviously," Gary said.

"Not aliens," Eddie said. "Uncle Sam."

"Why Moyer?" Maurice asked.

"We're guinea pigs, Mo," Eddie said. "Rats in a maze."

"But Moyer is so boring," Cory said. "Why pick us?"

"Because nobody cares about Moyer," Stevie said. "If the whole town disappeared, who would even notice we were gone?"

"Jeez, Stevie!" Reggie said. "That's dark, man."

"He's off his meds," Gary said. "Pop some of the happy pills, Stevie."

"I'm not on meds," Stevie said.

"That's the problem!" Gary exclaimed and laughed.

Sally said, "Darkness."

"Stevie's new nickname," Cory said, chuckling.

"Mo!" Sally yelled, pointing at her own computer screen. "What the hell is that?"

"What?" Maurice asked, scanning his screen, his image and the seven thumbnails for whatever had alarmed her.

"Behind you!" she shouted.

"Seriously?"

"Yes! Look!"

A sudden feeling of dread overcame Maurice. He whipped his head around and saw an ink-black shadow gliding across his dark room, floating mid-air, as if it had detached itself from a wall or the floor and become a separate entity. Strangely, it was shaped like a human silhouette, but he couldn't have cast the shadow and he was alone in the room. It shouldn't exist, but it eased toward him.

Petrified, he watched as it crept closer, his gaze intent on the shape and the substance. He sensed an uncanny depth to it, ripples on the surface of the darkness, as it neared, but from certain angles it almost vanished.

When it was inches away, he shoved his executive chair back with a convulsive effort, rolling on the chair's casters deeper into his nook. He wanted to stand but had the sense his legs would betray him. If it came any closer, he would dive away, somehow scramble past it and out the door of his room, locking it inside. But that thought triggered another. *How the hell did it get inside my room?*

"Mo?" Reggie called. "Talk to us!"

"What is it?" Sally said.

"I—I don't know," Maurice said.

The silhouette glided closer, into his broadcast booth, almost cornering him in his nook. He cast about for weapons. He had an old baseball bat in his room, but he kept it in his closet, well out of reach. A pocketknife on his keychain— hanging on a hook downstairs.

The silhouette slipped between him and his desk. He couldn't see through it, couldn't see the laptop or the concerned faces of his friends. It was a shadow but completely opaque, unaffected by the ambient light coming from the laptop screen. Except, he noticed, at the extremities. Where a human would have fingers and toes, the silhouette became fuzzy, almost wispy. Like a visual trick it hadn't completely pulled off. Look closely and you could see the fail.

"It's an alien, guys!" Gary said, completely serious for once. "A freaking alien!"

Whatever it was, Maurice tensed, ready to dive to the side once it got close enough. Maybe he could slip past the fuzzy edges.

But as it passed under the black light lamps he'd set up for his webcast, he noticed something happening to its surface. Almost instantly, the fuzziness vanished. Wispy extremities solidified with clearly defined edges. The transformation mesmerized him. And he forgot to duck and roll past it.

A black-shadow hand with slender fingers and pointed fingernails reached toward him.

"It's a she," Maurice said. "It's female."

"What?" Stevie asked.

"It's just—darkness," Sally said. "Get out of there, Mo!"

"Can't you see," Maurice said. "It's—"

The feminine silhouette-head canted slightly, revealing a brief flash of twin red orbs—eyes! Suddenly the silhouette-hand darted forward and brushed against his skin, raising the hairs along his forearm like a static charge.

"Whoa!" Maurice said, instinctively yanking his arm away from the strange contact.

"What happened?" Reggie asked.

"It touched me," Maurice said. "I felt it and—"

Again, the hand darted forward, this time aggressively, not content to graze his skin. This time it tried to penetrate his skin. And it felt like a black razor blade slicing into his flesh. Where the black edge of the silhouette pushed, blood flowed, running down his arms to his fingertips.

Maurice screamed in pain.

He shoved himself backward with such force that he

toppled over in his chair again, felt it flipping over, striking his back, pinning him. Throwing it off him with one frightened surge, he scrambled to his feet, staggered toward the right wall of the nook, caught his balance even as he trembled in fear, and braced himself for the next attack—

NINETEEN

A new wave of emergency calls flooded the Moyer Police Department with reports of sleepwalking injuries, car accidents involving people driving in their pajamas or underwear, missing spouses and children and, strangest of all, sightings of dark ghosts. Some police officers still hadn't finished writing their reports following the second round of midnight blackouts, and now had to respond to numerous calls. And unlike the blackout accidents, the new batch involved willful negligence.

"More Moyer residents behaving badly," Gruber said.

"With amnesia chasers," Dean added.

After determining his motel room had no unwelcome visitors hiding in the shadows, Dean had joined Sam and Gruber at the police station to interview a suspect who seemed immune to the town-wide blackouts and not above a little larceny on the side when the opportunity presented itself. While the Winchesters wanted to know how the man had acquired his immunity and if he had any involvement in causing the blackouts, Gruber seemed more concerned with the man's penchant for thievery.

The missing persons reports were troubling, especially those involving children, but most of those were resolved when the missing person turned up miles from home with no idea how or why they had wandered away. None had any idea what they'd done during those periods of lost time. Without evidence, eyewitnesses or security cameras, they faced no consequences, but those who had been observed or recorded faced charges.

As Gruber led the Winchesters to the interview room, a uniformed officer approached him.

"What's up, Dunn?" Gruber asked. "Wait. Do I even want to know?"

"Hear about Brady?"

"No. What?" Gruber asked. "Isn't he off-duty?"

"I'll say," Dunn replied. "Climbed out of bed buck naked, got in his car and rolled over his neighbors' lawns—four of them—tried making figure eights. Ripped up all the landscaping, left rooster tails of mulch, then took out all of the mailboxes and the corner stop sign."

"Jesus!"

"Brady's one of yours?" Sam asked.

"Unfortunately," Gruber said, embarrassed.

"Responding officers found his car idling in the middle of some hedges," Dunn added. "Apparently, he abandoned the car, walked home in the buff, got in bed and fell asleep. Has no clue what happened."

"Please tell me he failed a breathalyzer," Gruber said.

"Nope," Dunn said. "Stone cold sober. Brought him in a half-hour ago."

"Moyer's finest," Gruber said, shaking his head. "People are losing their damn minds!"

"Something like that," Dean said.

Not so much losing their minds as losing control of their minds. If the shadows took control and committed the act, the suppressed humans were innocent. Yet the Winchesters lacked any way of proving that to Moyer law enforcement, certainly nothing convincing enough to counter physical evidence and witnesses. Maybe now that the possession had affected one of their own, the police would allow for the possibility that the accused had no control of their actions.

Gruber escorted the Winchesters through the investigations office to the interview room. After peering through the narrow window slot, he unlocked the door and they filed in. Gruber took the seat facing the seated suspect, Albert Kernodle. The Winchesters hung back, standing on either side of Gruber.

Kernodle wore a knit hat, a pea coat with missing buttons, fingerless gloves, frayed jeans and scuffed work boots. His sallow complexion created a stark contrast to the dark circles under his bloodshot eyes. His forearms rested on the table between them, his fingers twitching.

Gruber placed a manila evidence folder on the table and said, "Hello again, Albert. You already know me. These gentlemen are from the FBI. We have some questions for you. You've been read your rights and have agreed to talk with us. Correct?"

"You bet."

Gruber tapped the folder. "Gotta say, Albert, you've been busy."

"No more than usual." Kernodle shrugged. That simple motion triggered a cascade of tremors and twitches culminating in him swatting his own ear and checking his palm for a squished insect. Even though his hand was empty, he shook away the nonexistent pest. After what Sam had told him about the footage of Kernodle, Dean had wondered if the man saw things that weren't there. He seemed to notice the shadow creatures but apparently suffered hallucinations as well.

"So, it's usual for you to steal from people?" Gruber asked.

"Don't steal," Kernodle said. "Never stole nothing."

Gruber opened the folder and fanned out several eight by ten glossies printed from the security footage, showing Kernodle taking cash from wallets and a purse. "What do you have to say about these?"

"You need a better camera," Kernodle said. "Besides, that don't look like me."

"You're wearing the same clothes."

"From a thrift store," he said. "Anyone can shop there."

"Oh, we have photos of your face," Gruber said and took out a shot of Kernodle smiling on the park bench. "That man is you."

"Maybe," Kernodle allowed. "But I didn't steal that money. They gave it to me."

"They were unconscious!" Gruber said, offended. "You rifled through their pockets!"

"Don't matter," Kernodle said. "Law says finders keepers."

"That's not a law, Albert," Gruber said. "And you didn't

find that money. You took it from unconscious people. At least one of them injured, bleeding at your feet."

Kernodle shrugged again, but clenched his hands together this time to fight off the trembling that raced down his spine. "What if I thought they were dead? Or dying? Everyone falls over like that, you assume they're dying. Can't take it with you, right?"

"Not everyone," Sam said, then pointedly, "Not you."

"What makes you special, Albert?" asked Dean.

"Tick tock, tick tock, my time's coming," Albert said. "Soon enough."

"But you didn't black out with everyone else," Sam said. "Not tonight. Or the night before. Why not?"

"Lucky, I guess," Kernodle said, chuckling until it triggered a coughing fit. "Ain't—that right—Off-Officer—Gr-Gruber."

Gruber leaned out the door and asked Dunn to bring some bottled water for the suspect. Less than a minute later, Kernodle downed half the bottle and wiped his mouth with the back of his hand.

"What did he mean?" Sam asked Gruber.

"Bad luck," Gruber said. "The worst luck, really. I know Albert because his situation is very unique."

"Homelessness?" Dean asked, confused.

"Bad genetics," Gruber said. "True, he's been living on the street for a couple years and can't hold down a job, but it's not his fault. For the most part."

"Why?" Sam asked. "What's wrong with him?"

"Fatal familial insomnia," Gruber said. "An incurable

genetic condition. Prevents sleep, can cause dementia and, eventually, leads to death."

"Life leads to death," Kernodle said.

"He's got a point," Dean said.

"Well, he's refused medical care all this time."

"Incurable, remember?" Kernodle said.

"Two for two," Dean said.

"He's been living off handouts."

Kernodle nodded. "The kindness of strangers."

"And scaring children," Gruber said. "Although that's due to his symptoms, not malicious intent."

Kernodle spread his arms, palms up. "Out of my control."

His neck spasmed, forcing him to drop his hands to the table and grip the edges. Once he regained some control, he took another gulp of water.

"Overall, he's been an occasional nuisance rather than a lawbreaker," Gruber said. "Until now."

"Old rules don't apply," Kernodle said.

"The law hasn't changed, Albert."

"End of the world, Gruber," Kernodle said, tapping the table with his index finger. "You just don't see it."

"What do *you* see, Albert?" Sam asked.

"All sorts of things, big and small," Kernodle said. "Some things aren't real. I know that. My symptoms, as Gruber says. But it all feels real. Like the bugaboos."

"Bugaboos?" Dean asked, glancing briefly at Sam.

"Yes, sir, in the dark," Kernodle said, nodding. "They ride in the dark. Seen them all over town."

"Dark?" Sam asked.

"Look like shadows," Kernodle said, "unless you pay attention."

"Let me get this straight," Gruber said. "You're afraid of shadows?"

"They're not shadows," Kernodle said. "They hide in the shadows. But they're alive."

"How long have you been seeing these living shadows?" Sam asked, ignoring Gruber's skeptical sidelong glance.

"First time…" Kernodle thought it over, scratched his jaw stubble with black-crusted fingernails. "Same day everyone fell down at once."

"After the blackout?" Dean asked, wondering if the cause of the blackout somehow released the shadow creatures.

"No," Kernodle said. "Earlier that night. But there's more of them now."

"How do you feel when the blackout happens?" Sam asked. "Any different?"

"Don't know," Kernodle said. "Never feel good or right. Guess I felt… surprised. First time it happened, I thought it was a blessing. Something finally going my way, you know? A little bit of payback for the crap sandwich that is my life."

Dean could understand. Guy had been dealt a lousy hand. No hope. Nothing but the ticking clock of his own mortality.

"But it doesn't really matter," Kernodle said after a few moments of silence. "End of the world's coming."

"You keep saying that," Sam said. "Why?"

Kernodle glanced around the room, checking all four corners, under the table and even inspecting the ceiling, all of which gave Dean a strong sense of déjà vu. *Try that in a dark motel room with a flashlight,* he thought.

Finally, Kernodle directed his attention to the three humans in the room with whatever phantoms haunted his mind. "They come from another world," he whispered at length.

"The bugaboos?" Sam asked.

Kernodle nodded. "They come from another world, but they want to take over ours." He tapped the tabletop. "Moyer is ground zero."

"Why Moyer?" Gruber said.

"Who knows? Maybe it's a weak spot in the space-time continuity."

"Continuum," Sam said.

"What he said," Kernodle said, chuckling. "This is only the beginning. That's why they're hiding from us. It's a gradual process. They're still learning how to defeat us. By the time we know they're here, it'll be too late. The war will be over before we knew it began."

"But *you* know," Gruber said. "Big flaw in their plan."

"Ha! Who will believe me? Everyone thinks I'm crazy," he said. "But I'm a freak of nature. Never sleep. I see everything. Even stuff that isn't there."

"You're right about one thing," Gruber said. "Nobody believes you."

"One night, you'll all fall asleep and never wake up," Kernodle warned, waving his fingers toward them dramatically. "They'll replace all of you. And I'll be there to see it. The end of the world. Our world—but not for long." He lowered his trembling hands to the table and muttered, "Tick tock, tick tock…"

TWENTY

With Kernodle's dire warning echoing in their ears, Dean, Sam and Gruber stood silently around the table, none of them sure how to proceed. Sam had told Dean he wanted to tell Gruber what they suspected, but when the moment was right. Kernodle had stumbled onto a kernel of the truth—Dean seriously doubted a worldwide invasion had begun in a small Missouri town—but Dean couldn't imagine a more unreliable witness.

The Winchesters had hoped to replicate Kernodle's immunity to the blackouts, but short of altering their DNA to incorporate a rare, fatal disease, the task seemed impossible. Hard to defeat an enemy who could render you unconscious from afar.

"Well, if that's it, gentlemen," Gruber said to the Winchesters as he helped Kernodle to his feet and slipped cuffs on him. "I'll take our prophet of doom here back to holding."

"Fine," Sam said, distracted. "Hey, when you're done,

maybe we should review that footage again."

"Why?"

"Thought I saw something."

Gruber frowned. "Don't tell me you believe this guy's nonsense."

Not one to leave Sam out on a shaky limb, Dean said, "I—We've seen stranger things."

"Yeah," Sam said. "You'd be surprised by some of the stuff."

"Okay, whatever," Gruber said. "I'm already half delirious."

As Gruber tugged Kernodle through the doorway, Sam caught Dean's shoulder to hold him back and spoke softly, "Dean, that footage—those dark shapes—we could run it by the British Men of Letters. I don't know. Maybe they—"

"This is about us, Sam," Dean said, fighting to keep his voice low. "You and me. Working a case. The Brits? They're a last resort—beyond a last resort. And I'm not stumped yet. Are you?"

"No, but—"

"Then, it's settled."

They heard a burst of excited shouting outside the interview room.

Dean and Sam exited the room at once, brushing past Gruber who tugged Kernodle along by his elbow.

With Sam a step behind him, Dean passed between the conference room and the chief's vacant office, then between records storage and the clerk office out into the lobby where an agitated teenager stood, holding out his left forearm wrapped in a blood-spotted t-shirt.

Officer Dunn attempted to calm him, but the kid's eyes

were wild, and he wasn't hearing anything the cop was telling him. "C'mon, man, she cut me!"

"I'll take your statement," Dunn said.

"My parents don't believe me," the kid said. To reveal his injury, he'd shrugged halfway out of a studded black leather jacket he wore over a Green Day sweatshirt and torn jeans.

"We'll get to that."

Exasperated, Gruber said, "Dunn's got this. I'll be back after I show Albert to his temporary lodging."

"Dude, you don't understand," the kid said to Dunn. "She came into my home. Sliced open my arm. You gotta stop her!"

"Who?"

"How can I sleep when she could be hiding anywhere?"

"Who cut you?"

"The shadow bitch! That's what I've been trying to tell you!"

"A woman cut you?"

"She wasn't a woman," the kid said. "Just female. Some kind of—I don't know—freaky shadow monster."

Dunn approached the Winchesters. "Don't mind him, agents," he said softly. "He's tripping balls."

But the kid overheard. "I'm not high!"

"Oh, no, not judging by the smell coming off your clothes."

"One joint, okay," the kid admitted, maybe forgetting for a moment where he stood. "Half a joint, if that."

"I'll take your word for it, Mr.....?"

"Hogarth," the kid said. "Maurice Hogarth—and I have witnesses!"

"Your parents? You said they didn't believe—"

"No! They were sleeping. They slept through everything.

I'm talking about my online friends. They can collaborate everything I'm—"

"Corroborate?"

"Yeah, man," the kid said. "They saw everything. Well, almost everything. They saw enough to prove I'm not lying!"

"Okay," Dunn said. "Let's see this wound."

Maurice unwrapped the t-shirt, wincing as he pulled the cloth away from the tacky blood around the laceration in his forearm. "See? No joke!"

"It's not that bad," Dunn said. "Clean cut. Doesn't look deep."

"Hurts like hell!"

"Son, I need you to come down from whatever cloud you're circling and begin at the beginning."

Maurice rolled his eyes and, had he been a few years younger, might have stomped his foot in frustration. "Seriously, I—am—not—high! And what if she's still in my house? She's dangerous. And my parents are freaking clueless."

Dean stepped forward and placed a hand on Dunn's shoulder, "We've got this."

"They can creep into our homes!" Maurice exclaimed. "Slice our throats while we sleep."

"You want this headache?" Dunn asked.

"No problem," Sam said.

"All yours."

Dean checked one of the interview rooms off the lobby, found it empty and motioned Maurice forward. Sam brought up the rear. Maurice and Sam sat opposite each other across a table, while Dean leaned against the wall on Sam's side of the room.

"Who are you guys?"

"FBI," Sam said. "Special Agents Blair and Tench."

"That's more like it!"

Sam smiled. "Okay, Maurice, do me a favor," he said. "Take a deep breath."

"What?"

Sam followed his own instruction.

Maurice nodded, followed suit. "Okay, now what—?"

Sam glanced at Dean, who guessed what he had in mind and nodded.

"Maurice, we know about the shadows," Sam said. "Agent Tench encountered one a few hours ago."

"So, why are the police pretending they don't—?"

"You're not talking to the police," Dean said. "Agent Blair and I are a bit more... open-minded about some things."

Sam asked to see the wound again. "Shouldn't need stitches," he said. "A shadow did this to you?"

"Yeah," Maurice said. "Like she wanted to slice me open."

"What kind of weapon?"

"Her hand—thing," Maurice said, raising his own hand. "I don't know, maybe it was one of her fingernails."

"What? Like Freddy Krueger?" Dean asked.

"No," Maurice said. "Normal fingernails but sharp."

"You could see them?" Sam asked. "Fingernails?"

"Yes—No—I mean, she was a shadow—an outline. Like a silhouette of a person."

"And you could make out individual fingernails?"

"Not at first," Maurice said. "But after it—after *she* came past my computer monitor, the shadow shape came into focus, like changing from low definition to high definition. You notice details you couldn't see before."

Sam turned aside to whisper to Dean, "The ones I spotted on the surveillance cameras varied. Some clearer than others. Many fuzzy or wispy around the edges. D—Agent Tench," Sam said, glancing at Maurice. "Could you see that level of detail with the shadow in the club?"

Dean thought back to the shadow that had emerged from Jasper James and the few moments of their standoff before it fled. He'd had the overall impression of a human silhouette, but not the kind of detail Maurice described. "No," he said. "The outline was clear, but not what I'd call high-def."

"Well, the one that attacked me definitely changed, like adjusting the focus knob on a pair of binoculars."

"We haven't heard of the shadows physically assaulting anyone," Sam said. "Until now."

"At least not directly," Dean said, because possession assaults were mounting. "So, what? We think they're escalating their attacks now?"

Sam turned back to Maurice. "We need to understand what triggered the attack."

"Nothing!" Maurice exclaimed, offended. "I was video chatting with some friends and this thing showed up in my room and came after me."

"After the blackout?" Dean asked.

"Yeah," Maurice said. "Everything was fine until midnight. I live-stream my reviews of hard rock albums, classics and new stuff, you know, while we listen to the tracks. I was in the middle of reviewing *Skull Town* by Morpheus Adrift—

you guys heard that one? No? You really should check it out. It's all about this fictional—sorry—where was I?"

"Midnight," Sam prompted.

"So, at midnight, we all blacked out—except for Sally."

"Wait," Sam said. "Sally didn't black out?"

Intrigued, Dean stepped forward. Had they found another immune person?

"She lives in Bakersburg," Maurice said. "The rest of us live here, in Moyer. I don't think anyone in Bakersburg zonked out."

"Unless they were in Moyer when it happened," Dean said, disappointed.

"Well, she was at home at midnight," Maurice said. "We all zonked out for two minutes. She thought we were goofing, at first."

"And after you woke up?"

"We were all still connected online," Maurice said. "But kind of freaked out by the blackout. Didn't feel like finishing my *Skull Town* review, so we hung out and talked."

"That's it?" Dean asked.

"After the blackout, I checked on my parents, but they slept through the whole damn thing. Or did they? If you black out while you're asleep, how would you even know? Like that riddle about the tree falling in the forest but not making a sound if nobody's there to hear it. But the tree still fell, right? Anyway, I wasn't hurt or anything. No damage to the house. So, I let them sleep."

"And that's when the shadow appeared in your room?" Sam asked.

Maurice nodded. "Out of nowhere," he said. "We were talking. Then Sally saw it through her computer screen, moving toward me. That freaked her out. She yelled a warning and then I saw it."

"And it appeared female to you?"

"Not then," he said. "Only after it switched to high-def."

"When it came after you?" Sam asked.

"Yeah, when it got close. It—She approached slowly at first," Maurice said. "I backed away, but she had me cornered in my room. When she got close she—touched me—and I freaked out."

"That's when it cut you?" Sam asked.

"Not at first," he said. "She brushed against me. And I felt her. You gotta understand how weird this was—this thing." He turned to Dean. "Well, you know. You saw one."

"Saw one," Dean said. "But it didn't touch me."

Dean had made a point of avoiding its touch. He'd seen how it oozed out of Jasper's pores and Dean had no interest in becoming its rebound host. But it had touched the kid. Without possessing him. *Was it trying to communicate? Or something else?*

"Well, trust me, it's freaky," Maurice said. "It's this floating darkness. Shouldn't be able to move through the air like that. And you shouldn't be able to feel it. But I did. And I yanked my arm back."

"When did it cut you?" Sam asked again.

"After I pulled away, she seemed... I don't know, confused, at first. But then she... charged me, basically. Her hand pushed against my skin hard. Right away I felt it cutting through my flesh. I freaked out."

"I can imagine," Sam said sympathetically.

"Then what?" Dean said.

"I was shouting," Maurice said. "And my friends were yelling through my laptop. Woke my parents up. They came rushing in. I tried to explain—well, you know how that went—wanted to search my room for drugs. They convinced themselves I had a nightmare or was high. Along with my friends. Hallucinating. Refused to believe some… creature had invaded our home and attacked me."

"What about the shadow?" Dean asked.

"Honestly, I don't know," Maurice said. "Between me freaking out and all the commotion, she disappeared. I mean, I never saw how she entered my room and I never saw how she left. For all I know, she's still there, hiding somewhere in the shadows. What if—What if, you know, after my parents went back to sleep, she came out and—oh, crap…"

"Maurice," Sam said after a quick glance at Dean. "Maybe we can help with your… peace of mind."

"Mo," Maurice said.

"What?"

"My friends call me Mo," he said. "How can you help?"

"We'd like to see where the attack happened," Dean said. "And we have a device—something that will tell us if it—she—is still in your house."

"That's great, man," Maurice said, visibly relieved. "Let's go!"

TWENTY-ONE

Before the Winchesters left the interview room to visit Maurice's house, Gruber poked his head in and told them he needed to stay at the police station and would catch up with them later. Sam suggested he watch the surveillance footage again and look for any unusual movement in the shadows. Dean could understand why he simply didn't tell Gruber to look for autonomous shadows gallivanting around town and invading homes. The cop would never take either of them seriously ever again. But if Gruber discovered for himself the many incidents of anomalous movement in the shadows, and the free-flowing darkness, he might start to accept that something unnatural was at work in his town.

Sam left him with a final bit of advice, "Consider the possibility that your fellow police officer, Brady, may not have been in control of his actions when he tore up his neighbors' lawns."

"Numerous eye witnesses put him in his car," Gruber said. "It was Brady, all right."

"That seem like something he would do?" Dean asked.

"No. But he did."

"Before tonight? Would you have imagined the possibility?" Sam asked.

"Again, no."

"And these other people," Sam added. "The ones you know."

"Before today—yesterday—no," Gruber said. "What are you suggesting? Mind control?"

"Just…" Sam said. "Be open to the possibility there's another explanation. Look at that footage."

Gruber threw up his hands. "Okay. Sure. Why not?"

Until they found hard evidence of supernatural possessions, something law enforcement could accept, advising Gruber to keep an open mind was the best they could do. But, deep down, Dean worried no amount of evidence would satisfy the police, the prosecutors or the courts. People would serve jail time for crimes they had no control over.

Sam had borrowed a first-aid kit and bandaged Maurice's arm. Then Maurice drove home with Dean and Sam following in the Impala. By the time they turned down his suburban street, dawn arrived with a retreat of shadows. Curious, Dean scanned the area to locate any of the shadow creatures who might have left themselves exposed. Sam greeted the new day with a jaw-cracking yawn.

"You okay?" Dean asked.

"Haven't slept."

Dean had grabbed a few hours before the EMF detector

woke him from his shadow invasion dream. "Good thing I'm driving."

"Roles reversed," Sam said, "would it make a difference?"

"Not really."

Maurice's beater bypassed the driveway to park in the street, so Dean pulled in behind him. As they climbed out of the car, Sam said, "Maybe he'll come around."

"Gruber?" Dean said. "Unless something happens to him, not likely."

"It's like that Arthur Conan Doyle quote," Sam said. "'Once you eliminate the impossible, whatever remains, no matter how improbable, must be the truth.'"

"Far as Gruber's concerned," Dean said, "anything but personal responsibility is impossible. Some law enforcement types only see black and white. No shades of gray."

Maurice led them into his house, taking care to close the front door quietly. His parents wouldn't wake for another half-hour, he said, and they were already mad at him for interrupting their sleep with a crazy story. He had no desire to explain to them why he'd left home in the middle of the night or returned at dawn with two FBI agents.

Waving the EMF detector before him, Sam said, "We need to sweep the whole house. Only way to be sure."

"Right, well, they'll be awake soon enough."

The morning sunlight filtered through the first-floor windows. Dean caught himself checking shadows in corners, and behind doors and furniture for any signs of roaming darkness. Maurice turned left at the top of the stairs and led them to his room at the end of the hall. His closed door was painted black with a bumper sticker that advised visitors to "Rock On!"

Inside, rock band posters were plastered across every square inch of all four walls and the ceiling. The two windows and the carpet offered the only visual relief from the promotional assault. When Maurice shut the door behind them—again with utmost care—the room produced a dizzying effect, as if they stood in a pocket dimension.

Maurice led them to a half-concealed corner of the room.

"This is my broadcast booth," Maurice said, pausing to hastily shove a frog-on-a-lily-pad bong and some wrapping papers into a desk drawer. "Where I, um, where I live-stream my album reviews." He flashed a crooked smile that seemed to suggest they should pretend the last few seconds hadn't happened. "And... keep my various props."

"Props," Sam repeated as he switched on the EMF detector and began a circuit of the room.

"Yeah, you know, gotta look the part," Maurice said. "Hard core and all that."

"Where were you when you saw the female shadow?" Dean asked.

"At my desk," Maurice said, happy to change the subject. "Sitting in my chair, facing the laptop screen. But only after Sally pointed it out."

Dean sat in the executive chair and looked across the room. Many of the posters had black as a dominant color. Others were variations of black-and-white or shades of gray. The whole room, at eye level, offered a lot of camouflage for a black creature to go unnoticed, especially if it remained still.

"Everything's the same?"

"Basically," Maurice said. "Except the laptop was on and my friends—fans—were on the screen."

As Sam continued to scan EMF readings, Dean said, "Recreate everything."

"You think it will come back?"

"Worth a try," Dean said.

"If it left," Maurice said. "Not sure I want it to come back."

"Could come back when we're not here."

"Fair enough," Maurice said. "I was playing *Skull Town*." He walked to his stereo, turned on the receiver and turntable and dropped the needle on the vinyl album. Immediately, he twisted the volume knob down so the music faded into the background. "We were talking, so I had it low. Otherwise, you know, I crank it up."

Maurice returned to his desk, spun the laptop around and loaded the video chat software. "Should I contact those guys? For real?"

"Why not?" Dean said. "They were witnesses."

"Maybe they saw or heard something you missed," Sam said, opening the closet door to scan inside. He paused, reached for a pull chain and yanked, bathing the closet in the light of a bare sixty-watt bulb. "She's not in here."

Maurice stared at the laptop screen and shook his head. "Looks like only two are online… Reggie and Sally." The laptop emitted some beeping and chime sounds.

"Hey, Mo," Reggie said. "What's up?"

"Maurice? Are you okay?" Sally asked.

"Not bleeding anymore," Maurice said, flashing his

bandaged arm. "Went to the cops and came home with two FBI agents."

"What?"

"FBI? Seriously?"

Maurice lifted the laptop off the desk and turned it in a slow arc for the webcam to pick up Dean and then Sam, who stood across the room with the EMF meter in his hand. "Special Agents Tench and Blair," he said.

"So, the cops believed you?" Reggie marveled.

"Cops thought I was high," Maurice said. "But these FBI agents believe me. Agent Tench saw one of those shadow freaks before me!"

"Cool," Reggie said.

"Well, not cool that it happened," Sally said. "But—what now?"

"We asked Maurice to recreate the circumstances before the shadow appeared," Sam said as he approached the desk, satisfied they were alone in the room. "That's why he contacted you."

"We were just talking," Reggie said.

"Maurice was in the chair."

Dean stood and indicated Maurice should take the chair.

Maurice sat, looked from one Winchester to the other and shrugged his shoulders. "This is it. Nothing special."

"We're missing the others," Reggie said. "Gary, Stevie, Fig, Cory and Eddie."

"No answer," Maurice said. "Everything else is the same. We were talking. And then Sally noticed the shadow coming near me before I did."

"What did you see, Sally?" Dean asked.

"At first, I thought his webcam was glitching," she said. "This black shape or streak or something at the edge of the frame. But then it started moving toward him. Kind of floating. Couldn't see all of it. Maurice said it had the shape of a person, but I could only see the top half of it on the screen."

"Maurice said it changed," Sam said. "From low to high definition."

"Yeah, that came later, after it cut off our view of Mo," Reggie said.

"He backed up," Sally said, "and then it came across the screen, almost blotting out the rest of the room."

"I rolled back on the chair," Maurice said. "Back into my broadcast booth. It had me cornered."

Dean looked around the room, from where Maurice sat, past the desk and across the room, taking in the field of posters across the walls and ceiling, confirming his first impression that the shadow creature had enough camouflage to stay hidden while motionless. They lacked much depth at all, so that when seen from the side, they almost disappeared. Maurice had been distracted, talking to friends. It would have seemed that it came out of nowhere, but it could have been in his room for minutes before revealing itself. Or it could have slipped through the keyhole or through a gap in the windowsill seconds before Sally spotted it. Dean looked at Sam and nodded toward the EMF detector. "Nothing?"

Sam shook his head.

"Everything else is the same?" he asked Maurice and his friends.

"Yeah," Maurice said.

"Identical," Reggie said.

"No," Sally said. "Something was different."

"What?"

"The lighting."

"Yeah, it's morning now," Maurice said. "Hours ago, it was dark."

"No, not that," Sally said. "Your broadcast booth lighting. Even though you stopped your review, you left the black lights on after."

"She's right!" Maurice said. Around the entrance to the nook, he had several strips of black lights mounted to the wall. With all the visual chaos of the tiled rock posters, the strips disappeared into the background. "I use them to set the mood."

The power cords for each of the light strips came to a master power switch on the floor by his desk. Maurice tapped the orange rocker switch with the tip of his shoe and all the black lights flashed on at once. Bathed in black light, many of the posters took on new life and detail.

"Cool, huh?" Maurice said.

Dean nodded. If he stepped outside the nook, the lighting was normal. Back in, the black light shone on his arms and clothes. "Would you say the shadow switched to high-def when she came back here?"

"Soon as she passed the laptop and my desk."

"When she was bathed in black light?"

Maurice rolled his chair back and reached out his arm, nodding. "Definitely."

Sam joined them behind the desk, standing under the black lights. "At the police station, you said she seemed confused after she touched you the first time."

Maurice nodded again. "When she touched my arm, she seemed confused."

"Something surprised her," Sam said. "Something unexpected happened. Or failed to happen."

"That's when she became angry?" Dean asked. "She charged you?"

"The second time, yes," Maurice said. "Felt like I'd made her mad the first time. But I didn't do anything. I was, like, in shock. Panicked."

"He did freak out," Reggie said, chuckling.

"Thanks, bro," Maurice said.

"Whatever she tried, didn't work," Sam said softly to Dean.

"So, she tried to force it," Dean replied.

"Second time was when she sliced my arm open," Maurice said. "That's when I really freaked out."

"One guess what didn't work," Sam prompted.

"Possession," Dean said quietly, nodding.

Maurice caught the end of their side conversation and his eyes opened wide. "What was that? What didn't work?"

"Nothing," Sam said quickly. "We were discussing another case."

"The shadow at the club oozed out of that man's pores," Sam said to Dean. "With no physical trauma. This one tried to get in, but couldn't. Did you notice any black light at the dance club?"

"Maybe," Dean said. "On the dancefloor. Hard to tell

with all the moving spotlights and strobes flashing. And the possess—the bad guy never got that far. The shadow came out by the table."

Sam turned to Maurice. "Do you remember exactly how you reacted after it cut you?"

"Like I told you," Maurice said. "I freaked out."

"He screamed like a girl," Reggie said, chuckling again.

"Really, Reggie?" Sally said, rolling her eyes in exasperation. "Or did Cory join this chat?"

"Oops! Sorry, Sally!" Reggie said quickly. "Removing foot from mouth."

"Okay, maybe I yelled," Maurice said. "And I—I…" He raised his arms, palms out and froze. "I… shoved her away."

"You mean, you tried to shove her?"

"No," Maurice said. "I actually shoved her… She kind of sailed backward toward the middle of the room. And she became… fuzzier around the edges."

"No more high-def?" Dean asked.

Maurice shook his head.

"Once she was out of the black light area."

"And then she darted away, toward the door," Maurice said. "Her… I don't know, attitude, changed. Confused… or, maybe, surprised again."

"What if the black light not only makes their appearance more defined," Sam said softly to Dean, "but gives them too much substance to take over a human host?"

"Makes sense," Dean said, voice low. "She came here thinking possession, but couldn't complete the hijack, got mad and tried again."

"And when she realized Maurice could shove her away, she freaked out and fled."

A quick knock on Maurice's bedroom door preceded the door opening far enough for his father to poke his head in. "Maurice, I thought I heard—voices," he said, noticing Dean and Sam and trying to reevaluate the situation. He opened the door all the way and entered the room. "What's going on here?"

"They're with the FBI," Maurice said quickly.

"FBI? Maurice, what have you done?"

"Nothing!" Maurice said indignantly. "I was attacked and reported—!"

"Special Agents Tench and Blair," Dean interrupted, pulling out his fake ID since neither he nor Sam were dressed the part. "We were at the Moyer police station when Maurice reported the attack."

"There was no attack," the elder Hogarth said. "He was alone. He had a nightmare. That's all it was."

Maurice held up his bandaged arm. "Did a nightmare do this?"

"You said you fell out of your chair at midnight," Hogarth said. "You probably cut yourself and only noticed it later."

"Agent Tench and I are investigating the strange incidents happening in Moyer," Sam said to try to extricate them from a family spat. "What your son witnessed is consistent with other reports around town."

"I don't understand any of this."

Sam held up the EMF detector. "I'd like to check your house with this," he said. "Elevated EMF readings are consistent with some of these... unusual events."

"Will that cause any damage to our home?"

"The detector?" Sam said. "None at all."

"Do you need a warrant for that?"

"We're guests in your home," Dean said. "Not looking for evidence of any crimes. We want to make sure your house is not vulnerable."

"Let them check, Dad," Maurice said.

"If it's okay with your mother," Hogarth said. "I don't have a problem with it."

Maurice's mother, though startled to find two FBI agents in her home, consented to the full scan. Room by room, almost treating the floor plan of each story as a grid, Sam scanned the Hogarth home for elevated EMF. Over a half-hour later, Sam declared the home safe. Clearly relieved, Maurice shook both of their hands vigorously in thanks.

Back in the Impala, Dean looked at Sam, whose demeanor matched his own. The kid had been upset, with good reason. And his relief was warranted, but the EMF all-clear was no guarantee that the shadow creature wouldn't return the next night. Or five minutes after the Winchesters left.

Dean's parting advice to Maurice had been to expand the black light coverage to his entire bedroom. That precaution would protect him from the threat of possession—while he remained in his bedroom—but didn't guard against the possibility of physical harm. The black-lit shadow had no problem slicing open human flesh.

If they want us dead, Dean thought, *slicing our throats is a brutally efficient way to get it done.*

TWENTY-TWO

As the sun rose over Central Avenue in Moyer's business district, the shadows compressed, faded and disappeared, but not all were banished. Beneath awnings and trees, along alleys and driveways, beside trashcans and under cars and outdoor tables, traces of darkness lingered. Inside every store, behind doors and under counters, they remained. In basements and closets, they persisted.

During the day, the free shadows of Moyer traversed two-dimensional planes among the living residents of Moyer, sliding up and down walls, gliding along floors and sidewalks, slipping under doorways, completely unnoticed. But many of the shadows had grown impatient with the wan existence. Once they had a sample of real life, however brief, they wanted more. As easily as humans slipped into a jacket, the free shadows slipped into humans. The briefer the experience, the more intensity they desired.

Harold Turnbaugh, an elderly man walking east along

Central Avenue slowed as he neared a middle-aged woman standing at a curb, carrying a shopping bag. As a panel truck delivering appliances rumbled through a green light and approached them, the man stopped behind the woman, waited a moment, then placed both hands against her upper back and shoved with all his might. The woman shrieked as she stumbled forward, losing her balance and tumbling face first. Before her body hit the street, the truck rammed into her. The driver hit the brakes hard, but too late. The dead woman rolled half a block before the shattered bones of her broken body came to a halt, oozing blood.

Harold turned on his heel and walked westward for almost a block before stopping, confused, checking street signs to determine where he had wandered since he'd come downtown. He failed to notice the dark streak that had spread beneath his feet and darted between two stores. Behind him people shouted, something about a woman having been pushed in front of a truck and killed. He stared at the scene of the accident, but couldn't make out any details.

Not wanting to gawk, he decided to cross the street to avoid the area when someone pointed in his direction and yelled, "That's him! Right there! That's the guy that shoved her!"

Harold looked over his shoulder, but he stood alone.

Craig Westerlund rolled his Audi to a stop in front of Sino Savings & Loan, windows rolled down, heavy metal music blasting from the speakers from a radio station that had never been one of his presets. Reaching over to the passenger seat, he picked up the lug nut wrench he'd removed from the trunk before leaving the parking lot at work. He climbed out of the car, idling in park, and set the wrench on the roof while he took off his suit jacket and tossed it through the window. In shirtsleeves, he marched into the savings and loan, cut in front of the line control stanchions and their retractable barriers and approached the first teller window.

The elderly woman standing there, with her checkbook out, along with a deposit slip and multiple rolls of pennies, saw the look on his face and the wrench in his hand. She emitted an involuntary squeak of alarm, grabbed her belongings and scurried to the other side of the lobby.

Taking her place at the window, Craig placed the wrench on the counter.

The teller, a thin man with a long face and pinched features, croaked out one word, "Sir?"

"Everything in your drawer or I split your skull open."

"Is this—Is this a—?"

The three other tellers and their customers had begun to stare at the confrontation. Several customers backed away and the old woman whispered to anyone who would listen, "He has a weapon."

Craig glanced at the brown nameplate on the counter that read, Jay Lauzier.

"Now, Jay!"

"Right, okay," Jay said, scooping out the bills one row at a time and stacking them on the counter.

When he reached for the coins in front, Craig said, "Keep the change."

"Of—Of course."

"Thanks, Jay," Craig said as he stuffed his trouser pockets with banded and loose bills. "I might try a real bank next. They have security guards and probably a lot more money."

As he walked toward the exit, an occasional loose bill falling out of his stuffed pockets, the grimy lug nut wrench resting on the shoulder of his white shirt, someone shouted. "Call the police!"

"I already pressed the alarm," Jay said.

With one hand poised on the door handle, Craig paused and shook his head. Whirling around, he loped back toward the teller window with a broad smile plastered on his face. "Had to ruin our moment, Jay!"

"I'm sorry—I won't—!"

"Actions have consequences, Jay," Craig said as he swung the lug nut wrench down like a hammer and crushed the back of Jay's left hand.

Screaming in pain, Jay clutched the broken hand to his chest.

"Sincerely hope that was the hand that pressed the alarm," Craig said, grinning. "Otherwise, we have to do this all over again. Was that the hand, Jay?"

Jay nodded vigorously. "Yes. Yes!"

Craig heard sirens and frowned. He raised the bloodied lug nut wrench and turned in a slow circle, taking in the customers, the tellers, and the branch manager who had poked her head out of her office upon hearing the commotion.

His voice abruptly deeper, Craig said, *"Let this set an example for all of you."*

For a second time, he walked to the exit, seemingly unhurried despite the imminent arrival of the police. He strolled to his car, climbed into the driver's seat and tossed the wrench over to the passenger side.

He placed his hands on the steering wheel but didn't shift the car into drive. Instead, he stared through the windshield, eyes unfocused. A few seconds later, he shook his head and looked around, confused, wincing at the music blasting from the speakers. Immediately, he switched off the stereo before the bass gave him a headache.

Last thing he remembered was stopping at the water cooler for a drink before heading back to his desk at work. At the sound of paper rustling, he glanced down and saw thick rolls of bills falling out of his trouser pockets. Fives, tens and twenties spilled onto the seat and fluttered onto the floor of the car. Without even counting the money, he realized it was much more than the maximum allowable cash withdrawal from an ATM machine. So, how—?

Glancing out the window, he read the sign for the Sino Savings & Loan, which explained the source of the cash. But he banked at Jefferson National. Even if he'd applied for a loan, he'd have to wait for the approval and they would have given him a check. *Why so much cash?*

As he sat at the curb, he debated walking into the savings and loan and asking them why he'd requested the money—

His gaze had drifted across the other side of the car, to the lug nut wrench, smeared with bright crimson—blood?

The sound of police sirens had become almost deafening. Looking through the windshield and then the rearview mirror, he understood why. Two patrol cars had pulled up on either side of his car, parking at angles to effectively box him in at the curb.

As the cops jumped out of their cars, guns drawn and pointed at him, Craig thought he must have been carjacked by a bank robber. If he'd been pistol-whipped, left unconscious with a concussion, that might explain the memory loss.

But why had the criminal left him with the money?

"Out of the car now!" one cop shouted.

"Hands where we can see them!" yelled the other.

Resigned, Craig opened the car door and stepped out.

Maybe they know what happened to me...

A few blocks from the Sweet Town Bakery, Jeremy Krepps walked along Central Avenue with the aid of a rubber-tipped wooden cane. Due to an unfortunate bout of clumsiness, he'd torn ligaments in his knee while playing tennis with an old college friend at one of the free courts in Penninger Park. After surgery and rehab, the knee had progressed to the point where he thought he could ditch the cane in a week or two, though it came in handy ascending stairs. Walking became a regular part of his rehab, so he tended to walk the route of his weekly errands.

After a trim at A Cut Above Salon, he walked toward the Red Rooster Tavern for lunch. Figured he'd grab a burger and a beer and walk it off on his way home. He had to cross over to the westbound side of Central Avenue, so made his way to the nearest crosswalk. Focusing on approaching traffic, he failed to notice the approaching rumble of polyurethane wheels. As he took a step toward the crosswalk, a teenager old enough to have been a dropout, but who had probably ditched school for the day, flashed in front of him. Jeremy flinched, tweaking his recovering knee as he recoiled from the collision. The kid's shoulder whacked Jeremy's left arm and the blow added another twist to the knee.

"Damn it!" Jeremy said.

The kid had to hop off the skateboard to keep from falling. That concession seemed to aggravate him more than the collision. "Dude, watch where you're going!"

"Me?" Jeremy said incredulously. "You cut right in front of me!"

The redirected skateboard rolled into the intersection a moment before a public transit bus cruised through the crosswalk. The bus's right front tire rolled over the middle of the skateboard and split it in half.

"Son of a bitch!" the kid shouted. "You're paying for that, gimp!"

Jeremy tried to ignore the throbbing in his knee. "How is that my fault?"

"You got in my way," the kid said. "That board cost me one-fifty. Pay up!"

"I'm not paying a dime for your negligence," Jeremy said. "You shouldn't even be on the sidewalk with that thing!"

Neither of them noticed that when the ripple of the bus's shadow passed, a darker shadow passed through it to their side of the crosswalk, momentarily settling under a nearby tree.

"One-fifty now, gimp," the kid demanded, right hand extended. "Or I beat it out of you."

"Get lo—!"

A wave of darkness blotted out Jeremy's vision and—

—his body convulsed, as if he were in the throes of a silent coughing spasm. When he straightened, a smile spread across his face.

"What's so funny, dumbass?" the kid asked.

Jeremy raised his cane, gripping it in two hands like a baseball bat, and whacked the kid in the head, splitting his ear open with the first blow. When the kid yelped and cowered in pain, Jeremy swung again, breaking his nose. A third blow toppled him.

With the kid curled into the fetal position and bawling in pain, Jeremy stood over him, a fiendish gleam in his eyes, and mercilessly continued the assault. One blow split open the kid's scalp, the next gashed his cheek, and a third knocked two teeth loose. The kid was unconscious when the cane cracked and split in half.

Jeremey studied the jagged end of the top half of the cane and looked down at the kid's bruised and bloodied face, settling on the closed eyes. Kneeling beside the kid to get a better angle, he raised the half-cane to strike and—

—someone sprinted across the crosswalk and caught his arm on the downstroke, the jagged tip of the half-cane inches away from the kid's left eyelid.

"Hey, buddy!" the guy said as he pulled Jeremy up and away from the unconscious skateboarder. "Anger management issues?"

Jeremy blinked rapidly, shook his head and stared at the stranger. He had the weird sensation he'd passed out. "Where—Where did you come from?"

"Red Rooster Tavern," the stranger said. "I saw you whaling on—"

"Oh, Red Rooster," Jeremy said, remembering his lunch plans. "What are the specials?"

"Specials? Seriously?" the stranger looked down. "You almost killed that kid."

"Kid? What—?" Jeremy looked down at the bloodied youth at his feet. "Who—How? I don't understand."

When he noticed the bloody remnant of his cane, still clutched in his hand, both of his knees buckled.

Near the edge of the commercial district, the Moyer Public Library existed as a quiet oasis. Unless a stay-at-home parent brought in young children or an elementary school class dropped in on a field trip, Bonnie Lassiter, the head librarian, spent most of the afternoon in contemplative silence.

She stacked returned books on the wheeled cart to take them back to their shelf locations. With each passing week, it seemed as if the number of returned books dwindled. Not because people forgot to return them, but because fewer people checked out physical books. Many adults who continued to read books rather than spend their free time on social media, had apps to download eBooks from the library's online catalog. Virtual patrons checked out and returned virtual books from a virtual library. A procession of ghosts in the machine, never initiating human contact.

In the evenings, various clubs and groups came in for weekly or monthly meetings, breathing needed life into the library. Others came in to use the computers and the free Internet connection. Where librarians had once fielded all sorts of questions, these days the answers were waiting at the click of a search engine's submit button.

Sometimes, though, the physical books stored on row after row of shelves seemed like an afterthought, remnants of a bygone era. Other than her college years, Bonnie had spent her whole life in Moyer, a small town with a pace geared toward those who consciously chose that environment over the frenetic, anxiety-laden life in a big city. And while they couldn't escape the inevitable march of progress, they were happy to follow behind at a safe distance.

Her wheeled cart filled with all the books returned in the last twenty-four hours, most via the drop box outside—yet another convenience that had the unfortunate side effect of discouraging visits—Bonnie rolled toward a bookcase on the far left of the library, hardcover fiction. Out of habit, she listened for a telltale squeak from the left front wheel, the one that continually needed a drop of oil to quiet its protests.

Instead she heard the whoosh of the automatic doors opening and closing, but no other sound. From where she stood with the cart, she couldn't see the entrance. "If you need assistance, I'll be with you in a moment!"

No answer.

She eased the cart to the end of the aisle, almost thought she heard the wheel squeak, but wiggling the cart back and forth produced no sound. The squeaky wheel reminded her of her troublesome left knee, though she had no quick fixes to quell its complaints. *First touch of arthritis there,* she thought with a melancholy smile, *a foothold in the knee.* But lately, her fingers had become a bit achy and stiff, less nimble.

Bonnie plucked the first book from her cart and was about

to shelve it when the thump and rustle of many falling books startled her. Alarmed, she almost dropped the book. The sound had come from across the library.

"Hello?" she called. "Are you okay?"

Again, no answer.

Generally, Bonnie assumed the best in people, but she had kept up with the news of people in town behaving not just badly, but criminally, in some cases. Streaking, vandalism, physical assault and, if she could believe the report, murder by an orderly after a riot in the emergency room at the county hospital.

She left her wheeled cart in the fiction aisle and walked cautiously toward the sound of the disturbance. Patting the pocket of her cardigan, she belatedly remembered that she'd left her cell phone on a shelf under the front counter. As she passed the corner of her office, she could see the counter and the front entrance. A few steps farther toward the other side of the building and she'd be able to see where the books had fallen.

At first, she failed to see the young man. Her eyeline had been too high. When she scanned for the books, she saw him sitting cross-legged on the floor beside the nonfiction bookcases, his head barely visible above the waist-high shelves. Sitting there, he appeared nonthreatening, as if he were resting or meditating in a quiet place. Curious, she walked around the low shelf and approached the open space where he sat staring straight ahead.

The books came into view, arranged in front of the man in the shape of a number, eighty-eight. But the glossy library slipcovers looked damp, with a few scattered drops of fluid on the floor around them. A thin aluminum can with a red plastic cap on the floor was next to the man's hip—

Lighter fluid!

The young man turned his head toward her, his faraway gaze finally locking on her, and his mouth opened slowly. For a moment, she thought he would speak, but his mouth closed and opened a few times without him uttering a sound. She had the weird impression that he'd forgotten how to speak.

With a resigned sigh, he struck a match and raised the flame over the mound of doused books.

"No!" she shouted, rushing forward to stop him.

Too late.

He dropped the burning match on the nearest book. The flames spread quickly, setting the number eighty-eight ablaze.

"Why?" she asked, shaking.

He waved his left arm over the flames, as if she could overlook a mound of burning books in the middle of her library. In a flash, her concern and confusion turned into anger and outrage. The young man looked at her again and smiled briefly, opening his mouth again in another attempt to speak. First a strained croaking sound came out, but another shaking, furrowed-brow attempt to speak produced a single word, "Re-remember!"

Remember what? Was it a threat? That he'd come back and burn down the whole building. Unless she—?

She gasped as he lowered his hand into the flame. Above the scent of burning books, she smelled the pungent aroma of burning flesh. Suddenly, he flung his body backward, away from the flames—

—and the fluorescent lights overhead crackled and flickered, creating a surge and retreat of harsh shadows. From his supine position, another shadow rose, like an inkblot stain. It hung motionless in the air above the unconscious man. Between the whorls of rising smoke and the motionless black shape, she blinked rapidly to clear her eyesight. Acrid smoke triggered a raw cough, prompting her to back up before it became an uncontrollable spasm.

Tears welled up in her eyes, blurring her vision.

Abruptly, the inkblot stain darted away. She imagined a frightened animal fleeing a forest fire.

With a sudden burst, the sprinkler head directly above the fire activated, spraying water across the floor and quenching the fire before it could spread. She hurried to the counter, grabbed the phone and dialed 911.

TWENTY-THREE

When his five-year-old sister screamed, Ethan had been in his bedroom, drawing dogs on a sketch pad his father bought for him. He'd decided to draw a different animal each day, but he soon learned a day wasn't long enough. He wanted them to look real, not like stick figures with blobs for their heads and bodies. "Practice makes perfect," his father had told him. But how much practice would it take for them to look good? "Because nobody's perfect," he muttered.

A sudden crash downstairs startled him, making him break the point off his pencil. Seconds later, Addie screamed. Pushing aside his drawing supplies, he jumped back, knocking over his desk chair, and froze.

The boogeymen flowed across his room, in through the windows, out through the doorway. Sometimes, if he really focused on an activity, he could tune out their presence. They never completely abandoned his house. They acted like they owned the place and Ethan and his family were the intruders. But his friend Barry had assured him multiple times the others would not hurt Ethan or his family.

"Addie!" he called. "Mom! Dad!"

Nobody answered. But he heard Addie sobbing downstairs.

The queasy feeling had returned. Ethan trusted Barry, but not the rest of them.

"Barry!" he called frantically. "Where are you?"

Barry had left the house earlier and hadn't returned. *What if something happened to Barry? What if it already happened? Would the others keep their promise?*

He ran into the hallway and down the stairs. Everywhere he looked, a shadow seemed to dart by. They moved around so much and looked so similar he had trouble counting them all. Were there five or ten—or twenty?

At the bottom of the stairs, he stopped and looked across the dining room. The table had been shoved from its normal location. Next to an overturned chair, his father lay sprawled on his back, eyes closed, one knee raised, a frying pan near his head and a bloody butcher knife a few inches from his open palm.

In shock, Ethan passed through the archway into the dining room. He saw his mother slumped against the unfinished wall. Blood oozed from a knife wound in her shoulder. At least he assumed the wound came from the bloody knife near his father's hand. Face pale, his mother fought to stay awake, her eyelids fluttering rapidly, occasionally revealing nothing but the whites of her eyes.

Sitting in a ball in the near corner, arms wrapped around her knees, head lowered to shield her own eyes, Addie sobbed, pausing only to wipe her runny nose on the sleeve of her white blouse.

"Addie," he whispered, but she refused to look up or answer him. "Addie!"

Nothing.

A dark shape entered the dining room, circled the table and left again.

Hugging the wall, Ethan scrambled over to his sister and tried to lift her face in his hands, but she fought him. Instead, he sat beside her and hugged her shoulders. Between the sobs and the sniffles, she released her own knees and wrapped her arms around him, burying her face against his chest.

Once again, he looked at his father and the knife by his hand, frying pan by his head. "Addie, what happened?"

"Dad—and then Mom…"

He wasn't dumb, but he was confused. Had his father stabbed his mother? Had his mother then hit him over the head with a frying pan to stop him? His parents had argued in the past, usually about something broken in one of the houses they stayed in before his father finished the repairs and they moved into another crappy house. But his father had never hit his mother. At least, he'd never seen him hit her. He had a thought that they finally saw the boogeymen and it drove them crazy. Somehow, he knew it was their fault. Maybe they scared his parents or made them fight. Since the living shadows first appeared in the house, Ethan wondered how they could hurt anyone. They couldn't open doors or windows, or lift anything. Not a knife or a gun. But he'd heard his parents talking about the news, about people in town hurting each other.

And now it had happened in his own home.

"You said you wouldn't hurt us!" Ethan yelled. "You promised!"

With his whole family in one room, more of the shadows entered and lingered nearby. More than six of them, he decided, almost ten. At first, he couldn't tell them apart, but the longer they stayed in the room, the easier it was to spot differences. Some of the smaller shadows were blurry with wispy arms and legs. They stayed far away from him, almost as if they were afraid of him or his display of anger. But the bigger ones had sharp edges, no blurry borders, and they hovered over him, trying to scare him, like the bigger kids on the playground who were bullies.

He was scared, but angry too. They'd lied. They'd hurt his parents.

Addie continued to sob quietly in his arms. Maybe she'd seen the free shadows, the boogeymen, and that explained why she refused to look up. You couldn't hear them or smell them or feel them. You only knew they were present when you saw them. If she didn't look up, she could pretend they were gone or that she had only imagined them.

Emboldened, he stared at the big one leaning over him, and shouted, "You said we were safe!"

Glancing across the room, he checked that his father was still unconscious. What would happen if he woke up? Would he try to kill Ethan's mother again? Would he attack Addie or Ethan next?

His mother's head lolled to the side, her hand fumbling toward the stab wound high on her left side, just below her shoulder.

"Mom?" he called. "Mom, can you hear me?"

She muttered something he couldn't understand.

A few of the shadows left the dining room. The big one who had tried to bully him, backed away without leaving the room.

"This is your fault!" Ethan said. "I'll tell Barry you broke your promise!"

Though he knew the threat was pointless, because Barry had no power over the others, Ethan sensed the need to put on a brave face, to not look weak in front of the bad shadows. But he had other concerns. Unlike the shadows, his father could hurt all of them if he woke up and decided he really liked stabbing people. Or, if it wasn't his fault, if the shadows had somehow made him do it, what would stop them from controlling him all over again, from forcing him to kill his entire family.

While he worried about what his father might do next, the blood stain on his mother's dress continued to spread. If Ethan sat there holding Addie and did nothing else, their mother could bleed to death.

A few shadows lingered in the room, floating around in no real hurry. Meanwhile, Ethan's heart pounded so hard he thought it might explode. And his growing panic made him tremble uncontrollably.

So that the shadows wouldn't hear, he leaned down and whispered into Addie's ear, "We need to get help!"

TWENTY-FOUR

Dean jumped from one browser tab to the next, checking the lore for information on shadow people, peripherally aware of sirens coming and going through town. He had a good idea the wave of vandalism and assaults continued to disrupt everyday life in Moyer. Gruber hadn't contacted them since they left the police station with Maurice, so Dean assumed he had his hands full.

They had to get ahead of the cycle of weird behavior and escalating violence and stop the reign of terror before Moyer became a ghost town.

The thought of ghosts triggered a quick glance at the activated EMF detector by the door, the best they could do for an early warning system. One thing at least that the shadow people had in common with ghosts. Dean wondered if salt-loaded shotgun shells could temporarily disrupt shadow people the way they worked on ghosts. Not a permanent solution, but maybe enough to buy them time to regroup.

Regular light had no effect on the shadow people, yet

black light changed their consistency and prevented them from possessing humans. Of course, black light also gave the shadows the ability to physically harm humans. "Double-edged light sword," Dean said as he skimmed sections of lore.

Exhausted, Sam slept through the rising and falling wail of the sirens.

Based upon lore, shadow people were most often seen in the periphery of human vision or during periods of sleep paralysis. They stayed near humans but preferred to remain unseen. Some were considered harmless while others seemed malevolent and induced feelings of dread. The physical descriptions and movement patterns matched what Dean had witnessed in the last two days. Unfortunately, the lore included little in the way of weaknesses or vulnerabilities.

"How do you gank a shadow?" Dean wondered.

He glanced toward Sam, who hadn't stirred since his head hit the pillow.

With a sigh, Dean reviewed his notes. The lore described the ineffectiveness of regular light against shadow people, but black light seemed to hamper them. Maybe that presented an opening.

He thought back to his encounter at Gyrations. That shadow had possessed a man and wanted to slice and dice a bunch of EDM aficionados. Yet it stopped before the assault began. Dean didn't flatter himself to think his presence had been a deterrent to the shadow knifer. So, something in the club had been an obstacle.

On the bedside table, Sam's cell phone rang.

Dean walked over and picked it up before it woke Sam.

Checked the caller ID. Gruber. "Yeah?"

"Blair?"

"Tench," Dean said. "What's up?"

"Several things," Gruber said. "None good. Luther Broady hanged himself in his cell."

"Damn," Dean whispered.

"Guess he couldn't handle the guilt over what he'd done."

Dean pressed a hand to his face. Though Luther hadn't been responsible for the murder, all the evidence pointed to his culpability. *Probably assumed he'd had some kind of psychotic break.*

"Chief Hardigan is on the warpath," Gruber said. "'How could this happen?' And all that, but we are stretched very thin, even with Bakersburg helping out."

"I hear non-stop sirens out there."

"Yeah," Gruber said grimly. His voice dropped as he continued, "So, I watched some of the surveillance footage again…"

"And?"

"And… something's there. Something I don't understand," Gruber said. "If it was one camera or one location, I'd chalk it up to an equipment malfunction or a trick of the light. But it's something else, isn't it?"

"Yeah," Dean said. Gruber had taken the first step. "Something else."

"Are they… Are they shadows?"

The conversation in the room roused Sam, who opened his eyes wide and pushed himself up into a sitting position on the bed, mouthing, "Gruber?"

Dean nodded and switched the call to speaker, so Sam could listen. "They only look like shadows," Sam said, raising his voice. "It's a mistake to assume that's all they are."

"Had a feeling you'd say that," Gruber replied with a sigh. "Somehow, those *things* are responsible for this—chaos, aren't they?"

"Almost all of it," Dean said.

"How is that possible?"

"The shadow people—"

"That what you're calling them?" Gruber asked. "Shadow people?"

"Good a name as any," Dean said, as if the name was a convenient label, rather than something recorded in the lore. "The shadow people poss—"

Sam reached for the cell phone. Dean frowned but handed it to him. Of the two of them, Sam had a better understanding of Gruber. Sam held the phone up and said, "These shadow people have the ability to… alter behavior."

"But how?"

"Like a drug," Sam said, holding up a hand to forestall Dean's vocal protest. "We know alcohol and narcotics can lower inhibitions, make people more compliant or angry, confused or depressed."

"Sure," Gruber said.

Good idea, Dean thought. *Give Gruber something he can wrap his head around.*

"Well, the shadow people have a more direct effect on people," Sam said. He took a deep, silent breath before proceeding. "Shadow people have the ability to control their actions."

"Again, how is that possible?"

"We don't know," Sam said.

Technically true, Dean thought. *We know they possess people but exactly how the possession works is something only they know.*

"More important question," Gruber said, having taken the supernatural aspect in stride. "How do we stop them?"

"We're working on it," Dean said, loud enough to be heard from across the room.

"While you're doing that, I have a favor to ask."

"Sure," Sam said, looking at Dean, who shrugged.

"Local librarian reported a book burning."

"Not that I approve of book burning, but—"

"Gets better," Gruber said. "Or worse, depending on how you look at it. She reported a strange shadow coming out of the guy who torched the books. And she insisted the burning books included a message of some kind. Maybe it relates to censorship, but these days, who knows?"

"We're on it," Sam said.

By the time the Winchesters arrived at the Moyer Public Library, a fire engine crew had determined the fire no longer presented a threat. They left behind an ambulance with two EMTs, one of whom bandaged the hand and forearm of the accused book burner, Robert Secord, by the front desk of the library.

They found the librarian, Bonnie Lassiter, a conservatively dressed woman in her late fifties or early sixties, standing over a charred mound of books at the center of a broad puddle of water. Around her, they heard a steady drip of water falling from soaked books and wet metal shelves. Judging by the covers and titles, twentieth-century American history had taken the biggest hit. Only one sprinkler head had been triggered, so most of the library had been spared water damage.

"Everything okay?" Sam asked.

"Oh! Hello," she said, almost startled to see them standing beside her. "Are you with the police department?"

"FBI," Dean said. "Special Agents Tench and Blair."

"FBI? Wouldn't have thought this crime deserved Federal attention."

"Long story," Sam said. "Were you injured?"

"No," she said. "I came over here to start cleaning up. But my mind wandered. Happens more often these days."

Dean peered up at the sprinkler head, then down to the floor and back up again. A bead of water dangled from the sprinkler for a moment until it finally fell, splashing right between the two soggy mounds of charred books. Dead center.

That's not a coincidence.

"We understand you saw a strange shadow," Sam said.

"Strange, yes," she said. "Everything about this was strange."

"Tell us what happened. From the beginning?"

"I was stacking returned books," she said. "Alone at first. Then Bob over there entered." She nodded toward the young man in the care of the EMT.

"You know him?" Dean asked.

"Never met him," she said. "Anyway, I heard books falling and came over to investigate…" She explained how she'd found Secord sitting on the floor, the books arranged neatly in front of him but doused in lighter fluid. Then the fire, his initial inability to speak followed by the utterance of one word before shoving his hand in the flame and passing out.

"'Remember'?" Sam asked. "Remember what?"

"I have no idea," she said with a shrug. "And it took him a long time to get out that one word. When he first tried to speak, he looked like a fish plucked from the water, mouth opening and closing."

"When you called the police, you mentioned a message of some sort," Dean prompted.

"The books," she said, pointing.

Dean and Sam looked at the books, too charred to read any titles or even make out what had been on the covers. "What were they?" Dean finally asked.

"I was too stunned to notice," she said. "American history, I imagine. That's the section he raided."

"So, what was the message?" Sam asked.

"The message wasn't the books themselves," she said. "But the way he arranged them. A number. Eighty-eight."

"Eighty-eight?" Dean asked.

"Look," she said. "You can still see it."

"Does that number mean something to you?" Sam asked.

"No," she said. "Sorry."

"He said 'remember' so there must be a connection to you," Sam said. "Was it a year—1988? Did something happen to you in 1988? Or here in Moyer?"

"Maybe a sports jersey number," Dean suggested. "Any famous sports figures from Moyer?"

"Not ringing any bells," she said.

"Robert," Sam called. "Mr. Secord? Does the number eighty-eight mean anything to you?"

Secord took a few steps toward them, looked over the low shelf at the burned books and shook his head. "She already asked me. I'm as confused as she is. I don't know how I got here. I don't remember pulling those books off the shelf or lighting them on fire—or burning my own hand." He sighed. "I have no idea why I would do any of those things."

Sam circled the two charred mounds of books, his boots sloshing water around, spreading the puddle outward. "Two eights…"

"Eighty-eight or two eights, it means nothing to me," she said, giving the puddle a wide berth as she crossed the room to a supply closet. "I really need to mop up."

"What if it's not a number?" Sam said. "What if it's two letters?"

"Letters?" she said. "Oh, you mean—?"

"Two Bs," Dean said. "An abbreviation? Or somebody's initials?"

"Of course!" she said, the mop forgotten as she walked back, right through the puddle to the destroyed books. A wistful smile spread across her face, making her appear at least a decade younger. "I'd almost forgotten. Our back-to-back Bs. Ah, but that was so long ago."

Sam glanced at Dean, who shrugged.

"Back to back?"

"That's how we wrote our initials," she said. "Bonnie and Barry."

"Who's Barry?" Sam asked.

"Someone I knew years ago," she said. Her gaze turned toward Robert Secord, who had wandered over, curious about their conversation. "Barry?" she asked, staring at Secord with tears welling in her eyes.

"No offense, lady," he said, palms raised. "But I've never met you before. And I don't know anyone named Barry."

"You couldn't have," she said, her smile lingering. "You're too young."

The EMT, who looked even younger than Secord, with a blond crewcut and a pierced eyebrow, touched the burned man's shoulder and said, "Need to take you to the hospital to have that burn looked at."

Secord nodded and left with the ambulance. Bonnie stared after him.

Sam looked at Dean again, confused by Bonnie's behavior, and walked over to the librarian. "You think he's Barry?"

"Oh, no, not him," Bonnie said, glancing up at Sam with a twinkle in her eye. "The shadow."

"The shadow?"

"It was him," Bonnie said. "Don't you see? It had to be him."

TWENTY-FIVE

"Barry was a runaway," Bonnie said. "Otherwise, we never would have met."

From the utility closet, she retrieved a mop and a wheeled metal bucket to clean up the mess left behind by the sprinkler. Sam took the mop from her and began the cleanup process. Dean carried over a large trashcan and dumped the burned books in it, then moved it to the wet shelves, where Bonnie could decide which books to discard. She handed Dean a legal pad to record titles, publishers and authors for her, making a list she would use to purchase replacements for the discarded volumes. While they worked, she told them about Barry.

She met a runaway boy in the summer of 1968. Bonnie was fourteen years old, and Barry was barely sixteen. Soon she realized he'd latched onto—or, more likely, fallen under the influence of—a local commune. Before long, the commune became more of a cult, with an enforced hierarchy of the founder and his leadership council.

"They called themselves the Free Folk of the Fields," she said, "or, simply, the Fields."

Barry had been one of maybe a dozen runaways and juvenile delinquents who found an unlikely home in the Fields. Some were good kids who fled abusive homes, or homes where one or both parents were in jail or addicted to drugs. Some of them were rough, repeat and violent offenders. So, some of them needed a safe space to live, while others needed a place to hide rather than a long-term home. But all of them craved structure, sometimes as simple as a place to sleep and regular meals.

But adults established the commune and many other disaffected adults gladly joined the Fields. Though they came from different backgrounds, they shared a profound sense of dissatisfaction. In a way, they were dreamers hoping to build a better way of life, separate from the confines and expectations of traditional society. Many were spiritual but adhered to no established faith.

"Some, I believe, hoped to establish their own religions," Bonnie said. "But I got the sense, from Barry, that they had a few too many spiritual seekers angling for the top spot."

"Too many chefs in the church kitchen," Dean said as he glanced down at the trashcan. A few more waterlogged books and he'd need to grab a second one.

Bonnie nodded. "The Fields had too much internal discord to survive long-term. Back when I was a young girl, it was more of a mystery to me, but from the outside it seemed like a confused mess. I never understood the appeal. I guess I was fortunate to have a stable home environment."

Sam had mopped up most of the excess water. He wrung

the mop out one last time. "How did the commune survive?" he asked. "Economically?"

"Well, Barry always told me the Fields grew and sold soybeans, corn, sorghum and vegetables to feed and support themselves. And that was the common perception in Moyer at the time."

"But?" Sam asked as he wheeled the sloshing metal bucket to the utility room where he could empty it in the sink.

"But Barry kept some of the unsavory details from me," she said. "So I wouldn't worry about his safety. The commune became a victim of its own success, in a way. They couldn't grow enough food to feed everyone, so they turned to other income sources."

"Bet I can guess what," Dean said.

Bonnie nodded. "I began to hear rumors around town," she said. "They were selling illegal drugs to supplement their income. Everything from marijuana and magic mushrooms to LSD."

"And the cops didn't find out?" Sam asked.

"I believe, initially, the spiritual leaders intended for the drugs to stay within the commune, and only for aiding the Free Folk in achieving higher spiritual awareness or altered states of consciousness or... something. Part of their expanding and sometimes contradictory religious ceremonies. They maintained the secret by selling strictly to tourists and out-of-towners."

"Tourists?" Dean asked.

"Sure," she replied. "Back then, Moyer was a bit of a tourist destination. In the late Sixties, Lake Delsea was scenic and pristine, a perfect place for renting a cabin, boating and swimming. And the Free Folk took advantage of that. They supplemented their income by roaming through the crowds selling beads and trinkets and tie-dyed shirts. Everyone assumed that was the only way they were generating income, myself included. We didn't know that along with those open public transactions, they were selling various hallucinogens and some marijuana."

She walked into the utility closet and returned with some rags. She gave one each to Sam and Dean, kept one for herself, and together they wiped down the wet shelving.

"During peak season, the Free Folk had no trouble keeping their underground economy hidden, there were so many tourists," she continued. "But in the off-season, everyone still needed to eat, and they had far fewer customers."

"They began to sell to locals," Dean guessed.

"A handful, at first," Bonnie said. "But word gets around, people start to seek them out instead of the other way around, and it becomes hard to discount the rumors."

"So, drugs were the downfall of the commune?" Sam asked.

"Today, some people say Pangento Chemicals brought jobs at the cost of tourists and that was the reason. Personally, I preferred the tourists. Who knew a few toxic chemical spills could ruin a lake's reputation?" She chuckled bitterly. "But Pangento came years after the Free Folk were gone. No, toxic leadership was the real reason for the downfall of the Fields."

"Not sure how Barry figures into this," Sam said.

Bonnie collected the wet rags, squeezed out the excess water over the utility room sink and hung them over the edge to dry. "When I first met Barry, he seemed carefree, happy to be away from foster families and a court system that dictated his life and living arrangements. We were both young, kindred spirits but in an opposites-attract way. My mother managed a lakeside souvenir shop and I hung around, sweeping floors, doing odds and ends for her.

"One day, Barry saw me sweeping out front and tried to sell me a bead necklace," she said, her wistful smile once again on display. "I told him I'd buy it—if he bought something from my mother's store. He said he had no money and I confessed the same. We laughed together. He offered the necklace as a gift instead, which I accepted. But I promised to buy him something from the store later. He said to save my money. He didn't need a tourist trinket since he lived in Moyer. When I wondered where—he was awfully cute, and I had never seen him in school—he told me about the Free Folk. Well, that seemed very exotic and adventurous and I was kind of smitten."

She sighed. Dean sensed her story was about to take a turn.

"As the summer wore on, Barry's eyes became haunted," she said. "I suspected something had soured for him in the Fields. Barry insisted nothing illegal was happening. He'd say, 'Nothing to worry about, my Bonnie Lass.' That was his nickname for me, because of my last name. He knew it always made me smile. But I started to wonder if he was lying for my peace of mind."

"You think he knew?" Sam asked. "About the drug business?"

"In hindsight, I think he had his suspicions," she said. "I'm sure he heard the rumors. But, I'd like to think he wasn't involved, even if he did know. What seemed to bother him the most during that time was Caleb."

Dean and Sam each grabbed a handle of the overflowing trashcan and walked it into the utility room. "Caleb?" Dean asked as they followed her to the front desk.

"Caleb was the founder and de facto cult leader," she said. "By then, the Free Folk had become more cult than commune. Anyway, Caleb started preaching about a doomsday event. He'd been… psychologically scarred by the Cuban Missile Crisis. He believed the world would end in nuclear fire. Literal hell on earth. And that became incorporated into their complex religious beliefs. That righteous men and women would not abide on the Earth. To him, the string of assassinations in the mid- to late Sixties were signs that he needed to prepare the Free Folk for the 'ascended life' before doomsday came. He regularly used psychedelic drugs and his hallucinations or 'visions' confirmed his fears. On a regular basis, he preached to the Free Folk about these visions and his plans for them. Caleb preached that only by achieving an altered state of consciousness could they 'ascend' and save themselves from the doom set to befall mankind."

Bonnie walked behind the front counter, looked down and straightened some papers and a stapler, her hands trembling slightly, before she looked up at them again. "Barry told me about this. Tried to make a joke about it. But I could tell it troubled him. Our friendship had grown deeper over the course of the summer and he confided in me more often. I begged him to leave the Free Folk several times, but he said he had nowhere to go, no better options. And he believed Caleb was simply using scare tactics to keep the Free Folk in line. Some of the adults had begun to chafe under his authoritarian rule and discussed leaving for good. Those who talked openly about defiance or disobeyed his orders had to spend time in underground detention rooms, symbolic graves, to realign their thinking. And by 'rooms' I mean narrow holes dug in the ground lined with plywood, with hinged wooden roofs camouflaged with sod, so outsiders wouldn't notice them."

"Symbolic graves?" Sam asked.

"Remember, he believed hell on earth was imminent," she said. "Those who refused the path to ascension would die with the outsiders. He convinced the Free Folk that realignment time in the detention rooms was beneficial for their troubled members."

"Sucker born every minute," Dean said, shaking his head.

"Barry told me once that the Free Folk also used the underground rooms to hide members whenever law enforcement came looking around."

"Why?" Sam wondered.

"Caleb believed their true number would frighten the town," she said. "And the town would pressure the police to harass them and chase them out of Moyer."

"How many were there?" Dean asked.

"The town believed there were twenty, two dozen at most," she said. "The Free Folk always gave the impression that people passed through, stayed for a while and moved on. That's why we would see different faces. The reality is that most who came stayed until the end. Barry said once he counted forty to fifty during one religious service. But they had multiple spiritual leaders, and each preached a slightly different gospel, if you want to call it that. And each leader had their own following, though some overlapped. My impression is that Caleb began to discourage individuality, consolidate all the splinter groups and force everyone to follow his own vision."

"Is that why they disbanded?" Sam asked. "Conflicting ideologies?"

"Oh, no," Bonnie said. "You don't understand. They never disbanded."

"So, what happened?" Dean asked.

"Caleb—or, rather, his irresponsibility—killed them all," she said, her voice quavering as tears welled in her eyes. "Even my Barry."

TWENTY-SIX

Somehow Ethan had managed to disentangle himself from his five-year-old sister, ignore the free shadows who continued to float and dart around his home, and scramble across the dining room to search his unconscious father's pockets. Once Addie discovered Ethan's plan she not only released him but agreed to stay in the far corner of the room.

To Ethan's horror, his father had begun to stir, fingers twitching inches from the knife that had stabbed Ethan's mother. Acutely aware of the streak of blood on the knife, Ethan reached into his father's back left jean pocket. In hindsight, he should have kicked the knife away, across the room or under the table, maybe hidden it somewhere. But he couldn't bear the thought of touching it after it had been used to hurt his mother.

In his mind, he imagined the news report resulting from his simple mistake. The newscaster would read the story in a serious voice, "House-flipper Daniel Yates stabbed wife, Susan to death before murdering the couple's two young children, nine-year-old Ethan and five-year-old Addison. Mr. Yates then abandoned their big, crappy house without a trace to top the FBI's most-wanted list. He will be remembered in campfire horror stories for years to come. Turning to other news…"

When Ethan glanced up, he saw that Addie had shoved herself along the baseboard to place herself next to their now unconscious mother, still bleeding from the shoulder wound. Before his father regained consciousness, Ethan scurried under the table to join Addie and his mother, clutching his father's cell phone in his hand. Leaning against the wall, he exhaled the breath he'd been holding for what felt like ten minutes. Then his father moaned—and Ethan held his next breath.

Daniel Yates, rubbed his head, wincing, "Susan? What— What happened? Did I fall?" He hoisted himself into a seated position against the wall, looking around in confusion. His hand brushed the bloody kitchen knife at his side. More confusion as he frowned and picked up the knife, staring at the blood. "What the hell?"

"Dad?" Ethan said, hoping his father had returned to normal. "Why did you hurt—?"

Before he could finish the question, the large shadow man who had loomed over Ethan earlier swooped into the dining room, sailed under the dining room table and crashed into Daniel Yates.

Ethan's father jerked, his torso rising, jaw thrusting forward then up, as if an electrical charge had surged through him. The boogeyman had poured into him, a darkness that overlapped his father's head, torso, arms and legs and submerged in an instant, right through clothes and flesh.

If Ethan hadn't suspected the truth, he might have thought that his father had battled the boogeyman and won. But Ethan knew better than to be fooled by what he'd seen. He realized this was how they made his father hurt his mother. *They go inside,* Ethan thought. *They go inside and make us do bad things.*

As if Ethan needed confirmation for this theory, his father's eyes momentarily flashed red, a soft glow indicating his father was no longer in charge of his own body. The shadows couldn't move things or hurt people—unless they got inside a real body.

Then they could do whatever they wanted.

His father's hand tightened around the handle of the knife, knuckles turning white with effort. For the moment, the thing occupying his father's body hadn't looked at Ethan or his sister.

Maybe it needs a minute or two to take over completely. Maybe less…

He grabbed his sister's small hand in his and tugged her. But she resisted, clinging to their mother's body. Right then, their mother couldn't protect them. And only Ethan could protect Addie. But they had to hurry.

"C'mon!" he whispered fiercely in her ear. "We have to go!"

"What about Momma?" she whispered back.

"We'll call for help," he promised. "Right now, we have to hurry!"

"Okay," she said, reluctantly releasing their mother's arm.

Ethan pulled her to her feet and tugged her along, stumbling out of the dining room. As they ran up the steps, he stayed slightly behind her in case she lost her balance. "Go, go, go!"

From behind them, he heard the squeak of a chair sliding across the floor, the creak of the floorboards as his father—his father's body—climbed to his feet. At the top of the stairs, Addie stopped and turned around. For the first time, she noticed the continuing movement of the shadow people. She squealed in terror as one shot past her on its way down the staircase.

"What are they?"

"Ignore them," Ethan said. "They can't hurt us."

It wasn't the complete truth, but it wasn't a lie either.

"Hurry," he said and led her to his bedroom. Once inside he closed the door as quietly as he could, turned the lock, then pushed his desk in front of the door.

Scared and confused, Addie leaned against his bed.

He joined her, facing the door. Wondering how long it would hold, how long it would stop their father from killing them.

"Are we safe?" Addie asked, reaching out to clutch his hand.

A free shadow slipped into his room through his windowsill, circled his room twice, as if making a mental list of everything he owned, then ducked low under the desk and out through the crack beneath the door.

"Ethan, are we safe?"

He swallowed, afraid to tell her he'd made a big mistake coming upstairs. His first thought had been to run to his safe place, the place where Barry had told him over and over that he and his family wouldn't be hurt. His bedroom. But none of that mattered now. Barry had lied. His family wasn't safe. And Ethan's bedroom was no more than a trap—a dead end.

The shadow people had acted as if they owned the house and resented Ethan's family living there. So, now Ethan knew they wanted it for themselves. And they were willing to kill every member of the Yates family to take it.

Ethan couldn't admit that to Addie. But anything else would be a total lie. And she would know it, would sense that he was lying to her, and she would panic. She would cry. And their father would hear her crying and he would come. He would break through the door, knock over the child's desk and he would raise his bloody knife and...

"We need to stay here until help comes," Ethan said.

He reached into the pocket where he stuffed his father's cell phone.

At that moment, he heard slow and steady footfalls ascending the wooden staircase.

"What are you doing?"

"I'm calling 911," Ethan said. "They'll send help. That's what they do."

"Good," Addie said, comforted. She knew about 911.

Ethan's throat went dry. He couldn't swallow. His hand began to shake.

A hand rattled the doorknob.

"Call them!" Addie whispered. "Why are you waiting?"

No matter how hard he stared at the phone display, the words stayed the same: ENTER PASSCODE

A fist slammed against the door, shaking it on its hinges.

Startled by the booming sound, Ethan almost dropped the phone.

"It's locked!" he whispered. "It's locked—and I don't know his code!"

TWENTY-SEVEN

"How did Caleb kill them?" Dean asked. "By spiking the Kool-Aid?"

"Indirectly," Bonnie said. "By his actions. The choices he made put them all in danger. From growing and selling drugs. To criminal carelessness. Technically, the explosion killed them."

"Explosion?" Sam asked incredulously.

Dean had a similar reaction. An explosion would not have been high on his list of expected endings for a late Sixties commune or cult.

"That's where the carelessness comes in," Bonnie said. "When it happened, I was shocked, naturally, and for a long time after that I was simply... numb. Deep down, I was in denial, hoping that Barry had escaped the cult before the accident, even if he had to leave without saying goodbye. But he..."

Her voice faltered, and she fell silent for a few moments before regaining her composure. She reached under the counter for a bottle of spring water.

"We didn't have to wait long for the official police report," she said. "I watched the news and read the newspaper account. According to the police, the explosion was caused by unstable dynamite. For some reason, Caleb stored it close to where they conducted their midnight communal gatherings. Unlike the religious meetings, where attendance changed and overlapped, depending on which spiritual leader in the group spoke, everyone had to attend the communal gatherings. Caleb and the council discussed commune affairs, business issues, the harvest, rules changes. They also welcomed new Free Folk members during these meetings. Attendance was mandatory. Several times when Barry and I hung out late, he would have to leave to attend one of these meetings. Called it his midnight curfew and rolled his eyes."

"Why midnight?" Sam wondered.

"Caleb believed midnight was a magical moment in each day, a 'bridge between the past and the possible.' He considered it a mystical gateway. Barry never explicitly told me this, but after Caleb started having visions, I believe he made the council and, eventually, all the Free Folk take his psychedelic concoctions at these meetings. Another rule he enforced. He wanted them to see what he saw. Barry didn't want me to know he'd been forced to use the drugs to stay in the commune. But I think that's when his mood began to sour."

She took another sip of water. "RFK's assassination may have pushed Caleb over the edge. The midnight meetings became almost a nightly occurrence. Caleb told the group they would ascend to a new world order, free of the sins of the past, but ascension was only possible during an altered state of consciousness and all the Free Folk must see and believe what he saw to ascend. But no two people hallucinate the same. That clearly frustrated him. In the end, none of it mattered," she said. "I made Barry promise me he would get out of there. But he wanted to convince some of the others his age, mostly the runaways, to leave with him. He thought their best chance to escape would come after one of the meetings. They would have at least a twenty-four-hour head start before the Free Folk realized they had gone. Even so, some were afraid to leave. Barry either waited too long or recruited the wrong person, who betrayed him. And they ended up in the wrong place at the wrong time on July twentieth."

"Why were they storing dynamite?" Dean asked.

"Before they turned to the drug trade," Bonnie said, "they expanded their planting area by cutting down trees and blowing up stumps. According to Barry, the Free Folk took advice from Old Man Warhurst, who owned a nearby farm. He sold them dynamite from his own stock. Probably turned a bit of a profit at their expense."

"Wait a minute," Sam said. "Warhurst? Martin Warhurst Sr.?"

"Martin, yes," Bonnie said. "But we all called him Old Man Warhurst. Crusty old bastard."

Sam turned to Dean. "Dynamite exploded during a thunderstorm on the afternoon before the blackouts."

"Right," Dean said, recalling the article. "Long before midnight. A dead end."

"Maybe not," Sam said. "That explosion occurred on the Warhurst farm."

"Okay, good to know," Dean said, guessing it was no more than a coincidence. Not many farms in the immediate area. And regular suburban homeowners wouldn't be stocking dynamite.

"So, get this," Sam said. "Martin Warhurst Jr. inherited that farm when his father died forty years ago but never worked the farm. He left everything as it was when his father died."

"You're suggesting—"

"The dynamite that exploded during the thunderstorm could be part of the same batch that killed the Free Folk."

"So, maybe there is a connection," Dean said, frowning, "but damned if I can figure it out."

"It's a puzzle piece," Sam said. "Not sure how it fits yet, but…" He turned to Bonnie. "You were saying—about why they needed the dynamite…"

"Once they started selling drugs, I guess they no longer needed dynamite. But it was unstable, and blew up during one of the midnight meetings."

"You believe someone betrayed Barry?" Sam asked.

"They found Barry's body and a few others in the detention chambers. Maybe they were caught trying to escape or somebody told one of the leaders what they were planning, and Caleb decided they needed to be realigned for 'their own good.' Because it was always for their own good. But some of them must have escaped before the explosion. I only wish Barry had been one of those who got away…"

"What makes you think some escaped?" Dean asked.

"The police only found twenty-three bodies," she said. "Barry never had an exact count, but there should have been close to twice as many. It's possible Barry inflated the size of the group to make me believe he was safe, less exposed to Caleb and the council…"

"It's been a long time, and I'm sorry for your loss," Sam said, "but why do you believe the shadow person who came here was Barry?"

"Because of those back-to-back Bs," she said. "And because he told me to remember. Back then, I couldn't tell my parents about Barry. They never would have approved of him. I worried daily my mother would have the police grab him and send him back to the foster family he fled in Kalamazoo and I would never see him again. But when I was home alone, and thinking about him, I started doodling the Bs. I showed that to Barry. He laughed, but then he carved it into a tree and a picnic bench and other places. He would take me around town and show me the Bs, acting surprised, as if he hadn't carved them himself. Nobody knew we were an item—not my family or the Free Folk—but we were together everywhere, like those back-to-back Bs. Our little secret. Because, if Caleb found out about us, he would have pressured Barry to have me join the Free Folk." She took a deep, shuddering breath. "After Barry died, I grieved, crying at the oddest times. My parents asked me about it, and I told them I had met some of the Fields kids and thought about how horrible it was they'd died that way. That was the closest I came to the truth. Maybe deep down, I knew it wouldn't last with Barry, but I never imagined how it would end. And yet, now, after all these years, he's really come back to me…"

"You're a librarian," Sam said. "If this shadow person cares about you, why would he burn your books?"

"You're right," she said. "I was scared at first. Book burning is kind of a librarian's go-to nightmare fuel, but I believe the fire was another message. I know what's been happening in town, the craziness. Barry knows too. And I think he wants them stopped, that he wants to help us stop them. He made me watch him burn his… host, to expel himself from the body."

"He could have left the body on his own," Dean said. "I've seen it."

"But this way, he revealed something that hurts them or forces them out. Fire."

"Thank Barry for the tip," Dean said, "but torching the possessed townspeople of Moyer is not gonna be Plan A, B or C. We need something else."

"The Free Folk died communally and violently," Sam said. "Based upon the time of the explosion, they were all drugged, experiencing an altered state of consciousness."

"And instead of straight-up ghosts," Dean speculated, "they became shadow people, all linked to this town and that one event."

"Who knows? Maybe the communal altered state of consciousness somehow linked them at that shared moment of death, creating a metaphysical loophole," Sam said. "It would explain the sheer number of shadow people in town. And definitely rules out an alien invasion."

"You seriously considered aliens?" Bonnie asked.

"Anything's possible," Dean said, tilting the flat of his hand back and forth.

"What if the midnight blackouts are some sort of paranormal echo of that explosion and the moment they all died?" Sam said.

"But why now?" Bonnie asked. "After all this time?"

"Albert Kernodle first noticed the shadow people before the first midnight blackout," Sam said. "Something 'awakened' them."

"Of course," Dean said. "The explosion – caused by Old Man Warhurst's dynamite."

"You're right," Bonnie said. "People assumed it was a transformer explosion during the storm. Nobody was hurt. I'd forgotten about it already."

"Bonnie, do you remember where the commune house was?" Sam asked.

"Was?" she said. "It's still there."

"But the explosion—?"

"Only the outdoor communal area was destroyed, along with the closest detention rooms," she said. "Next to the storage shed where Caleb stored the dynamite. The house and the planting fields survived intact."

"That property is ground zero," Dean said.

"If the shadow people have been dormant in Moyer all this time," Sam said, nodding in agreement, "they must be tied to the house."

Dean turned to Bonnie. "Have you seen the house since the craziness began?"

She shook her head emphatically. "I haven't seen it in decades," she said. "Once I got past my grief, I couldn't bear the thought of seeing that house again. All these years, I've avoided walking or driving down that street."

"I understand," Sam said. "You wouldn't want to relive those memories."

"I have no memories of that house with Barry," she said.

"We avoided being seen anywhere near there. I visited the house once, after the explosion, to say my private goodbye. But even then, it was torture. Knowing he spent his final moments trapped in a hole underground—what amounted to a vertical coffin—before his life was snuffed out by Caleb's paranoia and carelessness. So, I told myself, never again."

"We'll need some local perspective," Sam said. "Do you remember the street address?"

Bonnie nodded. She scribbled an address on a sticky note and handed it to Sam.

"What do you have in mind?" Dean asked.

"Gruber," Sam said, dialed his phone, and waited for an answer. "It's Blair. Any better?" He listened for a moment, gave Dean a head shake. "We're working on it. Have a lead, actually. Wondering what you can find out about the cult house in Moyer and the explosion that killed the Free Folk of the Fields on July twentieth, 1968… I understand. Any old-timers on the force? Okay, here's the address…" Sam read the address from the sticky note. "Yes," Sam said. "We believe it's very important to ending this."

"What did he say?" Dean asked after Sam disconnected.

"Before his time," Sam said. "But he'll make inquiries, check records, all that."

"Regardless of what he finds out," Dean said. "We don't go in cold."

"Agreed."

"What are you planning?" Bonnie asked.

"Like I told Gruber," Sam said. "We end this once and for all."

TWENTY-EIGHT

Senior Patrol Officer Tom Gruber stared at his computer screen. He ignored the waves of chaos that swept through the department with every new round of dispatch calls and focused on something that had happened in Moyer long before he'd been born.

Chief Hardigan must have thought his department had transformed into a bunch of Keystone Kops. He'd stormed into the station, glowering at anyone who dared offer a greeting or even glance his way. Slammed the door to his office to catch up on the endless reports and called them in one by one to grill them about everything they'd done, were currently doing and planned to do for the foreseeable future. Any whiff of a mistake or perceived incompetence and the walls shook with his enraged voice.

During the early stages of the chief's epic blowup—or meltdown, depending on your perspective—Gruber had tried to explain how the number and severity of the calls had continued to escalate. But Hardigan couldn't get over his embarrassment that the Bakersburg police force had come to Moyer to help get the chief's town under control.

Forcing himself not to dwell on the chief's fury, Gruber skimmed through the few short articles with sparse details about the Free Folk commune and the accidental explosion that wiped them out back in 1968. A mix of free-love types and societal drop-outs, teenaged runaways and some juvenile delinquents had been killed. All twenty-three bodies identified, next of kin notified. Cause of the accident identified as well: explosion of unstable dynamite the cult used periodically to clear tree stumps from their harvest area. One unusual detail mentioned that some of the recovered bodies had been in small underground chambers, which were described as meditation rooms. A crude form of an isolation tank or sensory deprivation chamber, Gruber supposed.

He leaned back in his chair and scratched his jaw.

Something about the articles, other than their brevity, troubled him. He couldn't put his finger on it. They listed the facts, but refused to identify the victims until next of kin had been notified. That made sense. But something was off. He checked for follow-up articles about the mass death and, again, details were scarce. A brief piece about the remains shipped back to the victims' relatives. And then the story dried up. No human-interest pieces about the victims. No details about the commune's time or activity in Moyer. Then it occurred to him that what bothered him was that nothing seemed to have bothered the reporters who covered the story. Minimal details about the incident. No speculation or follow-up.

What disturbed him weren't the details he read, but the details that had never been recorded for posterity. *As if they wanted the incident forgotten as quickly as possible,* he thought. But maybe that made sense. Back then Moyer thrived only with the influx of tourist dollars from Lake Delsea.

Last thing you'd want to do is poison the tourist well. Unless, of course, you're Pangento, in which case you don't really give a damn.

And yet...

Blair had mentioned talking to old-timers on the force, but most who were old enough to remember the Free Folk explosion had retired. Not quite true...

Gruber left his desk and walked toward the chief's office. He raised his fist to knock on the door, but somebody yanked it open before his knuckles fell against the wood. He took a reflexive step back as a red-faced rookie emerged, excused himself and hurried away as if a grizzly had caught his scent.

"Was that blur Gurevich?" he asked Hardigan from the open doorway.

"One and the same," Hardigan said. "Threatened him with crossing guard detail for the next twenty years." The chief straightened the nameplate at the front of his desk. Gruber thought it had probably shimmied a little closer to the edge each time Hardigan pounded the desk with his fist.

"Chief...?" Gruber began hesitantly. *No easy way to ask.*

"What is it, Gruber?" Hardigan asked, irritated, then sighed. "For Christ's sake, you look constipated. Speak up!"

Okay, then, jump in the deep end. "You've been in the department for a while," Gruber said. "Here in Moyer."

"Since my rookie days," he said with a quirked smile. "Used to be Gurevich. Though never that fainthearted."

"So, you were on the force during the commune days."

Hardigan frowned. "Commune?"

"The Free Folk of the Fields."

"Oh, that." The last trace of the nostalgic smile vanished. "Look, Gruber, in case you haven't noticed, I don't have time for a trip down memory lane. If that's all, I suggest you get back to—"

"That's not all, sir," Gruber interrupted. "I'm following up on a lead."

The frown deepened. "A lead on what, exactly?"

"Everything," Gruber said. "I believe all of the pranks and vandalism and violence are related."

"I admit, the timing is suspicious," Hardigan said. "But how can any of this relate to a nonexistent cult?"

"But it did exist," Gruber said. "At one time." Gruber took a deep breath before he insinuated the presence of evidence he couldn't be sure Tench and Blair possessed. "The FBI agents found a link between an incident at the library and something that happened at the commune."

Hardigan's eyes narrowed suspiciously. "What sort of link?"

"Something related to the fatal explosion."

Defensively, Hardigan came out of his seat, leaning over the desk with his knuckles resting atop it. "The *accidental* explosion?"

The body language screamed intimidation. Gruber realized with surprise that Hardigan wanted him to drop the topic altogether. *He's hiding something.*

"Was it an accident?"

"Of course, it was an accident," Hardigan said, pushing off his desk and turning around to look out his window at the parking lot in front of the building, refusing to meet Gruber's gaze. "They stockpiled dynamite to blow up tree stumps, expand their planting area. And it went bad, blew up during one of their woo-woo communal ceremonies. Simple as that. Was in all the newspaper accounts."

Hardigan clasped his hands behind his back. They were trembling. Even with his buzzcut of white hair, like a steel brush, the chief had always appeared younger than his age, not exactly trim, but energetic, powerful and forceful. Now, standing there with his back to Gruber, Hardigan visibly sagged, his shoulders hunched instead of held at attention. All at once, the man seemed out of his depth.

"I've read the articles," Gruber said.

With a dismissive wave of his hand, Hardigan said, "Well, there you go."

"They're hiding something," Gruber said. "I need to know what that is."

"You're grasping at straws, Gruber," Hardigan said. "Conspiracy theories? None of it matters now. Hasn't mattered in a long time. Just… let it go."

"Want to know the last incident report I read?" Gruber said, anger blooming inside him. "One of our patrol officers pulled over a motorist for rolling through a stop sign."

"As he should."

"He nearly beat the man to death!" Gruber said. "Our citizens are assaulting and, in some cases, killing each other.

And it's happening to us now. Nobody is safe from this. And somehow, it all leads back to that damn cult!"

Hardigan sighed, turned from the window and returned to his desk. After a moment, he dropped into the executive chair in resignation. "What's happening here, Tom?"

"I don't know… sir," Gruber said. "That's what I'm trying to find out."

"You want to know the truth?"

"Of course."

"It won't help," Hardigan said. "Trust me."

"Let me be the judge."

Hardigan arched an eyebrow. "All high and mighty now, Gruber?"

"I… need to know," Gruber said. "Anything could be helpful."

"Was there a cover up?" Hardigan said. "Yes. But not in the way you suppose."

"I don't—"

"Bullshit," Hardigan snapped. He pointed an index finger at Gruber. "You stand there, all self-righteous, thinking we murdered those cult members and covered it up."

Gruber stared at him. He prided himself on having an open mind. Maybe he had suspicions about what had happened back in 1968, but he hadn't made the leap to mass murder committed by the Moyer police department.

"Admit, it," Hardigan said. "I might even think the same thing—if I hadn't been there."

"So, what did happen?"

"Dynamite and an explosion," Hardigan said. "But the

explosion was intentional, engineered by Caleb Fells, the cult leader, along with some of his high council members. Dynamite hidden around their entire gathering area, on timed fuses to blow at midnight."

"But…"

"Why?" Hardigan asked and Gruber nodded. "We'd heard rumors that part of Caleb's message included the end of the world. Today, I guess you'd call the Free Folk a doomsday cult, choosing mass suicide. We'd also heard rumors of drug experimentation, but we thought it was contained to the hippy-dippy group. And not worth rooting out. They seemed mostly harmless and we had no complaints about them. But we miscalculated. We had no idea they had a thriving drug business catering to tourists and…"

"What?"

"And just how many loopy bastards lived on that land."

"Papers said twenty-three were killed."

"Twenty-three," Hardigan nodded. "That was a good number. Less than two dozen, but more than a handful. Believable. That was the main thing."

"What are you saying?"

"We found more than three times that number."

"But how?"

"This was years before Pangento propped us up," Hardigan said. "Moyer's lifeblood depended on our tourist trade," Hardigan said defiantly. "When we found out how wrong we were about the extent of the drugs, the sheer number of them… Let's just say an unfortunate accident involving an isolated group played better than… the reality of the situation."

"Who knew about this?"

"Everyone," Hardigan said. "Anyone who mattered. The nature of the commune gave us the idea. All their secrets, their cultivated anonymity. We lived right next to them and we missed it. How would anyone outside Moyer know any different? The mayor, the chief, the town council and chamber of commerce, along with the cooperation of the local press… we decided on a narrative that would hurt Moyer the least." He took a deep breath and seemed relieved by the confession. "You could say we respected the cult's right to privacy."

"But the bodies…" Gruber had so many questions, but at that moment, all he could focus on was the discrepancy in the number of dead. He grabbed the armrests of one of the two chairs in front of Hardigan's desk, and lowered himself into it. "The articles talked about returning the remains of the twenty-three."

"Mass grave for the rest," Hardigan said. "Pauper's funeral under cover of night."

"But next of kin?"

"Anonymity," Hardigan said. "Most of them rejected the conventions of regular society. That included paper trails and bureaucracy. Changed their names to Moonglow and Starshine and Shepherd. Nonsense basically. We looked for IDs, ran prints. If they weren't in the system, they stayed that way."

"Everyone went along with this plan?"

"We had to think about the living," Hardigan said. "Our livelihoods. We reported what we needed to report. Nothing more. Everyone moved on. Don't look at me that way, Gruber. Most of those people disappeared from society voluntarily long before we made it permanent."

Hardigan stood again, resumed his position looking out the window, hands clasped behind his back. But they no longer trembled. "History is written by the victors, Tom," he said. "The survivors. We did what was best for the town."

Gruber sat silently, trying to understand how the past tragedy and cover-up could be responsible for the chaos happening in the present.

"I told you," Hardigan said. "The tourists are gone. We have Pangento. The other stuff was long ago. None of it matters now."

TWENTY-NINE

Ethan stared down at the display of his father's locked cell phone, guessing one random six-digit number after another, while his father—or rather the boogeyman who had flowed inside his father's body to take control—tried to kick in his bedroom door. The wood around the lock had begun to splinter. With each thunderous impact, Ethan's student desk, which he'd pushed in front of the door, wobbled.

Clutching his arm, Addie whispered urgently, "What's taking so long? Call somebody!"

"Can't. Don't know the code."

Another violent kick and the door broke free of the doorjamb. The legs of the desk squeaked an inch across the hardwood floor. Addie shrieked in panic, scrambled up onto the bed and pressed her back to the wall. "Hurry!"

Daniel Yates pushed hard against the edge of the door, causing the desk to rumble across the floor, on the verge of toppling over.

Grabbing Addie with his free hand, Ethan pulled her

toward the far side of the room. One glance through the window revealed a second-story drop to the stone walkway circling the back of the sprawling house. Not a good option. But it was their only option.

With the door half open and the desk pushed aside, Daniel Yates stalked into the room triumphant, a fevered gleam in his eyes. A wide, sick grin was plastered on his face as he raised the butcher knife in his white-knuckled hand.

We're out of time.

Ethan turned to his sister and whispered, "Addie, I need you to be brave! Okay?"

After a heart-stopping moment, she nodded.

Ethan shoved open the window, trying not to think about the two-story drop. *It's the fall or the knife,* he thought. *It's gonna hurt bad, but we gotta take our chances with the fall.* "Follow me!" he said. "Climb over the ledge, hang there and then let go!"

"I don't wanna fall!"

"Be brave, Addie!"

Shoving the phone in his back pocket, he urged Addie onto the ledge. A quick glance back at his father—what only looked like his father—revealed that he was enjoying their fear. Could've rushed them with the knife, but he savored the moment, creeping forward, running his index finger along the bloody blade.

His father spoke in a voice not his own, a deep voice intended to intimidate. *"Some need to fall in line,"* he said, tapping the blade against his palm. *"But some won't listen."*

Though she shook uncontrollably on the windowsill—

clutching Ethan's arm so hard it hurt—Addie yelled, "Leave my father alone!"

Even she realized what looked like her father was something else now, something that enjoyed hurting and scaring people. Ethan hoped she knew their father would never hurt their mom. None of this was his fault.

"Addie, we need to go now," Ethan said, his voice quavering despite his efforts to sound brave for her. "Okay?"

She pinched her lower lip between her teeth, eyes wide, and nodded at him.

"Ready, set—"

At that moment, another shadow, smaller than the one that controlled Daniel Yates' body, flew through the doorway and slammed against and then into his back. Yates staggered forward and fell to one knee, as if from a physical blow.

Ethan clutched Addie to prevent her from falling, and braced himself against the windowsill. His father looked at them and his eyes again flashed momentarily red. A moment later, his body trembled and shook violently. More importantly, the butcher knife fell from his hand.

A croaking, gasping voice rose from his father's throat, completely raw and unlike the threatening voice they'd heard moments ago. The words came out as if every syllable was a struggle. *"Run... Ethan, run! Can't... hold him... long..."*

"Barry!"

Ethan grabbed his sister's hand and pulled her down from the windowsill, urging her past their shaking father, around the desk and through the doorway. As they ran down the stairs, he heard the scary voice shout in rage,

"You need… to fall in line, boy!"

Somehow, Ethan knew the bad shadow voice spoke to Barry, not Ethan. And that Barry, who had promised safety to Ethan and his family, was losing the fight against the evil shadow.

"Fall—in—line!"

Ethan heard a crash from his bedroom, almost certain Barry had lost the battle for control of Ethan's father.

He pulled Addie along, toward the front door, but too many shadows slipped in and out of the doorway, some through the doorjamb, others underneath the door, and a few through the keyhole. Instead, he reversed course and ran through the back door and out into the wide yard.

After they'd first moved into the house, his father had discovered buried lengths of wood, some charred black from fire, and narrow underground chambers topped with trapdoors secured by padlocks and chains. They were hidden under layers of grass and dirt to conceal their existence.

Ethan remembered his father talking to his mother at breakfast one day, saying those narrow chambers may have been root cellars. But Susan Yates had been skeptical. "Who makes root cellars barely wide enough for one person to stand in?" she'd asked him. "And why dig so many instead of one large one?" Dan Yates had no answer. He'd simply shrugged and said, "Guess we'll never know."

One day he'd gazed down into some of the underground pits, which was what he'd decided to call them, and he agreed with his mother. They hadn't been dug to store produce. Something about the padlocks and chains unsettled him. For several nights, he'd had bad dreams about someone—a stranger whose face remained hidden in shadow—throwing him into one of the pits, slamming the trapdoor shut and locking it with an old padlock and chain.

His father had been concerned with the pits closest to the house, and most of those had crumbled as the charred wooden walls disintegrated. Safety hazards, he'd said, and started to fill them in.

Ethan, however, had become morbidly fascinated by the pits hidden all over the backyard. He'd taken pages from his sketch pad and made a reverse treasure map of sorts. Instead of a map with one X indicating the location of buried treasure, his map had multiple Xs on it where he could someday hide something valuable. What sort of treasure he might want to hide in one of the pits never occurred to him, other than the standard pirate's chest of gold coins. Because of the nightmares, he'd never considered hiding himself in one of the pits. Until that moment.

The pit located farthest from their house, almost where the planting fields began, had been in good shape. His father had snipped the padlock from the chains with a bolt cutter, looked inside to make sure it was empty, before closing the trapdoor again.

Ethan envisioned his sketchpad map and zeroed in on the pit he remembered. Kneeling, he brushed off the dirt, shoved the rusty chains aside and pulled open the trapdoor. The wooden sides stretched down into shadows and darkness. To Ethan, it looked like a coffin lifted onto its end and dropped into a hole in the ground. *When cemeteries become too crowded, will they save space by burying people standing up?*

For a fleeting moment, a chill ran down his spine. He imagined that he had brought his sister to their actual grave. That they would wait at the bottom together, trapped in the pit, until the boogeyman controlling their father arrived and killed them. He wouldn't have to stab them. Just fill the pit with dirt until it covered their mouths and noses. Kill them and bury them in one step.

Addie backed away, her eyes wide. "I'm not going down there!"

"It's the only way," Ethan said urgently, trying to convince himself as much as his little sister. "We have to hide. At least until I figure out the phone code."

With that, he pulled the cell phone out of his back pocket and stared at the stupid lock screen prompt.

Reaching for the phone, Addie said, "Let me try."

"This is serious!"

"I know," she said, reaching again.

"Then leave it alo—!"

"I know Daddy's code."

THIRTY

Something had been bothering Dean since his encounter with the shadow person at Gyrations. The lore had been woefully lacking in any information about how to defeat shadow people, so he'd been forced to examine individual encounters with them in Moyer. First, Sam's hunch had paid off. The Winchesters knew shadow people triggered the EMF detector. Made sense, because spirits of dead cult members ticked the paranormal spectrum checkbox. Second, Maurice Hogarth had accidentally discovered black light made them more substantial—and physically dangerous—while blocking their ability to possess humans. Third, based upon Gruber's apprehension of the possessed orderly who snapped the neck of a disgruntled patient, a taser hit expelled a possessing shadow from its human host. Fourth—and useful only as a worst-case scenario—burning the host's flesh also expelled shadows from their hosts. But what had Dean learned from the Gyrations encounter?

A possessed human with a knife intent on launching

a killing spree had balked at the last moment. With the host relegated to the back seat of his own consciousness, the shadow person had aborted the assault. Normal light had no effect on shadow people. Couldn't even penetrate their shadow form. That ruled out the tracking spotlight at the dance club, since it was simply a bright light. If Dean discounted his somewhat biased opinion that EDM might have sent the spirit packing, that left one possibility.

When Dean described the Gyrations encounter to Sam for the third time, looking for clues, he'd mentioned that when he moved toward the dance floor the shadow had frozen before recovering and darting away. The shadow had stopped at the edge of the conversational nook, beneath an overhang, right before it would have been exposed to the barrage of strobe lights. Dean figured strobe lights were simply normal lights, blinking fast and wouldn't work as a deterrent. But Sam made a good point.

"People with photosensitive epilepsy have seizures triggered by flashing lights," Sam said. "Strobe lights definitely qualify."

"So, creatures made of shadow could be, what, mesmerized by strobe lights?"

"Definitely," Sam said. "From what you describe, the strobe lights may have had a hypnotic or paralyzing effect. To our eyes, the rapid interchange of light and shadow creates gaps in movement. To a shadow person? Maybe, I don't know, fractured reality."

With his notes and a shopping list, Dean drove around town to purchase shadow hunting gear, before hopping on the interstate to visit a department store and a party supply warehouse for the last few items.

When he returned to the Moyer Motor Lodge, Dean found Sam on his bed, sitting next to an impressive pile of salt rounds for the two shotguns he'd removed from the trunk of the Impala before Dean left. "Both loaded," Sam said. "With plenty of rounds to spare."

"Two-man war?"

"Town's riddled with shadows."

"Don't even know if the salt will have any effect."

"They trip the EMF detector," Sam said, nodding toward the bedside table.

Whether the last intruder had been a random encounter or a scout sizing up a potential enemy, neither of them could guess. The possibility existed that the shadow people knew about hunters. Some of them had possessed cops, so they might know of the arrival of two FBI agents. But none of the cops had an inkling that the Winchesters were hunters or anything other than government agents.

Dean assumed the prior visit was random. The possessions had become more brazen, the shadow people themselves less secretive, allowing themselves to be observed by numerous eyewitnesses. More than likely, they assumed they were immune to any countermeasures the humans might employ. They wouldn't expect an assault on their home base.

Sam began to fill two leather pouches with the salt rounds. "Better too many than not enough," he said. "You find everything?"

Dean slid the strap of a stuffed duffel off his shoulder and tossed the bag on his bed. "It's all there," he said. "Tasers, stun guns, portable black light flashlights and portable strobe lights."

Sam's cell phone buzzed. "Gruber," he said as he picked it up and put it on speaker. "Go for Blair."

With raised eyebrows, Dean mouthed the same words at Sam, who shrugged.

"Sorry it took so long," Gruber said. "No time-outs in Crazy-town. Arrested two neighbors for robbery."

"Working together?"

"One robbed a bank," Gruber said. "With his hunting rifle. Warning shot in the ceiling. Demanded singles only. No large bills."

"Strip club plans?" Dean asked.

"Hadn't thought of that," Gruber said. "The other went next door and robbed Calloway's Crullers—with an aluminum tennis racket."

"Donut place?" Sam asked, surprised.

"Yes, but nothing from the cash register," Gruber said. "Only donuts. Specifically, jelly donuts."

"Any warning serves?" Dean asked.

"It's not all fun and games," Gruber said. "A pair of off-duty cops who happen to live a few houses apart, decided to have an old-fashioned duel, Glocks at twenty paces. One took out another neighbor's headlight. But he wasn't so lucky. Lost his spleen. And, of course, none of them remember anything." They heard a sigh over the line. "But that's not why I called."

"Find something out about the cult house?"

When Gruber spoke next, his voice was lower. "Newspaper account glossed over the explosion and the loss of life. Hardly any coverage or follow-up articles. Seemed odd. But guess who was on the force way back in 1968."

"Hardigan," Dean said, recalling the chief of police, who had the military bearing of a law enforcement lifer.

"Got it in one," Gruber said. "I pressed him about it and he finally caved. After the explosion, the police found a stockpile of marijuana, LSD, magic mushrooms, you name it. They also discovered the population of the commune numbered about three times what they expected. And, get this, the whole gathering area had been intentionally wired with dynamite set to explode at midnight. Over seventy victims, though they only reported a third of that. Anyone whose prints weren't in the system got tossed in a mass grave at night. Other than a few samples to fit their narrative, the drugs were destroyed and never mentioned. They explained it all as an unfortunate accident rather than a mass cult suicide."

"Mass suicide? But, why?" Sam asked. "If their illegal operation had gone undetected, why check out?"

"The cult leader, Caleb, believed the world would end. The Robert F. Kennedy assassination was a sign or portent or something. The whole group took his psychedelic concoction at one of their gatherings or sermons. Caleb had planted dynamite around the whole area, under the outdoor communal dining tables and so on, with timed fuses to detonate at midnight. Some underground... holding cells were also rigged to blow. They found some of the bodies in those underground rooms."

"Wow," Sam said softly.

"From the forensic reports, it's likely they were all tripping out of their minds when the dynamite went off," Gruber said. "Even if they weren't stoned three ways from Sunday, with the simultaneous explosions, they wouldn't have known what hit them."

"But the house is still there, right?" Dean asked, wondering if Bonnie had her facts wrong. At her age, faulty memory was a possibility.

"Still standing," Gruber said. "Changed owners several times over the years but remained unoccupied and fell into disrepair. Whether the explosion was an accident or mass suicide, a lot of people died there."

"Guess the stigma of all those deaths hung a black cloud over the place," Sam said.

"Until a couple months ago," Gruber said. "Previous owner sold off most of what had been the commune's farmland, leaving the house and a sizeable backyard. Marketed the house as a fixer-upper—which was a massive understatement—and sold to Daniel and Susan Yates, married couple in their mid-thirties with two kids."

"Is it possible the Yates family has a connection to the Free Folk?" Dean asked.

"I reviewed the list of twenty-three official victims," Gruber said. "Nothing jumps off the page. Of course, we have no records for the victims buried in the mass grave, so all bets are off there."

"They moved in months ago," Sam said. "If they had a connection to the shadow people, something would have happened before now."

"Humans living there again could have been a trigger."

"Maybe," Sam said. "But something would have sparked

sooner." To Gruber, he asked, "Was the Yates family told about the cult before they bought the house?"

"Doubt it," Gruber said. "The house suffered no damage in the explosion. They're out-of-towners. Or were. Possible they've heard something about the house's history since moving in. But the husband is a house-flipper. Don't expect them to hang around after the fixing-up is done."

"Telephone number?" Dean asked.

"Checked," Gruber said. "No landline."

"Thanks," Sam said, raising a finger to disconnect the call.

"Wait!" Gruber said. "I bluffed a confession out of Hardigan, but you never said how the commune from the Sixties is connected to whatever the hell is happening in my town."

"You wouldn't believe us if we told you," Dean said.

"Try me."

"Do you believe in ghosts?" Sam asked.

"You're telling me that Moyer is haunted?"

"In a manner of speaking."

"What now?" Gruber asked, clearly frustrated by a threat he had no rational way to neutralize. "We hold a séance? Burn incense?"

"We have something more... offensive in mind," Dean assured him.

"Well, whatever it is, hurry," Gruber said. "It's tearing the town apart."

As Sam disconnected his call, Dean's phone rang. He showed the caller ID display to Sam before taking the call: Bonnie Lassiter.

"Go for Tench," Dean said, trying it out with an overly dramatic nod toward Sam. "You have something?"

"Oh, you bet I do," she said. "He's back."

"You mean…?"

"Yes," she said. "Barry's here."

THIRTY-ONE

Since Addison claimed to know their father's cell phone passcode, Ethan made a deal with her. They would only hide in the underground room until the police rescued them. No time at all, really. Because, if they didn't hide, they'd have to keep running, and then the police would never find them.

Though shaky on his logic, Ethan only had to convince a five-year-old that it made sense. They were too exposed above ground. And if they had to keep running, Addie would grow tired a lot sooner than their possessed father. He recalled one of his teachers talking about how humans and animals reacted to extreme fear with the fight or flight response. So far, they had chosen flight because fighting their father—a grown man with a bloody knife—was out of the question. Neither option worked for them. Ethan knew they couldn't outrun their father. So, the time had come to hide instead.

The pits were deep enough for a grownup to stand in and not bump their head on the trapdoor. For children, that meant a drop into darkness that could result in a sprained or broken ankle if they weren't careful. Ethan couldn't risk Addie getting hurt and crying, trapped in a pit with him, at the mercy of their possessed father. Ethan flashed on his nightmare of being buried alive in one of the pits and shuddered.

He dropped to his stomach and told her to take his hands before swinging her legs over the pit. Braced against the ground he supported her weight, inching forward to lower her down as far as he could.

"Don't drop me!"

"It's not far."

"It's dark," she said. "I'm scared!"

"The bottom should be close to your feet," Ethan said. "You could probably feel it with your toes if you had big clown shoes."

She laughed at the image. "Really?"

"Just a little hop down."

"Okay."

"On three," he said. "One, two…"

"Three," she said and let go of his hands.

He heard an *oomph!* Then a low, "Ow!"

"Are you okay?" he whispered.

"Fell on my butt," she said. "But, yeah."

"Told you," Ethan said.

"It's dark down here," she called. "Don't leave me alone!"

"Coming," he said, swinging his legs around to lower his body over the edge. He almost let go—

"Oh, crap!"

"What's wrong?"

"Forgot the door!"

Fingers digging in the dirt, he had to scramble up the rough wooden surface of the chamber wall, the toes of his sneakers slipping a couple times before he pulled himself back over the edge. He flipped the door over on its hinges, propping it up with a stick, high enough that he could slither through the gap. With his left forearm circled around the stick, he lowered his body again. The fingers of his right hand clung to the edge.

"Stand back!" he called.

"Don't fall on my head!"

"Watch out!" he called as he yanked his left arm toward the hole, which pulled the stick out from under the door. At the same time, he let go with his right hand and dropped into the pit. The door slammed shut a moment before he landed with a thud. His momentum caused him to stagger backward, brushing Addie before he thumped against the far wall.

"You okay?" Addie asked.

"Bit my cheek," Ethan said. He ran the tip of his tongue over the cut, tasted his own blood. "I'm fine."

"It's darker now," Addie said plaintively.

With the door shut, they were trapped in almost complete darkness. Ethan stared up at the trapdoor, the ceiling of their tiny underground cell. A few tiny cracks in the wood let through some light from above, but he couldn't escape the spooky feeling that he'd buried them alive with no help at all from their possessed father.

"Makes it harder for him to find us," Ethan said, attempting to sound more positive than he felt.

His mother always said, *"You choose if the glass is half full or half empty. Nobody else.* " They had lived in a bunch of crappy houses the last few years. His mother had always found something positive to say about each one. And every time they moved into another bad house, she told them it would get better each day as their father continued to fix it. And someday they would move into a great house and it would be theirs for good. He would make friends he could keep and finally get a dog.

As Ethan stood in the dark with his sister, hiding from something evil that wanted to kill them, he focused on the positive. His father had no idea where they were, so they were safe. And he believed his mother was alive and would get better, once they called for help. One simple phone call.

Ethan took those few moments to calm himself. *Be brave so she'll be brave.*

Reaching into his back pocket, he handed Addie their father's cell phone. "Okay," he said. "Enter the code."

She took the phone from him, looked at the lock display and began tapping numbers on the onscreen keyboard.

With his arms spread, Ethan could touch opposite walls of the pit. Turning ninety degrees, he reached out again and found the distance the same. *Wide enough to lie down,* he thought, *but not comfortably.*

"Once you unlock it, we'll call for help," he said. "And we'll use the flashlight app, so we can see down here until the police and ambulance come for us and Mom."

But Addison was frowning. He hadn't counted the taps, but she'd entered way more than six numbers. "What's wrong?"

"It's not working."

"You said you knew it!"

His calm had already started to evaporate. He could feel panic rising from his stomach. "Tell me the number," he said. "I'll try it."

"Daddy said it was a secret," she said. "Not supposed to tell anyone."

"I'm not anyone, doofus," Ethan said impatiently. "I'm your brother!"

She tried the number again, and again.

He snatched the phone from her hand. "Tell me," he said. "Let me try."

With a dramatic sigh, she said, "Okay, but I better not get in trouble."

Ethan laughed. Couldn't help himself. They were hiding in an open grave from their father, who was possessed by an evil shadow creature that wanted to stab them to death, and Addie was worrying about getting in trouble for revealing a cell phone passcode.

"What's so funny?"

"Nothing," Ethan said. "*So* not funny. Tell me the code!"

"He told me it's our birthdays, but that's too long," she said. "They won't all fit."

Three birthdays, Ethan thought, puzzling it out. Their mother's, his and Addie's. Six digits. Two digits for each birth day, birth month or birth year. But which one? And in which order? Oldest to youngest? Or the opposite. Six possible combinations. He'd have to try each one.

From above, he heard his father's voice, the scary shadow voice, like an animal growl, calling out to them. "Ethan!" he called. "Addison!"

Ethan entered their birth years, starting with their mother's, but for a few moments he couldn't remember the year she was born and the panic bubbling in his sour stomach surged.

"Ethan!"

Was it his imagination, or did the voice seem closer to their hiding place?

"Addison!"

Closer! Too close, already!

He heard a creak of rusty metal and the thud of a wooden door falling. "Come out of there!" the voice called. "I know you're hiding!"

Oh, crap! He's already checking the pits!

Nearby, a trapdoor slammed.

Hunched over the cell phone, Ethan feared he might vomit on the wooden floor. Addie was scared now, but if she knew how terrified he was, she'd panic.

The security code failed.

"Okay, try days," he muttered to himself.

"Did it work?"

"Not yet," he said.

"Told you it didn't fit."

"That's not the—!" He sighed. "I'll get it."

"Found something in the corner."

"What?" he asked. *Rotted food? Flashlight with dead batteries?*

"A stool," she said. "With three legs. It's short. I can sit on it."

"Do that," Ethan said. The three sets of two-digit birth days failed to unlock the phone from oldest to youngest, and again from youngest to oldest. "Okay, months now."

"It's wobbly," Addie complained.

"We'll fix it later," Ethan said.

Last two digits, Addie's birth month.

The lock screen vanished, revealing the phone's home screen. "Thank God!"

"What? It worked?"

"Yes," Ethan said.

SQUEAK—THUD!

Another trapdoor yanked open and slammed shut.

"Come out, come out, wherever you are!"

If Ethan closed his eyes, he pictured his father less than ten feet from their pit, heard the scuff of his shoes on the ground as he strode toward them. Bile climbed his throat. He grimaced and swallowed hard.

Quickly, he dialed 911. But nothing happened.

No dial tone! "Crap!"

"What's wrong?" Addie asked. "Battery dead? Momma's battery always di—"

Ethan tuned her out. The battery icon showed half a charge, but the other side of the screen showed a weak signal, only one bar. *No!* he thought angrily. *Not after everything we...*

"Let me have the stool!"

"Finders keepers," Addie said in a maddening sing-song voice.

"Just for a minute," Ethan whispered urgently. "I'll give it back."

"Okay."

Ethan climbed onto the seat of the wobbly stool, balancing himself precariously as he raised the cell phone over his head, high enough to brush the underside of the trapdoor. The single bar transformed into two bars, flickered to three for a second then back to two.

Should be good enough, he thought, and dialed 911 again.

When he heard the operator's voice, he almost fell off the stool in relief. She wanted to know the nature of the emergency. *So many,* he thought. *Where to start?*

"Hello?"

"Yes, yes, we need help," Ethan said quickly, afraid the signal would cut out before he finished. "This is Ethan. Ethan Yates. Me and my sister need help—fast! But my mom's hurt bad. He stabbed her. Our father—in our house and he's gonna… hurt us, if he finds us." Ethan had been rambling, but caught himself before he said anything that might freak out Addison. Well, freak her out more than she already was. "We need the police—and an ambulance for our mom—but tell the police not to hurt my dad, because it's not really him doing the bad stuff. Something's inside him. That's the bad thing."

"Where are you?"

"Hiding in a pit, in our yard," Ethan said. "But he's coming—he's close!"

"I need your address, Ethan."

Ethan gave her their address, something his mother had always made him and Addie remember, but it changed so much, sometimes Addie mixed up street and town names. Ethan always made an extra effort to get it right, repeating it to Addie in case she ever got lost.

He climbed down from the stool, careful of the wobble, and gave it back to Addie. She sat on it. He sat on the floor beside her. They waited in the silence of the pit, while above, another trapdoor thumped shut on squeaky hinges. Any minute, he would find their trapdoor and yank it open…

His mother always said, "You never know when an emergency will happen."

This time, the emergency was in their own backyard.

This time, it was their father who was lost.

THIRTY-TWO

When the Winchesters returned to the Moyer Public Library, Sam grabbed the loaded duffel bag from the trunk and followed Dean inside. Other than the Impala, the visitor parking lot remained empty. *Too much chaos rolling through town for anyone to consider quiet time with books.* Assuming Bonnie had parked her car in the employee lot in back, he expected at least one other car out front, whatever Barry's new host drove. Unless...

Dean looked over his shoulder at Sam. "Wonder if it's burning man again," he said, echoing Sam's thought.

"Any reason why it wouldn't be someone else?"

Dean shrugged. "Familiarity?" he said. "Each new rental car, you gotta figure out how to work the headlights and wipers all over again."

The automatic doors *whooshed* open. The library seemed deserted.

"Bonnie," Dean called.

The office door behind the front counter opened, and

Bonnie emerged. "Good," she said, smiling. "You're here."

Sam set the duffel bag on the counter.

After glancing around at the freestanding shelves and the computer island, Sam asked, "Barry?"

"He's here and wants to help," she said. "But he's very agitated." She turned to face her office, the door half open, as she'd left it. "Barry, come out."

The overhead fluorescent lights flickered once.

Then Sam realized why the parking lot was empty.

Barry had come as himself—a shadow person.

Unnerving. If asked, that's how Sam would describe his reaction upon seeing the dark human silhouette, undisguised and ghost-walking toward them, out in the open under the uncompromising glare of fluorescent lights. With no attempt at visual subterfuge, the shadow person calling itself—himself—Barry, seemed to distort reality, a willful darkness, rippling through the air, through the human world, completely out of time and place.

"Whoa!" Dean said, reaching for the duffel.

He had a shotgun half out of the canvas bag before Bonnie raised her hands, palms up. "Wait! He won't hurt you!" she said hastily.

"Guy with the burned hand might disagree," Dean said skeptically.

"He wants to help," she pleaded. "Just hear him out."

"Shadows talk now?" Sam asked.

Eerily, the mostly two-dimensional being turned toward each of them as they spoke. Even if shadow people couldn't talk, they could apparently hear, or at least interpret meaning.

They had been human once. Maybe that was enough.

"We had something else in mind," Bonnie said, grinning. "Practiced a bit while we waited for you."

"Practiced?" Sam asked, then glanced at Dean.

"Shadow puppets?" Dean suggested, shrugging. "That's all I got."

Shadow Barry glided forward from his position beside Bonnie.

Instinctively, Sam tensed, ready for a hostile move. Unlike Dean, he hadn't encountered a shadow person up close, only via surveillance video, and the visual experience was much more disturbing in person, even in perfect lighting.

Barry pivoted to face Bonnie. For a moment, Sam saw only the narrow edge of the shadow body, which almost vanished, but appeared instead like a hairline fracture in reality or a visual fault in his field of vision. Then the broadside appeared and expanded again, Barry's relative back to the Winchesters as he faced Bonnie. She smiled and gave a slight nod. Barry eased toward her.

They were similar in height, but Shadow Barry expanded and contracted where necessary to match her physical dimensions. Briefly, the darkness coated her from head to toe, as if her whole body had been dipped in India ink, her face rendered in obsidian by a master sculptor. But the moment passed, and her body seemed to absorb the shadow with no ill effects.

Bonnie stared at them, almost blindly, her body frozen in place.

Then her eyes glowed, a pulse of red that faded as quickly as it appeared.

"Bonnie?" Sam asked.

Her mouth opened and closed. She nodded her head once, slowly. Her fingers curled, hands clenching and releasing. "Bonnie… can't answer…"

"Have you hurt her?" Dean asked.

His hand still rested on the stock of one of the shotguns in the duffel. As a bluff, it failed. No way would Dean shoot Bonnie, even with a salt round. But Dean probably felt as helpless as Sam at that moment.

"Would never… hurt my… Bonnie Lass." Bonnie's voice, but with a strained edge and hesitant. "She is… beneath, but aware."

"You're a shadow person?" Sam asked. "You're all shadow people?"

"We are… what we are. Not sure… why we are… here. Now."

"Where were you before? All these years? Trapped in the Veil?"

"Veil?"

"It's a plane of existence on earth but—" Sam began.

"Where ghosts, hellhounds and reapers hang out," Dean said. "Like a supernatural holding tank but without a door. It's complicated."

Bonnie's body shrugged, almost a pantomime of a shrug. "No Veil… for us. Alone but linked together… our minds… in darkness. Like dreaming… drifting… no sense of time."

Sam nodded. "There's speculation in the lore that shadow people are extra-dimensional, inhabiting another universe or alternate reality."

Dean was skeptical. "Wouldn't that make them aliens?"

Sam smiled. "No, but what if the circumstances of their simultaneous deaths—the altered state of consciousness combined with the explosion—created, I don't know, a metaphysical pocket universe. And when these types of souls break free, they bypass the Veil and manifest here on earth as shadow people."

Bonnie's head nodded slowly. "Second explosion fractured... no more dreaming. Rushing back... to energy. Hungry for... life."

"You enjoy possessing people?" Dean asked. "That it?"

"Some... addicted. Like new drug. I would not... chose not... but danger to you. Everyone. Moyer. Can't ignore."

"No offense," Sam said. "You don't seem very good at it."

"Takes practice... to control. Only works with those... when we sense connection. A link... open minds. The rest... locked."

Obviously, Barry had a connection to Bonnie. And many older residents of Moyer had known about or interacted with the Free Folk. If not them, their children and grandchildren. Connections beyond Moyer would be limited. And yet, Sam sensed he was missing a final piece of the puzzle...

"I waited, refused. Others repeat many times. Some want... possession permanent. Right host... never leave. Live again."

"Your people—the shadows—want to take over human hosts permanently?" Dean asked, outraged.

"Is that possible?" Sam asked.

"Not my people. Caleb and those... loyal to him. Council leaders. Others. Some believe... permanent possible. Caleb's mission... incomplete. Wants to try again."

"There's nothing in the lore about shadow people possessing humans," Sam said. "Incidents of paralysis, inducing feelings of dread, but not possession. Somehow, the Free Folk's connection to Moyer created an exception."

Again, Bonnie's head nodded. "Only if we sense link... to us."

There's that word again, Sam thought. Then realization struck him. "That's it," he said. "The Free Folk were linked together when they died, linked in their pocket universe, and linked when they returned. The midnight blackouts are metaphysical aftershocks—diminishing echoes of the event that created them. Somehow, they create an altered state of consciousness in anyone within Moyer's town limits when they happen. Good news is, the echoes will fade out, limiting the number of potential possession victims. Bad news is..."

Dean frowned. "Blackout victims become honorary Free Folk."

"Or at least compatible minds," Sam said, doubtful the comment made Dean feel any better about it. *Maybe possession vulnerability would wear off when the blackout echoes faded away.* "But why the pranks? The vandalism? Why all the violence?" Sam asked. If practice made possession permanent—or even if some of the shadow people believed that—Sam understood why they would repeatedly take over human hosts. But why lead them to violence and suicidal acts?

"Many of us. Many reasons joined... Free Folk. Some... truth seekers, some free love, some freedom, some runaways and... criminals, wolves among sheep. Now free to hunt, kill, no... consequences."

"So, a few bad apples spoil the bunch?" Dean said unsympathetically.

"We… many disbelieved Caleb's vision… wanted only freedom, safe place, acceptance. Nothing more. Not Caleb's ascension. Or his end of world obsession. But he… wouldn't accept doubters, deniers. Those who refused ascension and his drug con-concoc—potion—were locked in detention rooms 'for their own good.'"

"He put you in one of those underground rooms," Sam said.

"Every gathering."

"Including the night the cult committed mass suicide," Sam added. "That's where they found your body."

Bonnie's body shuddered momentarily. *Barry confronting his own mortality from the other side,* Sam thought.

"*Lies*… not all suicide. Caleb chose for all, but many never knew his plan. Mass murder. All of us—snuffed out. Until now… back as shadows. Some angry… rage at life, at the living… feel cheated, lash out, want to hurt… But some possess only to… experience joy of life, freedom again, wind in hair, smell of flowers, warmth of sun. And yet… they know it's wrong. Stealing minutes or hours from others. Want to stop. But, for some, hard to stop…"

"They're addicted to life," Sam said.

Bonnie's head nodded, almost naturally this time. "Intoxicating… So, they want you to… find a way to stop them. For their own good."

"Gank them?" Dean asked. "How?"

"We don't know how to… end this unnatural existence. But we need to find a way. We want to… But some will never stop. Caleb's will… remains strong, demands allegiance, submission, obedience. As he was in life…"

"He wants to create a shadow cult?" Sam asked.

"Until possession permanent and hosts fade away." Another nod. "Some of us want to fight him. Stop him. Stop history from… repeating. Battle lines drawn. But numbers not… in our favor. Those who fight against. I tried to stop Caleb, but I was… ineffective, too weak to take control. I failed Ethan…"

Tears welled in Bonnie's eyes, spilled over her cheeks. But the grief causing them belonged to Barry.

"Who's Ethan?" Dean asked.

"Ethan Yates. His family moved into our former home… before the dreaming ended. I promised Ethan he and his family would remain safe… off-limits. Caleb agreed, so others agreed. But Caleb craves power… and control… He's become a mega-megalo—"

"Megalomaniac," Sam finished.

An improved nod. "Again. Possessed Ethan's father… Daniel… to kill whole family. Tried to stop him, but he controls hosts much better than I… He expelled me. Please help me stop him before more hurt… more die."

Sam looked up as the fluorescent light flickered again. To preserve battery life, he'd switched off the EMF detector before tossing it in the duffel. Too late now.

"Dean!"

A darkness rippled across the floor tiles, making a beeline for—Dean. The ink-like coating rose from Dean's feet up to his head, enveloping his face.

Dean threw his head back and managed to scream one word, *"Nooo—!"*

—before the shadow submerged.

His body convulsed, doubling over, then standing tall and stiff, almost vibrating for a moment before he relaxed.

Though Sam had little warning, he yanked the duffel bag along the counter, close enough to reach inside.

Wild-eyed, Dean glared at Bonnie, a malicious grin twisting his features. "Caleb had me follow you," he said. "Treasonous little bastard!"

"Deke," Barry said through Bonnie's mouth.

"Who's Deke?" Sam asked. Unlike Barry, Deke must have had a lot of possession practice. Not good. Sam's hand moved carefully through the contents of the duffel bag.

"Council leader," Barry said derisively. "Caleb's sock puppet."

"I've had it with you whiny runaways," Deke said through Dean. "Especially you, leader of the runt pack." Dean grabbed a stapler off the counter. "Cat's out of the bag. Your juvenile rebellion ends here!"

Dean backed up two steps, then rushed forward, and jumped on the counter.

Expecting an attack, Sam swept his right arm out, knocking Dean's feet out from under him. Dean collapsed to all fours, knocking the pencil holder and a folder tray onto the floor while maintaining his grip on the stapler. From his awkward position, he took a swing at Bonnie's head, but missed as she jerked backward.

Sam leaned over to press a stun gun to Dean's side, and pulled the trigger. With a wild spasm, Dean fell backward, off the counter onto the tile floor. As Sam expected, the electric charge worked as Gruber's taser had on Luther, the orderly. The darkness, expelled from Dean's body, rose upward.

Reaching back, Sam grabbed the shotgun stock protruding from the duffel bag and yanked it free.

Before the disoriented shadow could flee—or try to possess Sam—he flicked on the black light flashlight mounted to the end of the shotgun and fired a salt round center mass—or whatever passed for center mass in a shadow person. Sam half expected the shadow to flicker out, like a ghost would, knocked temporarily out of commission. Instead, the shadow silhouette shattered like a sheet of glass. Under the glow of the black light beam, a thousand shards of darkness fluttered downward. As they struck the tile floor, they began to fade, from deepest black to palest gray. Sam moved the black light beam aside and watched as they faded away, leaving no trace behind.

Sam worked the action, ejecting the spent shell casing and loading another round in the chamber.

Barry, still controlling Bonnie's movements, flipped open the counter gate and walked to the spot almost with reverence. Kneeling on the floor, he placed her palms where the pieces had faded. After a moment, her voice said softly, "You found a way."

"Is he gone?" Sam asked. "Gone for good?"

Bonnie stood and nodded, her gaze fixed on Deke's final resting spot. "That light... What is it?"

"Black light," Sam said. "Makes your kind more... solid. Figured I'd try it before Deke tried to possess me."

"He could not. Your mind is not... open to us."

"Only mine is," Dean said, annoyed.

"You blacked out… he did not. His mind remains sealed."

"Great," Dean groused. "I'm a liability."

To Barry, the vulnerability had been obvious, not worth mentioning. Which meant shadow people knew at once who they could and couldn't possess.

"That light… the moment it touched Deke… I sensed it. He seemed… more of this world. Hard to explain. Caleb believed in midnight as a gateway. This was a different kind of gateway… almost a bridge between the living and our… half-existence."

"Don't need an explanation," Dean said pragmatically. "If it works, I'm good."

"When the time comes, when Caleb is defeated, I ask that you… release me the same way."

This time, the tears welling in Bonnie's eyes might have been her own.

Sam's cell phone rang. Gruber again. "Blair here," Sam said, putting the call on speaker.

"Get this," Gruber said. "Weird call just came in from the cult house."

Bonnie took a wobbly step backward, grabbed the edge of the counter to steady herself. Barry bracing himself for bad news about Ethan.

"Kid and his sister say they're trapped underground, mother injured, father armed and dangerous," Gruber said. "Dangerously possessed, I'm guessing."

"Sam."

"Ethan? Ethan's still alive?" Bonnie's voice asked.

"Where are you?" Gruber asked. "Who else is on the line?"

"Librarian who gave us the cult house lead," Sam said, focusing on the call and momentarily ignoring Dean, who kept looking around as if he'd forgotten where he left his car keys.

"As of a couple minutes ago, both Ethan and Addison, his sister, were alive," Gruber said. "Hiding underground. On my way there now, with Chief Hardigan."

"Sammy!"

"What?" Sam asked, then followed Dean's gaze.

More than a dozen townspeople, men and women ranging in age from twenty-something to sixty-something, approached from all directions, some from across the street, others from more than a block away, all walking methodically toward the library. They carried guns, knives, baseball bats, shovels and anything else capable of inflicting serious bodily harm.

In front, a gray-bearded man in a trucker hat and bib overalls carried a lime-green gas-powered chainsaw. Sam heard the idling motor rumble. A step behind Gray Beard, a bald man wearing sunglasses and an orange safety vest over a plaid shirt, jeans and work boots carried a sledgehammer in a two-handed grip. None of them spoke to any of the others, but even from a distance, their single-minded purpose was evident.

"Yeah, I don't think they're coming to check out books," Sam said, his throat suddenly dry.

"Cat's out of the bag," Dean reminded him.

"Gruber," Sam said. "Looks like we've got our hands full. We're surrounded."

"What?"

"Angry villagers," Dean said. "Possessed and dangerous."

"We'll be right there."

"No!" Bonnie's voice cried. "Save Ethan and Addie!"

"He—She's right," Dean said.

"We'll handle this," Sam added with more confidence than he felt.

"Okay," Gruber said. "I'll send help. Whatever help I can…"

Before Gruber ended the call, Sam warned him, "Remember, everyone who was in Moyer during either blackout event—whether they were asleep or awake—is susceptible to possession!"

"Okay, that eliminates… almost nobody in town," Gruber said. "But good to know."

Gruber was safe from possession but, other than Sam, he might be the only one. Sam disconnected, raised his eyebrows and looked at Dean. "So…?"

"Our last stand will not be in a library," Dean replied. "Us or them, right? Kill or be killed."

"Dude, you're okay with killing civilians?"

"Of course not," Dean said. "But I'm less okay with them killing us."

"We'll drive the shadows out," Sam said. "Kill them one by one."

"They've got the numbers," Dean said. "And too many frigging weapons."

"I'll get help," Barry said through Bonnie. "My fellow runaways and some of the delinquents will fight them… for a chance to end this. Once and for all."

"Team Rebel?" Dean asked.

"Team Rebel. I like that." Bonnie smiled, nodding emphatically this time. "I'll see if I can get them to follow me away from here... away from you and Bonnie. But if they felt Deke... wink out of existence, they'll know you're dangerous."

"Good luck," Sam said.

"We thought we were free back then. Maybe this time... will be different."

Swaying, Bonnie's eyes became vacant—lights on, nobody home—and Sam readied himself to catch her if she fainted. Darkness spilled out of her, spread across the floor like a widening inkblot, then gathered itself, rose as a black silhouette and soared through a gap between the automatic doors out into the parking lot. He swooped around the parking lot, crossing in front of the approaching possessed mob, then soared away. Only one of the mob took the bait, an old woman with a meat cleaver. Her possessor pulled itself free from her and followed Barry. The woman, unburdened, staggered and fell sideways to the blacktop.

Bonnie, on the other hand, regained her balance and her focus. "He's gone," she said, stating the obvious—or lamenting the loss.

"He said you were aware?"

"Felt like eavesdropping on a conversation two rooms away," she said. "But I heard it all." She looked through the wide windows above the rows of study carrels and four-foot-high bookshelves, and the double glass doors, their only protection from a mob intent on killing them through no fault of their unwilling hosts. "Oh, no!"

"Lock yourself in your office," Dean said. "Wait for help

to arrive, in case things go sideways."

"I'll lock the front doors first," she said, rushing to the control panel and switching the doors from automatic mode to closed. "No need to welcome them with open arms."

As Bonnie retreated to her office, Dean unzipped the duffel bag and flipped it over on the counter, dumping out their anti-shadow-people arsenal. He handed one of the stun guns to the librarian. "Take this," he said. "It will expel a shadow from a possessed human."

Won't help if the expelled shadow decides to jump inside her next, Sam thought, but kept quiet about his concern.

For the Winchesters, the harsh reality was simple. They would be fighting innocent civilians, which meant they had to hold back to avoid maiming or killing the unknowing hosts. But the possessing shadows faced no such compunctions. Open season on hunters. Worse, Sam couldn't trust Dean to have his back. If a free shadow mind-jacked Dean, Sam would stand alone against the entire bloodthirsty mob.

THIRTY-THREE

A whole building protected only by glass—wraparound windows and plate-glass doors. And none of it bulletproof. With the installation of computers in the middle of the library, anti-theft security was a legitimate concern. For all Sam knew, every window and door into the library was wired. In their current circumstances, none of that mattered. Already stretched dangerously thin, the Moyer Police Department would deem a library theft the lowest priority imaginable, maybe one step above a recidivist jaywalker. Besides, Gruber had promised help with so little confidence in his tone, he might as well have said, "You guys are on your own."

Sam turned a slow three-sixty, counted more than a dozen townspeople. *Pay special attention to the few with guns,* he thought. The rest would need to come close to inflict damage. *Unless they decide to hurl shovels and pitchforks.*

"Circuit breakers?" Dean called to Bonnie, who stood in the office doorway, the door open wide enough for her to peek out—for now.

"Utility closet," she said. "Why?"

"Too bright in here," Dean said. "Need to cut the lights."

"You want to fight in the dark?"

Outside, the sun had set but dusk had not yet given way to night. Inside, the library was bright as a business office. Made the darkness of shadow people easier to spot, but might neutralize one of the Winchesters' weapons.

"Strobe lights," Dean said. "More effective in the dark."

"I'll flip the breakers," Bonnie said, starting toward the lobby again.

A series of pops sounded from outside. Metal clanged. One window cracked. Another shattered.

"Down!" Dean shouted as he crossed the lobby and took cover behind the low bookshelf. Sam crouched on the other side. Bonnie ducked, keeping her head below the counter, and scrambled back through the door into her office.

"Get inside and lock it!" Sam called.

Both Winchesters held shotguns rigged with black lights and loaded with salt rounds. Dean had stuffed a stun gun in his jacket. But Sam's remained on the counter, out of reach. Since their shotguns held salt rounds, neither could put down suppressing fire for the other. They had automatics with real bullets in the duffel but had decided to stick to anti-shadow weaponry rather than risk killing a possessed human.

Gray Beard with his chainsaw stood outside the double doors of the library, almost as if he expected them to part for him. Then he stepped aside for the younger, bald man with the sledgehammer. If the Winchesters had had more time, they could have barricaded the plate-glass doors—but not the windows.

"Sitting ducks," Dean muttered, loud enough for Sam to hear.

As if to emphasize that point, several more shots popped. Another window cracked, then shattered. A bullet thudded into a book on a shelf behind Dean. A second round blew out a fluorescent light over Sam.

"Hey, at least they're poor shots," Sam said.

With the blown light, a shadow fell across Sam. He noticed Dean staring at the shadow, wary, waiting for—

—the sledgehammer crashed into one of the front doors, blasting a shower of glass into the library where it clinked and clattered across the counter and tile floor.

A dark shadow raced along the floor, veered toward Dean.

"Not this time!" Dean shouted, shoving his hand into his jacket pocket as darkness raced up his legs. "Sam!"

Sam guessed what he intended and thought it might work.

Dean jammed the stun gun against his chest—darkness flowed up his arms, torso, neck and face, blotting out his face as he squeezed the trigger. His body spasmed, causing him to fall back off his heels and crash into the low shelf before he slid to the floor.

Sam's black light was on and waiting. He swung the shotgun barrel toward Dean, conscious of Mr. Sledgehammer ducking to step through the open lower panel of the door. As Dean stumbled and fell, the shadow shot upward, expelled from Dean's body mid-possession. After an agonizing moment waiting for a clear shot, Sam fired a salt round at the shadow, between its silhouette head and torso. Like Deke, it shattered in eerie silence and flutter-faded away.

The possessors of Moyer people paused in shock or consternation after one of their number died. In Gray Beard's hand, the lime-green chainsaw continued to idle. Risking gunfire, Sam stood and reached across the counter to where Dean had emptied the duffel bag, grabbing two tasers, and tossing one to Dean.

"Long range," he said. "Ready?"

Dean nodded, flicking on his mounted black light.

Sam fired the taser at Mr. Sledgehammer, who stiffened and trembled before he fell to the ground with his weapon. The electrical charge expelled a shadow and Dean took the shot, shattering another of Caleb's goons. The possessed townspeople roared in anger, charging the shattered door, with Gray Beard ducking through the opening first.

Sam pumped another round into the chamber as Dean tasered the old man through his overalls. A third shadow bit the dust. But the rest of the Moyer mob spread out, breaking windows and climbing through the narrow and jagged gaps. With blood-streaked faces, arms, legs and hands, the mob looked like extras in a zombie movie. The possessed with guns stayed back, firing into the library, but they either lacked the patience or the skill to hit targets from a distance.

Crouching behind the low bookshelf, Sam pressed his stun gun to a woman in a business suit wielding a large pair of scissors like a dagger. As she dropped, Sam scooped up his shotgun, tracked the shadow person flung from her body and drilled it with a salt round. A man behind her attempted to spear Sam's side with a pitchfork. Rolling across the aisle, Sam evaded the rusty tines and scrambled behind the computer island.

A fireman in full gear swung an ax at one of the front windows. He lost his helmet pushing through the broken glass, and the dark streaks on his clothes indicated that he'd abandoned a fire to join Caleb's goons. As soon as his boots hit the floor, he bull-rushed Dean, who fired a salt round at his chest to no effect.

The fireman swung his red-bladed ax in a wide vertical arc, bringing it down with enough force to cleave Dean's skull down to his collarbone. Dean twisted aside and crashed into one of the metal shelves, snagged between split metal.

From one knee, Dean fired his taser at an awkward angle. One prong caught in the turnout jacket, the other missed the mark. The fireman knocked the taser from Dean's hand. He freed the ax and tried to ram it into Dean's face. Swinging his arm up, Dean batted the handle aside and ducked under the blow.

Dean circled around the end of a bookshelf to put it between him and the aspiring ax murderer. Out of the corner of his eye, he spotted Sam tangling with two teenagers swinging hockey sticks like clubs. Dean clawed in his jacket pocket for the stun gun. He'd need contact with the fireman's skin to expel the shadow, but the turnout gear protected most of the fireman's body. Fortunately, he'd lost his helmet, exposing his face, and he wore no gloves. Dean had a portable strobe light in his other pocket, but the bright fluorescent lighting nullified the paralyzing effect of the strobe.

Through a gap in the bookshelf, Dean saw the fireman backing away. Dean looked up at one of the fluorescent panels, only a few feet above the top of the bookshelf. Without a second thought, he climbed the shelves like a ladder. Bracing himself, he drove the stock of the shotgun up into the panel, breaking the plastic, then shattering the long tubes inside. Take out enough of the lights and the strobe light would—

The fireman roared as he charged the tall shelf, slamming his shoulder into it. Clinging to the top, Dean felt it begin to tilt. Dean would be pinned between his shelf and the next, or crushed beneath it if he dropped to the floor. Twisting around, he leaped to the next shelf, almost losing his grip on the shotgun. He scrambled on top and flattened himself as the falling shelf collided with his, striking it hard and high.

"Crap!" Dean said as his shelf began to fall, and the domino effect took over.

Dean jumped from one tumbling shelf to the next. He swung at the fluorescent light panels at every chance he got, but his luck was hit or miss. The fireman scrambled after him, climbing up the fallen shelves like steps and jumping between the bookcases.

Before the last shelf stuck the wall, Dean raced ahead of the chain reaction and dropped behind the last shelf. That shelf would stop when it hit the wall, leaving a gap for him to wait.

Dean swept the books off the shelves. He needed a clear view, no obstructions for his arm or the shotgun. As expected, the last shelf hit the wall and shuddered to a stop. He swung the barrel of the shotgun through the shelves, swatting one of the fireman's legs out from under him mid-leap. The man missed his mark, toppling backward.

Dean hooked an arm under the man's shoulder and pulled him close, but lost his grip on the shotgun. He snagged it by the black light mounted at the front of the barrel and jammed the stun gun against the fireman's exposed neck. The shadow welled up from within the man's body, moments away from darting clear. If Dean shifted his grip on the shotgun barrel, he'd lose the black light effect—and the shadow would possess Dean. If he kept the black light trained on the shadow, it could use its increased substance to slice Dean's throat, as the other shadow had lacerated Maurice's arm.

Dean stretched past the fireman, pushed the stun gun against the hovering shadow and pulled the trigger.

The shadow whipped around, its silhouette stretching like taffy, flexing and doubling over. Holes began to gape inside it, stretching and resealing themselves. Dean tugged the groaning fireman out of his way, tossed the shotgun barrel upward and caught it by the action. He grabbed the stock and fired a salt round. The shadow blew apart, raining down like black fireworks before fading away.

Nearby, Sam grabbed one hockey stick in both hands and yanked backward into a somersault, heaving the hockey player holding it into his teammate behind Sam. They crashed together in a heap.

Sam zapped the first one, reaching back for his dropped shotgun, but Dean had approached and blasted the expelled shadow. Sam zapped the player underneath and

Dean took out the second shadow.

In a few minutes they took out the remaining possessed townspeople, but not before Dean had to stun himself again to shake off a possession in progress. Sitting on the floor, he asked, "That the last of them?"

Over a dozen dazed and injured townspeople cradled bruised or lacerated limbs, wondering what the hell had happened to them and why they had gathered in the town's library of all places. The woman in the business suit, rubbed her head and said, "Somebody call 911…"

"Yeah," said Sam. Then he noticed movement outside the shattered front doors; two men in uniform. "Little late, but cavalry's here."

"Cops?"

"Two of them, but—" Sam frowned.

"What?"

"Pulled their guns," Sam said. "And they look…"

"Like extras from *Night of the Living Dead*?"

Sam considered for a moment, and nodded. "Sure. Let's go with that."

"With friends like these…"

those who succumbed to the blackout were vulnerable
ossession. Gruber had been on vacation during the first
out, and in Bakersburg during the second one. But
digan had never left Moyer. Even if he'd been home in
both nights, he was compromised. For all Gruber knew,
entire force could turn on each other at any moment.
those who had been out of town during the blackouts
d be immune.

rst, they checked the foyer and living room. In the dining
n, they found overturned chairs and bloodstains on
ight wall—fresh drywall—along with bloody handprints
he hardwood floor. Glass shattered in the kitchen,
ling them.

ey rushed to the kitchen doorway. Gruber peeked
nd the doorjamb, saw a woman hunched over the
en counter. A trail of blood drops marked her path to
ounter. Gruber waved Hardigan forward, then followed
into the kitchen.

usan Yates?" Gruber asked.

—I…"

ipping the counter with one hand, she turned toward
, revealing a blood-soaked blouse. She'd been stabbed
v the clavicle. "Help… Addie and Ethan," she said,
acing in pain and exhaustion. "He's trying to… kill them."
r knees buckled—

rdigan tossed his taser on the table as he rushed to help

caught her from behind, her weak body trembling.
you!"

THIRTY-FOUR

Senior Patrol Officer Gruber double-checked the address.
"This is it."

"I'm aware," Hardigan said drily, sitting on the other side
of the bulky computer console, in the passenger seat of the
police cruiser.

Of course, he knows, Gruber thought, *you don't take part
in a conspiracy to cover up the deaths of seventy people and not
remember where they died.*

As they strode toward the rundown farmhouse, Gruber
swept the peeling and rotted clapboard exterior with his
flashlight. The roving beam revealed the shadow people
haunting the place. Some darted away from the light, but
others ignored it. Gruber tried to count them, but their
strange movement—darting, shifting, flowing—and their
uniform appearance made any tally difficult.

"What the hell is this?" Hardigan asked nervously.

"A haunting or resurrection or mass possession," Gruber
said. "Whatever it is, we're not prepared."

"I'm not afraid of shadows, Gruber," Hardigan grumbled.

"You should be."

Flashing red lights swept into view and a second patrol car pulled up next to Gruber's.

"Who is it?" Hardigan asked.

"Backup," Gruber said. "Bowman and Morrissey."

"Good… That's good," Hardigan said, nodding slowly.

The chief hadn't heard them on the radio and now appeared nervous and a little guilty, confronting the past. When the two men joined them, Hardigan continued to stare at the house, almost entranced. Gruber wondered if he ever had nightmares about dumping the remains of fifty strangers in a mass grave. Meanwhile, Bowman and Morrissey awaited orders.

"Circle around back," Gruber told them. "We'll take the front." As they hurried away, Gruber called after them, "Tasers only! No guns!"

The two men exchanged shrugs and pulled their tasers out of their duty belts. Then they resumed their jog toward the back of the house, avoiding the weathered wraparound porch and its creaky floorboards.

"Ready?" Gruber said to Hardigan, who simply nodded.

"Morrissey! What the hell?"

"Wait," Gruber said, stopping. He swung the flashlight beam toward the side of the house and could just make out the two young cops facing each other. Morrissey stood frozen, his automatic pointed at Bowman's head, while Bowman stood with both hands up, his right holding the taser.

"Bowman! Taser him! Now!"

"What—?"

"Do it! Now!" Gruber yelled, moving tow

"What the hell—?" Hardigan said.

Bowman pointed his taser but, before he p blackness rippled over his face. The taser f and Bowman unholstered his own automatic Morrissey's head.

"On three," Morrissey said, grinning. Bo returning the amused smile. "One, two—"

"No!" Gruber screamed, running the rest o outstretched in his right hand. *Still too far…*

"Three!" Bowman and Morrissey said toget their triggers.

The twin gunshots overlapped, sounding pop. The backs of both their skulls blew apart, and brain matter in opposite directions.

"Jesus!" Gruber whispered, falling to his kn

A shadow emerged from each supine corp away, toward the backyard.

They don't die when we die.

He returned to a visibly shaken Hardig "What have we done?"

"We're here to save two kids," Gruber said all that matters right now. Lead the way, Chi

Hardigan stared at him for a moment, bu curt nod, removed his taser and hurried to th shoved it open while shouting, "Police!"

Gruber hung back, letting Hardigan tak could keep his eyes on the older man—and attempted to possess him. If Blair's inform

She shuddered and turned her face toward him, a grateful smile on her lips.

Gruber saw a flare and fade of red in her eyes. "Chief!"

"What now—?"

She twisted in his arms and shoved a butcher knife deep into his gut. Hardigan staggered back and crashed into the kitchen table, falling to the floor. Gruber aimed his taser, but the shadow inhabiting Susan Yates rose out of her neck like a cape caught in an updraft and vanished in the darkness. Susan collapsed, unconscious and probably minutes away from death by blood loss.

Grunting in pain, Hardigan pulled the knife free and stared at it for a moment before tossing it across the floor. After rifling through several kitchen drawers, Gruber found the dish towels and had Hardigan press one to the wound in his gut.

"Prolonging... the inevitable," Hardigan said, his voice strained.

Gruber radioed for help, told the dispatcher the chief was wounded. "Send only officers from Bakersburg! Nobody from the Moyer police force!"

"But—?"

"Bakersburg only!" Gruber repeated emphatically. He needed men he could trust. As far as he knew, anyone in a Moyer uniform was a ticking bomb.

The original call said the boy and his sister were hiding from their homicidal father underground. But not in the basement. In the backyard. *In one of the cult's underground chambers...*

A child screamed.

Gruber looked toward the back door. The scream had come from outside. The father must have found the kids! He turned back toward the chief. "I have to help—"

His eyes registered Hardigan holding his taser in a trembling hand, aiming it at Gruber—

Must have fallen off the table when he—

—and firing!

CRACKLE-CRACKLE-CRACKLE!

Gruber lost control of his motor functions, a terrifying paralysis gripping him as he toppled over—

THIRTY-FIVE

The two possessed patrol officers entered the demolished interior of the deserted library and paused. In front of them, they saw a wooden table on its side, the top facing them. Amid the destruction and chaos throughout the building, it garnered no special attention. They walked forward, their shoes crunching broken plastic, guns ready.

When they were within a few feet of the table, Sam popped up from behind it, a taser in each hand, and fired both weapons simultaneously. Both cops stood rigid for a second, before colliding with each other and falling over. Dean rose a moment after Sam, shotgun aimed above the men, waiting a beat for the shadows to eject from their hosts. Then, it was like skeet shooting, shattering the shadow on the left, working the action to pump another salt round in the chamber, tracking to the right and firing at the second shadow.

"All clear!" Sam called.

Townspeople emerged from the utility room and Bonnie's

office, the walking wounded. Of them all, Bonnie alone had survived the ordeal unscathed.

The business woman looked around at the complete mess of a library and all the wounded, confused people and spread her arms. "Can somebody please tell me what's going on?"

"You're all alive," Dean said. "Take the win."

The formerly possessed townspeople approached the two formerly possessed cops, helped them to their feet, then proceeded to question them. One said, "We were responding to a call—render aid at the Moyer Public Library and…" The other cop looked at him and shrugged. "I remember pulling into the lot… then nothing…"

"Lot of wounded here," Dean said to them. "Might want to call for ambulances. Plural."

Sam turned to Bonnie, who appeared shell-shocked by the state of her library. She walked out of her office, her legs wooden. "Sorry about the mess," Sam said.

She reached out to hand him the stun gun she hadn't needed.

"Keep it," he said. "Just in case."

Placing it on the counter, she stood beside him, too numb to speak. Sam waited as Dean flipped the table right side up and approached them. "Need to lock and reload for the cult house," Dean said. "Even if Gruber believes half of what we told him, he's punching above his weight."

"True," Sam said, turning to grab the duffel bag and gather the anti-shadow armory they'd brought into the library.

"Never got to use this," Dean said, pulling the battery-powered strobe light out of his jacket pocket and looking up. "Bonnie—?"

With a fierce look in her eyes, she pivoted toward Sam. A silver object slipped down from her sleeve into her hand. She raised her arm over him, a letter opener held like a knife ready to plunge into Sam's back.

Dean flicked on the strobe light, praying it worked in the pale light. "Hey! Parasite!"

Sam turned away from the duffel.

Bonnie glared at Dean—and froze facing him, red embers wavering in her eyes.

"Sam!" Dean called. "She's got a rider!"

Startled, Sam stepped back, putting some distance between himself and the possessed librarian. Of course, the office door had hardly been proof against something that could slip under it or pour itself through a keyhole.

"Stun her," Dean said, raising the shotgun he held in his right hand. "I got this."

Sam crossed in front of Bonnie to grab the stun she'd left on the counter. Momentarily released from the strobe effect, the shadow inside her decided against waiting for the inevitable electrical charge and subsequent disorientation and burst free of her body, flowing out of her eyes, ears and nostrils.

Belatedly, Dean realized he'd turned off the mounted black light after they'd subdued the cops. In his hurry to flick it back on, he dropped the strobe light, but never took his gaze off the fleeing shadow. With the substance addled by the black light, the shadow moved sluggishly, gliding toward the front door and freedom. Dean fired—and the shadow burst apart.

THIRTY-SIX

Dean parked the Impala next to the two police cruisers.

Against the evening sky and the wide-open space behind it, the cult house stood almost in silhouette, no interior lights glowing. Almost, because the inkblot shapes of the shadow people presented as unforgiving darkness that blotted out reality wherever they passed. Some of the shadow people came from blocks away, returning to the house where they had once lived.

"They need this place, Dean," Sam said. "Something about it brings them back."

"Maybe they come back to recharge."

He opened the trunk, unzipped the duffel bag. They each took a shotgun with a mounted black light, stun gun, taser with extra cartridges, and a portable strobe light. Lastly, they each grabbed a leather pouch filled with extra shotgun salt rounds and slipped the shoulder strap over their heads.

Cautiously, they approached the front door of the wooden house. The white paint had faded and chipped away, exposing bare and rotted wood. The gingerbread accents on the archways and sagging wraparound porch were broken and crumbling. The slanted roof had shed brittle green shingles like dandruff, pieces littering the front and sides of the house. Dean wondered if Daniel Yates had purchased a money pit rather than a fixer-upper. Even without a haunting by dozens of malevolent shadow people, the farmhouse had been a candidate for a bulldozer rather than a renovator.

"Dean!" Sam said, pointing to the left side of the house.

Dean saw a glint of metal, from a police badge. A few steps later, they found two corpses. "Recognize this one," Dean said. "Bowman, from the station."

"Shot each other at close range," Sam said. "Simultaneously."

"Both possessed," Dean said bitterly. "Mutual destruction."

"Let's end this," Sam said, the words a snarl of anger.

They strode to the front door, which hung partially open. A shadow swooped down from the second story and entered before them. Then a second shadow—or maybe the same one, it was hard to tell them apart—flowed across the floor, rose up to full height and eased away from them. Sam flicked on his mounted black light, and Dean followed suit, with a shudder. With so many shadows circling, entering and exiting the house, he felt particularly vulnerable to possession. As if the two dead cops hadn't been reminder enough.

"Tase me, if you have to, bro," Dean said, trying to lighten the dark mood.

"I will," Sam said immediately.

Dean caught his shoulder. "Dude, you don't have to enjoy it."

"No," Sam said, straight-faced. "Strictly business."

He waved his loaded taser in front of Dean. Even in the darkness, Dean thought he saw a fleeting smile on his brother's face. Or, maybe a grimace. Hard to be sure in the darkness.

Black lights crisscrossing in front of them, they cleared the foyer, living room and dining room. In the kitchen they found Susan Yates on the floor, pale and unconscious, her breathing labored. Dean knelt beside Hardigan who, in addition to a stab wound in his gut, had a broken nose and smashed lips. Alive… barely.

In the distance, Dean heard sirens. He listened for a few moments, but they seemed no closer. *No help coming. It's on us.*

"Dean!"

Dean looked up from Hardigan and saw them, shadows circling the kitchen, along the countertops and ceiling, through chair legs and under the kitchen table. Some alien quality about them reminded him of sharks.

With his black light sweeping the kitchen and his taser in his other hand, arm outstretched, Sam attempted to track them. Each time one approached Dean, Sam zeroed in on the threat and it veered away, sensing danger.

They know we can take them out.

Slowly, Dean removed the strobe light from his jacket pocket, placed it on the floor and angled it toward the back of the kitchen. "Sam…" he said, nodding toward the light on the floor. The shadows continued to make slow circuits of the kitchen, waiting for a moment of inattentiveness. Sam glanced at the floor and nodded. Laying his taser on the countertop, he reached into his own pocket and withdrew his strobe light. Eyes up, he reached down and let Dean take it from his grasp. Dean positioned the second light to face the front of the kitchen and the archway that led to the dining room. He positioned one hand on each light's power switch.

"Showtime!"

Instantly, strobe lights bathed the entire kitchen with stuttering light.

With only a split-second separating each period of darkness from light, every exposed shadow person froze in place, incapacitated. The effect could be permanent or only temporary. Would they adapt to the pattern? Best not to test the theory.

Standing back to back, the Winchesters aimed their black lights at one shadow after another—increasing their density or substance or simply their foothold in the world of the living—and dispatched each one with a salt round.

As he reloaded his shotgun, Dean exclaimed with grim satisfaction, "Like shooting fish in a barrel."

"That all of them?"

"Every damn one," Dean said, kneeling to switch off the strobe lights.

He froze. Under the table, shielded from both strobe light arcs, a single shadow person slid from side to side, trapped.

"Sorry, pal," Dean said, bringing the barrel of the shotgun to bear. "You picked the wrong guy to possess."

Blam!

"*That* was the last one," Dean said. Even so, he decided to leave one strobe light in place, the one facing the kitchen entrance, to prevent anyone possessed from following them out of the house.

"Dean," Sam called. "Blood."

They followed the trail of blood drops out the back door, which creaked with the protest of rusty hinges, Dean leading the way. Crossing the sagging, weather-beaten deck down to the backyard, Dean's skin began to itch again at the potential for a hostile takeover. He gripped the stun gun in his damp left palm, pressed awkwardly against the forestock of the shotgun, ready to zap himself at the first sign of mental invasion. Though, with Sam's black light shining behind him, any attempted possession might result in a brutal—possibly fatal—cut, depending on the attempted point of entry.

Dean dreaded the idea of losing control of himself. Even without the potential for murderous consequences, he shuddered at the prospect of becoming something's human sock puppet.

Beyond the backyard, encircled by a split-rail fence a few decades past its prime, the commune's former farmland stretched to the distant tree line. They walked through a gap where the rotted rails had fallen.

"Somewhere out there," Sam said. "Two terrified kids are hiding from their possessed father in a small underground room."

"Homicidal hide and seek," Dean said. "Hope we're not too late."

"Where the hell is Gruber?"

Dean had no answer, feared the worst.

They loped across the overgrown fields, their mounted black lights a poor substitute for flashlights. Here and there, they spotted the trapdoors, some flipped open to expose small underground rooms lined with plywood. Whoever had left them open had created an inadvertent minefield, though the doors themselves might have been too rotted and brittle to support the weight of a full-grown man.

Dean leaped over an open doorway—*floorway?*—as Sam said, "There!"

Near the trees, almost hidden among their crowded silhouettes, stood a dark figure, seemingly wracked by seizures as darker shapes plunged into his flesh, only to be expelled seconds later. No sooner had one lost the battle for control when another took its place.

Behind them, Dean heard the tell-tale squeal of the rusty back-door hinges. They stopped, turned. Whoever it was, they'd gotten through the strobe-lit kitchen, so hadn't been possessed. Of course, as Dean knew, that could change in an instant.

A figure ran toward them, favoring a knee—Bonnie. She'd followed them rather than remain behind at the library. They waited while she caught up to them, breathless. "I haven't been back since…" she began. "Barry brought me."

"Where is he?" Dean asked.

She waved an arm above her head, causing Dean to look up as a dark shape swooped down from the roof of the house and merged with her. For a moment her eyes glowed red. Then she said, "Right here. But hurry! They can't hold Caleb for long."

"Who?" Sam asked.

"Team Rebel!"

A young girl screamed.

All three of them sprinted for the tree line. Possessed by

a man who died young, Bonnie's spirit was certainly willing but her body, at more than sixty years of age, struggled to keep up with the Winchesters.

As she began to flag, Barry spoke to them—and her—through her breathless voice. "We dreamed of the chains breaking… dreamed of Ethan's father… reclaiming the land. Then the explosion that ended us… echoed again, taking us to the moment all was lost… and somehow, we awoke… as if the dreaming had preserved our lost moment in time… giving us a second chance… A strange new life—but free! We wanted to live again… the promised afterlife… we yearned for it."

She staggered, caught her balance, and continued. "Then the blackout… an echo *we* created, opened a door into their minds… for us to be truly free… Until Caleb ruined everything again."

"Save it!" Dean said, lacking sympathy for freedom obtained by hijacking others' lives.

Ahead of them, the seizing man—Daniel Yates—backhanded a young girl, who stumbled and fell over a body—Gruber, bleeding from a lacerated scalp.

Yates grabbed Ethan by the throat with his left hand, raising a butcher knife in his right above the boy's head. *"That's far enough!"*

Dean, Sam and Bonnie froze.

Too far away!

"You promised!" Ethan screamed. "Fight him, Dad!"

The possessed father remained out of range of their black lights and tasers. Even shotgun salt rounds were useless at this distance.

"Sammy! No choice now!"

Holding the shotgun in his left hand, Sam pulled a handgun out from the back of his waistband. Because he was vulnerable to possession, Dean hadn't trusted himself to carry a gun with real ammunition, but Sam had no need for such self-restrictions. And yet, the distance rendered the automatic dangerously inaccurate. Sam took aim, as likely to hit the boy as his father. But if he did nothing, the boy would surely die.

In her Barry-possessed voice, Bonnie said, "I promised."

As his shadow withdrew from her body, Bonnie moaned in pain, clutched her chest and fell forward. After the briefest pause, Barry's shadow flew across the remaining distance and plunged into Daniel Yates.

The doubly possessed man staggered, his arms spread wide as if tugged apart, releasing Ethan. The boy scrambled away from his tormented father and joined his sobbing sister on the other side of Gruber's motionless body.

Inside Daniel Yates a battle raged for control of his mind and body. His arms jerked and swung independently of each other. The left leg lunged forward, while the right swung to the side. He bent forward, then threw his head back, slipped and fell, then scrambled back to his feet, with Caleb ascendant.

"You are weak, boy! Just like the others. Now—fall—in—line!"

A second, desperate voice erupted from Yates' throat.

"Nooo! You don't—control me—anymore!"

A shadow began to emerge from one side of Yates' body, then sunk back, while a second shadow lost control, pushed out from the other side, before surging inward again. Blood trickled from Yates' ears, nose, and eyes. In turn, his wild eyes focused on the Winchesters, in seething anger—then on Bonnie's fallen form, in deepest sorrow. While Barry retained control, he turned toward the Winchesters.

"*Burn it all!*" he yelled. "*Only way to end this. Now! Before it's too late, before I lose—!*"

The entangled shadows continued to struggle, half inside, half outside Yates' body.

Sensing that Barry had lost ascendancy, Dean reached into his jacket pocket for the strobe light he'd taken from the kitchen and flicked it on, which revealed and froze the rebel shadows who had attempted to thwart Caleb before Barry returned.

Sam swung the barrel of his shotgun toward Yates, the cone of solidifying black light touching upon the man and both partially emerged shadows. Immediately, Daniel Yates screamed in agony, then doubled over, gagging. The partially expelled shadows had become like large shards of glass, slicing open Yates' flesh.

"Dad! No!" Ethan screamed.

Yates convulsed in pain, blood flowing down his torso and arms.

"Dean!"

Sam tossed the taser toward his brother in a looping arc. Dean dropped his shotgun and snagged the taser out of the air, aimed it at Yates and—hesitated.

If he zapped Yates while the shadows were solidified, expelling them might slice him in half right in front of Ethan and his sister. Aside from killing Yates, who was completely innocent in all the mayhem his body had caused, he'd give those kids a lifetime of therapy bills and endless scream-yourself-awake nightmares. Instead, he lowered the strobe and fired the taser. Yates' body stiffened, vibrating from the five-thousand-volt charge. Both shadows lost substance a split-second before the electrical current expelled them from Yates' body.

Yates pitched forward, creating a clear shot.

"Can't tell them apart!" Sam shouted.

"Do it!" Dean advised.

Before either shadow person could recover from the momentary disorientation, Sam fired at the one on the left, worked the shotgun's action, and fired at the one on the right, shattering both seconds apart. Both Caleb and Barry were gone.

Dean switched off the lowered strobe light.

Then a curious thing happened. Multiple shadow people descended from the treetops, hovering at ground level before Sam and Dean.

"What is this?" Dean asked, his skin beginning to itch again. "They're creeping me out, Sam."

After a moment, Sam understood. "Waiting their turn," he said. "They're ready for it to end."

One shadow approached Sam slowly, in as nonthreatening a manner as possible, and hovered before Sam's shotgun, placing itself in the cone of black light. Sam raised the shotgun and aimed.

What do you say to someone willing to give up a second life, Dean wondered, *regardless of how strange that second life had been, for the greater good?*

"Thank you," Sam said. "For fighting to save the kids."

The shadow, displaying more definition under the violet glow of the black light, had a more defined face, a feminine face. Unable to speak, she simply nodded and waited for the end. Sam pulled the trigger, and she burst into a thousand pieces of fading darkness. Another took her place in line—a male face with a lined brow, the face of an elder. Perhaps the rebel contingent had included more than just the teenaged runaways after all. "Thank you," Sam repeated, and fired again.

Dean picked up his shotgun and aimed it toward the trees. At once, a shadow positioned itself in his black light beam. "Thanks," Dean said, echoing Sam's sentiment because it seemed appropriate after all. Before he fired, a few others hurried to join the first shadow in line. From their youthful faces, Dean could tell he had a batch of runaways and maybe a few reformed delinquents, all wanting to go out together.

His jaw tight with emotion, Dean raised a fist and said, "Team Rebel."

They smiled, nodding their approval. Shadow arms and hands draped around shadow shoulders, and they waited. Dean fired.

Others begin to gather in groups in front of both shotguns. But a few shadow people, afraid of the finality, fluttered away from the black lights, yet not too far away. Maybe they were afraid. Or maybe they wanted to hang around to see the end of it. Eventually, they all came into the light to say their final goodbyes, to each other and their shadow world.

After all the shadow people were gone, Sam knelt beside Bonnie's body, checked for a pulse they both knew he wouldn't find, looked at Dean and shook his head. The final pursuit had been too much for her heart. But she'd died willingly to save the children and to help her teenage crush, possibly the love of her life, finally find peace.

Dean checked on Daniel Yates, who bled from multiple wounds, most of them superficial. Where the shadows had remained within his body, they hadn't solidified under the black light. No internal damage, at least not of the physical variety. Dean had no idea how multiple and tag-team possessions might affect someone mentally. If Yates was lucky, he wouldn't remember any of it.

Sam helped Gruber to his feet.

Carrying the equipment, Dean led the way back to the farmhouse, steering them clear of the exposed underground chambers. Behind him, a recovering Gruber escorted the children, a hand on each of their shoulders. Sam brought up the rear, carrying the body of Bonnie Lassiter in his arms.

With everyone at the front of the house, the Winchesters returned to the kitchen for Susan Yates and Chief Hardigan. Somehow, despite considerable blood loss, both clung to life. Sam carried Susan out, mindful of her injured shoulder, so as not to reopen the clotting wound. Draping Hardigan's arm over his shoulder, Dean wrapped his arm around the chief's waist and hauled him up to his feet. The movement triggered a burst of pain that had Hardigan gritting his teeth and hissing every curse he'd ever learned in his long life. By the time Dean lowered him to the front curb, the old man had passed out.

While the Winchesters had been occupied, Gruber had

called for an ambulance and seemed confident it would arrive well before midnight. With the shadows gone and the possession-fueled violence over, the combined police forces of Moyer and Bakersburg would finally regain control of the town.

Dean stared at the decrepit house, a monument to lost dreams and mass murder, and a psychic fueling station for dozens of malevolent spirits, who belatedly raged against the dying of their light. "Barry was right."

Sam nodded. "Yeah."

They assumed all the shadows had been vanquished or surrendered, but what if some had fled before or after the final battle? Dean doubted any lingering shadow people would survive long after the destruction of the house.

He found a pair of two-gallon containers of unleaded gasoline in a small tool shed out back, intended for the riding mower. He splashed gas around the base of the house and poured a liquid trail from the kitchen up the stairs to the second floor, then lit it with a stove match. Meanwhile, Sam took the second container and a stack of newspapers, along with the box of stove matches and burned what remained of the detention rooms that had been rigged with dynamite during Caleb's failed ascension.

While waiting for the ambulance, they watched the house burn.

Sam knelt beside Ethan, staring intently at the flames, and said, "Sorry about your house, Ethan."

"Good riddance," he replied.

He turned his back on the house, and took his sister's hand.

As the flames raged and consumed the entire farmhouse, Dean continued to stare, wondering if they should dig up the mass grave and burn the remains of the bodies never reported to or claimed by any family. *What's the point? We'll never track down the twenty-three that were shipped home.* In the end, he deemed it unnecessary. The shadow people hadn't been true ghosts. Destroying them with black light and salt rounds seemed to remove the possibility they could ever return. *As good as burning the remains.*

The ravenous fire consumed old wood and aged shingles, shattering and melting glass, turning everything in its path to char and ash. And as the light shone brightest, even the darkest of shadows paled and faded away forever.

THIRTY-SEVEN

On the night the Free Folk commune house burned to the ground, Sam and Dean returned to the Moyer Motor Lodge and waited for the bedside clock radio to transition from 11:59 PM to…

12:00 AM.

"So far, so good," Dean said.

Sixty seconds later, 12:00 blinked to 12:01 and Sam sighed in relief. "All clear."

The shadow people were gone, the midnight blackouts over.

"Life goes back to normal in Moyer," Dean said, unsure if he meant the statement as a question. So many lives damaged, some lost. Going forward, *normal* would have many shades of gray. Like shadows.

"It's amazing when you think about it," Sam said. "All that metaphysical energy released decades ago, waiting endlessly. Then all those minds reawakening, willing themselves back to life, the only way they could."

"By taking the townspeople on a psychic joyride," Dean

commented sourly. "Not a fan. No matter what they went through all those years ago, they had no right to take control of others like that."

Sam nodded. "I think they came back a little crazed," he said. "But most of them—other than those blindly loyal to Caleb or whatever strange vision they had for the cult—most of them got that in the end. Did the right thing, bowing out."

"Not too soon for me," Dean said. "No Team Free Will without free will."

Dean checked the time again.

"You up for a long night's drive to the bunker or…?"

"Crash here, hit the road in the morning?" Sam said. "Room's paid for."

"Crash it is," Dean said, stifling a yawn.

Back in the driver's seat of his own mind, he felt the tension drain from his body, and with that relief came pure exhaustion. He fell asleep with no concern about shadows living in the darkness. But in his dreams, the street lamps projected cones of black light and all the cars had strobe lights, rather than headlights, mounted on either side of their grills.

Gruber called Sam in the morning and requested they stop by the Moyer police station for an update. Dean wondered if their FBI cover was blown, but Sam thought Gruber sounded upbeat, so they agreed to meet.

At the police station, Gruber looked as if he hadn't slept all night, his face pale, dark circles under his eyes. He'd received stitches for his scalp wound and wore a bandage that extended well past his hairline.

"Shouldn't you be in the hospital?" Sam asked.

"I was," Gruber said, frowning. "Long enough to get stitched up. Doc wanted to hold me for observation. Told him I'll come back today and he can observe me all he wants for the next forty-eight hours while I sleep it off."

"So, you wanted to see us?" Sam asked.

"First, I want to thank you for your help," he said. "Doubt we would have made it through the last twenty-four hours without you. Don't think I'll ever truly understand what the hell happened, but it's over, so I'm good."

"Just doing our job, man," Dean said.

"Above and beyond, so thanks," Gruber said. "I asked you here because I thought you deserved an update. Fortunately, the chief doesn't remember me punching him in the face after he tasered me. But I think he's okay with it, considering everything."

"Yeah. Sure," Sam said.

"He's done," Gruber said. "Tough old bastard, surviving a nasty gut wound, but he's officially retiring."

"Susan and Daniel Yates?" Dean asked. "The kids?"

"Susan lost a lot of blood," Gruber said. "Weak as a kitten, but will recover. Daniel's lacerations are superficial but, if you ask me, he's a bit shell-shocked from whatever battle raged in his mind. Again, I don't pretend to understand. Fortunately, his memory is Swiss cheese about the whole day, doesn't remember stabbing Susan or threatening Ethan and Addison."

"Wasn't him," Dean said.

"I get that," Gruber said. "Hard to wrap your head around it though."

"Not after it happens to you."

"I'll certainly take your word for it," he said. "After watching Bowman and Morrissey…" He shook his head, letting the rest go unsaid. "Anyway, Yates tells me the whole family will stay with his mother in Philadelphia. She'll help with the kids until they're feeling normal again. But he swears he's cured of house flipping. Going to find something in good shape and put down roots."

"Guessing Ethan's thrilled about that," Sam said.

"You bet," Gruber said. "First thing he said, he can finally make some friends and get a dog."

"What about Moyer?" Dean asked. "Lot of people here lost control of their lives, and a lot of lives went to hell as a result."

"Not to mention the legal consequences," Sam added.

"Yeah, about that," Gruber said. "Retiring or not, Hardigan is working on a new spin. Something about how the townspeople went briefly crazy due to the aftereffects of the train derailment chemical spill, combined with old narcotics from the commune leaching into the water supply mixed with whatever nasty stuff continues to brew in Lake Delsea."

"So, no one is at fault?" Sam asked. "No harm, no foul?"

"Except Pangento," Dean said. "If Lake Delsea is part of Hardigan's spin."

"Bet they won't be happy in the role of scapegoat," Sam said.

"There's an interesting postscript," Gruber said with the hint of a knowing smile. "Yates bought the commune house and yard, but the rest of the land had already been sold. Want to guess the buyer?"

"Not Pangento…?" Dean said.

"One and the same," Gruber said. "Last night I took some of our guys out there, had them comb through the fields, like a search grid. Told them to look for any wounded survivors, wanted to tag any underground chambers. But I had my suspicions about Pangento. That land isn't near their plant. And they never took full responsibility for the toxic spills in Lake Delsea, with their chokehold on our economy."

"I see where this is going," Dean said, smiling.

"Evidence of fresh digging back there," Gruber said. "Holes big enough to accommodate some dubious fifty-five-gallon drums. And, Hardigan may be retiring, but he has contacts there, and he knows some things that never came to light about Pangento from way back. Short of it is, we can link those drums to them. And Lake Delsea."

"With all the Federal agencies poking around," Sam said, "they might be feeling particularly… vulnerable."

"Massive understatement," Gruber said. "And, as a concerned corporate neighbor—without admitting any liability, of course—Pangento has agreed to set up a healthy settlement fund for the victims and families of the blackout incidents. The fund will cover all medical and funeral expenses, pay for any property damage, establish college funds for any kids who lost a parent, and establish annuities for anyone maimed or unable to work."

"And in return?" Dean wondered.

"Folks sign waivers. We keep a lid on the old and new toxic transgressions, figuratively speaking," Gruber said. "Not ideal. Nothing can make up for the loss of lives and limbs, but it will help the survivors cope and move on with their lives without facing financial burdens on top of everything else they've been through."

"And you're okay with another cover-up?" Sam asked.

"If Pangento holds up their end of the agreement, yeah, I can live with it," Gruber said. "But part of that agreement is they don't relocate, and they stop the toxic dumping. If we ever find out they've polluted our land or water again, everything goes public. So, they damn well better be good corporate neighbors moving forward. Moyer has the leverage this time, which means we have control over the future of our town."

Once they reached I-70 West, Dean spun the radio dial in search of a clear classic rock station. After a while the signal would grow faint and he'd search for the next station.

"Suppose it's the best possible outcome," Sam said at last.

"Better than I expected," Dean said, nodding. He'd expected lots of jail time and heartache for a bunch of unfortunate people, with no way to prove their innocence. Of course, all the money in the world wouldn't erase the heartache. "But Pangento skates again."

"PR win, but a big financial hit," Sam said. "To be fair, they had no hand in the blackouts or possessions."

"Doesn't make what they did right."

"True."

"Poetic justice, maybe," Dean said.

Sam nodded. After a while, he asked, "What about you? Feel any better about our current situation?"

Dean thought about willingly turning over control of

his life for a potential greater good versus literally losing control of his own mind and body to an invading entity. He'd never be okay with the Brits' condescension and their micromanagement style, but he'd signed on, no strings attached, and would continue the course while their goals aligned—but not for one second after they diverged. That remained his choice.

"Every day is a battle, Sam," Dean said. "Sometimes a series of battles. You face them head on. They knock you down, you get back up. You lose one, you damn well better win the next. You take the wins. Because tomorrow is a crapshoot."

ACKNOWLEDGMENTS

Writing involves a lot of time working alone, but books don't happen without the support of a great team. With that in mind, my heartfelt thanks go out to Joanna Harwood, Cat Camacho and Miranda Jewess at Titan Books in the UK. Closer to home, many thanks to Chris Cerasi and everyone at Warner Bros. I wouldn't get to play in the *Supernatural* universe (again) without all of you!

On the home front, I am thankful for the support of my wife, Andrea, along with Matthew, Luke and Emma. I promise to get to all the stuff I put on hold to finish writing this one.

Finally, none of this would be possible without the creative mind of Eric Kripke or the wonderful performances of Jensen Ackles and Jared Padalecki. You guys rock!

About the Author

John Passarella won the Horror Writers Association's prestigious Bram Stoker Award for Superior Achievement in a First Novel for the coauthored *Wither*. Columbia Pictures purchased the feature film rights to *Wither* in a prepublication, preemptive bid.

John's other novels include *Wither's Rain*, *Wither's Legacy*, *Kindred Spirit*, *Shimmer* and the original media tie-in novels *Supernatural: Night Terror*, *Supernatural: Rite of Passage*, *Supernatural: Cold Fire*, *Grimm: The Chopping Block*, *Buffy the Vampire Slayer: Ghoul Trouble*, *Angel: Avatar*, and *Angel: Monolith*. In January 2012 he released his first fiction collection, *Exit Strategy & Others*. *Supernatural: Joyride* is his thirteenth novel.

A member of the Horror Writers Association, International Thriller Writers and the International Association of Media Tie-In Writers, John resides in southern New Jersey with his wife, children and two dogs. As the owner of AuthorPromo.com, he is a web designer for many clients, primarily other authors.

John maintains his official author website at www.

passarella.com, where he encourages readers to send him email at author@passarella.com, and to subscribe to his free author newsletter for the latest information on his books and stories. To follow him on Twitter, see @JohnPassarella.

For more fantastic fiction, author events,
competitions, limited editions and more

VISIT OUR WEBSITE
titanbooks.com

LIKE US ON FACEBOOK
facebook.com/titanbooks

FOLLOW US ON TWITTER
@TitanBooks

EMAIL US
readerfeedback@titanemail.com